THE STRUGGLE CONTINUES

An arduous journey of hope

A NOVEL BY
CHRISTOPHER THOMSON

 FriesenPress

One Printers Way
Altona, MB R0G 0B0
Canada

www.friesenpress.com

Copyright © 2023 by Christopher Thomson
First Edition — 2023

All rights reserved.

No part of this publication may be reproduced in any form, or by any means, electronic or mechanical, including photocopying, recording, or any information browsing, storage, or retrieval system, without permission in writing from FriesenPress.

ISBN
978-1-03-915762-0 (Hardcover)
978-1-03-915761-3 (Paperback)
978-1-03-915763-7 (eBook)

1. FICTION, HISTORICAL

Distributed to the trade by The Ingram Book Company

The Struggle Continues is a work of fiction. All incidents and dialogue, and all characters, with the exception of some historical figures, are products of the author's imagination and are not to be construed as real. Where real-life historical figures appear, the situations, incidents, and dialogues concerning those persons are entirely fictional and are not intended to depict actual events or to change the fictional nature of the work. In all other respects, any resemblance to actual persons, living or dead, is entirely coincidental.

Much of the background to the book is inspired by actual events in the 1972-1982 period. The author has taken liberties in relation to timing, relative importance, and linkage of events for the sake of the setting of this story. The period in which this work is placed was one of extraordinary political, social, and religious complexity in Lebanon and elsewhere in the region. These issues are well beyond the scope of the author's experience and this work. Accordingly, many significant events and developments of the time are not dealt with.

For my wonderful family

CHAPTER ONE

BEIRUT, 1972

The mid-teenaged boys wore a range of expressions on their faces and in their eyes: nervousness, excitement, and some fire. Ali Hassan watched anxiously with four others from across the street as they huddled against the side of a concrete building, glancing around the corner. Half a dozen smartly dressed boys in school blazers, grey pants, and striped ties were coming toward them. The boys laughed, giving each other good-natured shoves, stepping into the street and back to the edge, as cars honked at them, and making faces to go with whatever stories they were telling.

The previous week, Ali and his Palestinian schoolmates had been harassed by students from the nearby Maronite Catholic school. This happened all too often as they left their dilapidated and poorly equipped Palestinian school on the fringe of a Christian neighbourhood in Beirut.

The early 1970s had seen a huge influx to Lebanon of displaced Palestinians who had first fled, or been pushed out of, what had become Israel and sought refuge in Jordan. Internal disputes among the Palestinians and conflict with the Jordanians came with a rise in militant activity by the Palestinian Liberation Organization (PLO). When the Jordanians pushed them out for their increasing militancy, many thousands moved to Lebanon, where the reception was no more positive.

Ali watched in apprehension as his friends across the street burst out of their hiding place, yelling and running toward the coming group. "Come on! Let's get them!" a friend shouted. Ali took a deep breath and joined in as his side did the same, shouting and waving arms and fists as they approached the others. Exchanges of insults soon led to shoving, and a fight broke out. Ali fell to the ground from a fist to his cheek, tearing his pants on the rough pavement and scraping a knee.

Three grandmotherly women at a fruit stand and four grey-haired men, drinking tea on a bench across the street, called out in fright.

"Stop that fighting, boys!" hollered two men from a construction site as they rushed into the street, waving shovels and shouting. "Break it up! Stop that!"

The boys disbursed, yelling insults at each other and threatening to get them the next time. *Oh no, I've ripped these pants again*, Ali thought, looking at the bloody knee. *Mother will be so annoyed, and I'll hear again that we don't have extra money to buy new ones, as she and my father always remind me.*

As the fight broke up, the Palestinian boys gathered themselves together, pleased that they had stood up against the kids from the smart Christian school, and moved off. Ali, sweating and feeling his sore knee and reddening cheek, waved to his friends and turned to walk the rest of the forty-five minutes home from his school near the Palestinian camps of Sabra and Shatila, where most of his friends lived.

Ali was headed for the upscale Raouché district, where his father was fortunate to have a stable job as a concierge and a small apartment in the building. Ali knew that his family was relatively well off compared to the conditions of the refugees in the camps, where most of his friends lived. They were certainly poor, he knew, and their accommodations badly serviced. Many were crumbling concrete buildings with only intermittent water and electricity. He had often gone after school with friends to the Shatila area and found that some even lived under tin shacks on building roofs or under frames covered with plastic sheeting in vacant lots or buildings, offering little protection from the elements. In that area, pieces of concrete in the street, having fallen from corners or around window frames, often showed the results of random firing in the ongoing Lebanese-Palestinian conflict. The stench of poor sanitation and refuse drifted throughout the area to the point that residents barely noticed it.

As Ali crossed street after street, the buildings and shops became more prosperous, and people were better dressed. *Why do any of us have to live like those in the camps?* thought Ali, looking in the window of an expensive menswear shop. *All the adult Palestinians talk about is returning to Palestine, a place I've never seen and probably never will. Many of them haven't seen it either.*

Ali cut through a garbage-strewn vacant lot on a dusty path between scrub and thorny bushes, calling out, "Mother, I'm home!" as he entered a door at the back of the building where he lived, opening straight into the area that served as kitchen and sitting room.

Zeina turned from the sink, a broad smile of pleasure on her face at hearing her son's voice. But it turned to a scowl as she saw him enter. "Hi, Ali. Are you hungry? Oh no, Ali! Look at your face and pants! What have you done now?"

"I'm sorry, Mother. We got into a fight with the Catholic school kids again, and I was knocked over. You know I don't like to get into fights with the Lebanese, but I have to stand up with my friends."

"Oh Ali, wash your face. Take off those pants, and I'll try to clean off the blood stains and repair them. You know you must take care of your clothes."

After giving him time to clean up, a short while later, Ali's father, Hani, called him. "All right, Ali, you can make up for tearing your pants by helping me in the building entrance. I can use some help polishing the marble floor."

Kneeling on his bandaged knee, Ali worked sullenly. Hearing a car, he looked up to see a familiar black Mercedes pull up at the front door. A teenager a year or two older than him got out, wearing the uniform of the prestigious Saint Paul's University School, and strode toward the entrance. Salim al Omeri lived on the top floor of the building with his mother, Amina, who was a lawyer, and this was her car and driver. *These are Palestinians who live in a different world,* thought Ali.

His father, who gave Salim a nod and welcome, had told him that the Omeri family was distinguished and wealthy. In fact, they owned the building they were in. Not only that but Ali also remembered they were important members of the community. Salim's father, Suleiman, an engineer who had been mysteriously killed on a construction site a couple of years earlier, was known to be a prominent member of the Beirut Committee of the PLO. His place had been taken by Amina when he was killed. *These people should be able to speak up for the Palestinians and do something instead of futile fighting,* thought Ali. *I can't see them getting into a struggle on the street for nothing, as we do.*

As the door to the elevator closed behind Salim, Hani said, "Ali, you should remember to be polite to Salim. Don't forget that our living is dependent on that family."

"Father, I don't see Salim often, but he always seems nice and friendly, even if he is older. Not like the wealthy Lebanese school kids on the way home, who are always giving us a bad time because they think we're all poor and from the Shatila camp. They say we are over-running Lebanon and don't have any right to be here. If only the Lebanese could realize that we Palestinians have nowhere else to go."

"You are right about that for the moment. It's not only our food and my job, Ali, but the future of the Palestinian community might depend on educated families like the Omeris. That education and their connections can be very important."

CHAPTER TWO

BEIRUT, APRIL 1973

Four heavily armed men, wearing faded and sweat-stained military fatigues and dusty, scuffed boots, slouched against a Jeep that was blocking a nearby crossroad, ensuring that no vehicles turned into the quiet side road near the Sabra refugee camp in south Beirut. Farther along the decaying, rubbish-strewn, ill-lit street, in a once prosperous merchant's house, light faintly shone through the breaks in the heavy velvet curtains. Smoke curled from the cigarettes of the two muscular men outside the door. Two others stood in the shadows across the street, leaning against the corner of a totally dark and boarded-up building.

Inside the house, in a sparsely furnished salon, were three of the most important and most wanted leaders of the Palestinian community in Lebanon. Muhammed Yusef al Najjar, known by the *nom de guerre* of Abu Yusef, head of the Higher Political Committee for Palestinian Refugees in Lebanon, talked at length in a low voice, hoarse from smoke. He rambled on about his responsibilities for the social and economic welfare of the refugee population, randomly inserting comments on recent military activities. "My friends, it is very late. Our people need work and food, and that's why we're here tonight. Those aid shipments the Saudis are paying for are already loaded on the trucks in Jeddah, but we need to determine which camps they should be sent to."

"Yes, let's move on," said Kamal Adwan, sitting on the other side of the table. "It is my job to organize military activities in the West

Bank, and I have new ideas to raise with you the next time we meet. But for now, can we bring this discussion of food to a close?"

On an old, creaking, wooden kitchen chair, against the wall where half a dozen others watched the discussion, sat tiring Amina al Omeri, an attractive woman in her mid-thirties. *It's always the same,* she thought. *These men all want to lead the military campaigns, but we can't feed our families with bullets or talk, and there are thousands of children and others waiting for us.* She shared Adwan's desire to bring this largely fruitless and seemingly interminable discussion to a close and was anxious to return to her home, where she lived with her fifteen-year-old son, Salim. Amina felt the pressure of being an only parent, and she deeply missed her late husband, Suleiman. The cause of his death a year earlier, in a mysterious accident, had never been clearly investigated, as was the case in so many likely politically related fatalities in Lebanon.

Her dark and intelligent eyes, slim figure, expressive face, and lively personality always brought her a good deal of male attention. Amina smoothed a crease on her black trousers and adjusted the flowered, silk scarf folded elegantly around her neck, feeling soiled from sitting for hours in the stifling air and dust of the smoke-filled room and the humidity of the spring night.

With an affluent family background and a long association with the Palestinian cause, Amina had taken Suleiman's seat on the committee. She worked closely with her boss, Kamal Nasser, who was quietly listening at the main table. Amina was a faithful, determined, and hard worker for the Palestinian people. Nonetheless, not a few thought her place in the PLO hierarchy and rumoured personal relationship with Chairman Yasser Arafat was based on his attraction to her as much as anything.

Amina's upbringing and years in excellent private schools in Beirut had developed her into an articulate woman with an innate media sense. These skills gave her ready access to the local (and increasingly, international) media, who sought her out. They could relate to this well-educated woman, who had access to the Palestinian leadership, looked good in the film clips, and perhaps most importantly, spoke English and French fluently, as well as Arabic, making the work of the usually unilingual journalists so much easier.

At long last, the men at the table agreed on which groups and camps should receive the supplies from the Saudis, and critically, who was to control distribution and get credit for it. The men rose and embraced like lovers parting. Amina stood, gracefully stretching out the cramps in her legs, while everyone moved toward the door to leave the house.

Three days later, Abu Yusef, Kamal Adwan, and Kamal Nasser were dead.

CHAPTER THREE

Assaults on Lebanese sovereignty were common enough, but tensions throughout the country increased sharply as the story of the deaths became known. Israeli commandos had landed in small, inflatable boats, covering the last ten kilometres from their naval vessel to the shore and landing on the beach at Ramlet al Baida, south of the city and close to the airport.

Four Israeli agents had arrived in Lebanon some days earlier, travelling on forged passports, which was a specialty product of the Israeli secret service—one claiming Belgian nationality, another Swiss, and two British—and stayed in different hotels. They moved quietly around Beirut, preparing for the raid and scouting the planned landing area. They rented vehicles, and on the night of the attack, under the cover of a conveniently planned air raid on an oil refinery at Sidon, some forty-five kilometres to the south, they simply drove up to meet the commandos at the beach.

Fouling the water in the quiet bay and across the sand was a layer of litter. Plastic bags, burned chicken bones, orange and grapefruit peelings, and papers were everywhere, mixed with clumps of oil. As the weather became warmer, the sand would eventually be raked. Summer bathers would still have to wash off smears of oil, using rags and cans of gasoline that municipal authorities occasionally supplied on the strand. The Israeli force of eight armed commandos waded in from their boats through the fetid, oily refuse.

Tires spun in the sand beside the road as the four vehicles and their passengers turned north onto the main road, heading into the residential area of Verdun and approaching the Sabra camp.

In little more than half an hour, the three Palestinian leaders were gunned down in their homes, along with several guards and Mohammed al Najjar's wife. This fuelled additional conflict between the PLO and Lebanese security forces, many members of which supported this attack on the Palestinians. Days of political feuding failed to overcome the embarrassment to President Franjieh of foreign intervention and conflict between religious factions.

CHAPTER FOUR

SHEMLAN

Alexander Matheson, a young foreign service officer on his first posting at the Canadian Embassy in Beirut, sat through the second day of a week-long course at the Middle East Centre for Arabic Studies (MECAS). The centre was in a complex of stone buildings in Shemlan, high in the hills above Beirut. He sat on an unforgiving chair in a traditional, pale-green-painted schoolroom with wooden tables arranged in a rectangle.

Along with a dozen colleagues from various embassies and agencies, he listened to the afternoon lecture on the convoluted political history of Lebanon since the Ottomans had been driven out in World War I. Paying attention was becoming increasingly difficult. The day was warm, and having only arrived in the country the previous autumn, Matheson wasn't acclimatized to the weather. He didn't feel properly dressed for it either, finding even the early spring quite warm in his too-heavy blazer and slacks. The substantial lunch they had enjoyed hadn't helped. His eyes drooped as the undoubtedly distinguished presenter droned on. The presenter had been through the same material far too many times, and it seemed he wasn't finding it very stimulating either.

MECAS had been established in the Lebanese mountains by the British Foreign Office in the 1940s, when it was moved from Jerusalem to Lebanon. It had built on an outstanding reputation for its Arabic language courses, with a range of others including history, contemporary politics, and cultural awareness. The centre, destined to be closed a few years later during the Lebanese civil war, was known in the region as the "school for spies." Generations of British security services officials had been trained there, including the infamous MI6 agent and traitor George Blake.

In an effort to focus his attention, Matheson took a drink of tepid water from a jug, adjusted his striped silk tie, and sat straighter. An administrator—overweight, grey-haired, and (notwithstanding the heat) wearing a tweed jacket and heavy flannel pants—hurried into the room and interrupted the speaker.

"Ladies and gentlemen, I am dreadfully sorry to disturb you, but we are forced to close the centre for the day. There has been an outbreak of fighting in Beirut, and we ask all non-resident students to return to the city. We have organized an army escort for you and ask that you remain in a convoy until you are close to your neighbourhood. Thank you for your cooperation. We will inform you when the course is to resume."

The students gathered their books and papers and hurried out onto the long stone terrace outside the lecture room. Down the mountainside, past the slopes covered with a canopy of graceful pines and toward the sparkling sea, was the city of Beirut. The magnificent setting was marred by half a dozen columns of black smoke rising from the city. They could hear the faint sounds of the detonation of rockets fired from and toward the southern sector, where Palestinian camps dominated the area.

Matheson thought anxiously of his pregnant wife and his daughter, who were at home in their apartment in the upscale residential and commercial area of Raouché. He went down the stairs with his colleagues to the courtyard in front of the main buildings, where four light army vehicles were waiting as escorts. After a brief discussion with the group about the route, Matheson got into his blue Volvo sedan and joined the convoy of ten vehicles, including the military units.

The army vehicles led the way, moving at speed along the road from the hills, down the steep, winding road away from Shemlan, and taking a sharp right to the village of Fsaquine, past unfinished, small concrete houses and apartment buildings. Matheson saw they were set into rocky hillsides with terraced olive trees and gardens showing their green with the spring rains. They sped through Aramoun, where the vehicles scattered a line of squealing little girls, in their light-blue school tunics, who were walking beside the dusty road. Minutes later, the vehicles dove down onto the coastal plain, joining the major Sidon-Beirut highway just south of the airport.

The military vehicles accelerated on the wide coast road and were waved through a roadblock, set up by the Lebanese military, near the airport. They closed quickly on the area where the Palestinian camps in the near distance were under fire, and rocket fire was seen coming into and leaving the camps. The convoy swept by and veered left up the hill leading onto the corniche along the seafront. All seemed suddenly peaceful amongst the glittering modern apartment blocks that promised the security of the city proper. As agreed with the escort, moments later, Matheson turned abruptly to the right around a corner and brought his car to a skidding stop behind his apartment building, scattering two frightened street cats rummaging through the fetid garbage piles nearby.

Why can't they pick up the rubbish? Alex thought. He got out of his car across the street from a malodorous, six-foot-high, forty-foot-long heap of refuse that had been there since they had moved in. Added to daily from the neighbouring apartments and businesses, the pile was reduced periodically when someone would set it on fire, but the stench of burning garbage lasted for days as the pile smouldered. "Beirut, the Paris of the East," he said to himself with a grin.

CHAPTER FIVE

BEIRUT

"Hello, sir. Have you heard about the events?" asked Hani Hassan, the Palestinian caretaker of the building, as he came into the lobby out of the back hallway. Hani was a short man in his forties, almost dumpy, and wore a pair of tan pants and a colourful shirt. On top of that, he wore a used, brown suede jacket that Alex had given to him a few weeks earlier.

"Yes, I have, Hani. Is everything quiet here?" asked Matheson, walking in the door and crossing the highly polished marble foyer.

"Oh yes, sir. The fighting is mostly in the camps. It will always be quiet in this district. The best in Beirut. Your family will be well in my building, sir."

"Thank you, Hani. *Insh'allah,*[1]" replied Matheson as he swung open the door of the small, carpeted elevator and stepped inside.

The two-person elevator rose slowly to the sixth floor, where it stopped with its usual solid *clunk.* Matheson opened the door with its complaining screech of hinges and stepped into the dark, small landing that served only one apartment per floor of the building. He pushed the button beside his apartment door for the hall light, fumbling for his house keys in his haste. Opening the door, he called out, "Elizabeth, I'm home."

"Yes, we're in here," said his wife from behind the light-brown marble wall that divided the entrance from the large living room. As he

---

1 God willing.

rounded the corner, he saw Elizabeth, coolly dressed in a pair of light green, shantung-silk maternity slacks and a loose white blouse. Smiling from beneath her short, blonde curls, she looked up from where she was sitting on the dark red sofa, reading to their almost-three-year-old daughter, Sarah. The little one was wearing a favourite t-shirt and blue shorts and had auburn hair, unusually thick and long for her age.

She squirmed off her mum's lap and ran toward the hall. Squealing, "Daddy!" she jumped into his arms, giving him a huge hug. Burying her head in his neck, Sarah laughed while Alex held her tightly and gave her a hug and tickle in return as her hair swirled around her head.

"Oh, it is so lovely to see you, my beautiful people. I guess you've heard all about the fighting this afternoon?" said Alex as he leaned over to kiss Elizabeth.

"We're just fine," she replied. "I'm not surprised that you're back early. The embassy called to say your course was interrupted and that you'd be coming home. Nadia, from the nursery school, called at noon, and I took a taxi to pick up Sarah, as they wanted to close. I've been quite concerned, but it's amazing how you get used to having these conflicts so close by. By the way, the office wants you to call when you get in. There've been lots of sirens on the corniche. From the balcony, we can see the rockets hitting the Sabra and Shatila camps, and the smoke going up. It's so horrible to think that there are people at that end. Come outside and have a look."

Elizabeth heaved herself up and walked to the wide glass doors, where she stepped out onto the terra-cotta-tiled balcony across the front of the apartment and sat on the bamboo furniture. "The Lebanese forces are really punishing the Palestinians today. There's been a lot of smoke, and you can see some fires. Of course, as a good Beiruti," she laughed, "while Sarah had her nap after lunch, I brought my tea out on the balcony to watch."

"It's a real concern, but fortunately, it hasn't affected this part of the city at all—yet, anyway," said Alex. "I'll call the office and find out the latest."

Alex called the embassy to say that he was home, and all was well. In exchange, he received a news update from Raymond, the duty officer. Raymond reported that fighting was dying down, as the Lebanese President, Franjieh, had convened a group of officials and security representatives to meet with a Palestinian delegation, at the presidential palace, to try to bring the fighting to a halt. Nevertheless, they advised that officers and family members should avoid going out until the situation cleared.

Alex poured two fingers of Famous Grouse blended whisky for himself. He and Elizabeth sat outside on the balcony while Sarah played with a jigsaw puzzle on the floor. The cool of the evening came in from the sea as they talked through the day, and Alex related the excitement of the escorted drive from Shemlan.

"They're really concerned at the embassy that this conflict will become more intense rather than be resolved, Elizabeth. We'll have to watch developments closely. Maybe we should think about you taking Sarah and going back to your family in Vancouver until the baby's born," Alex said.

"I hope it doesn't come to that." Elizabeth looked anxious. "I so want us to be together when I have the baby. Let's see how things go and not decide now."

Sarah went to bed about seven o'clock, and as usual, fell asleep while she was being read to. Alex and Elizabeth sat down to a simple dinner of broiled whole fish in garlic butter with asparagus and fresh, warm pita bread. Afterwards, they went back out on the balcony and sat on the comfortable bamboo divan. They enjoyed the spring evening while Elizabeth filled Alex's glass with a light, delicate, and smooth red wine from Chateau Ksara, heir to five thousand years of grape and wine production in the chalky soil of the Bekaa Valley. As she was just starting her eighth month of pregnancy, Elizabeth had to settle for yet another cup of tea.

Around eleven o'clock, the Mathesons checked on Sarah and went to bed to read.

CHAPTER SIX

As darkness fell, the city calmed after the afternoon of fierce exchanges of gunfire and rockets between the Palestinian camps in the south of Beirut and the Lebanese army. In unusually light traffic, no doubt a reflection of the troubles of the day, an old, sun-faded, grey and red Mercedes diesel taxi drove along the corniche toward Pigeon Rock and turned right, just before the Shell Building, into the residential area of Raouché. It slowed to a halt at the second cross street. A man got out wearing beaten and faded workman's pants and a filthy, collarless t-shirt under his flannel shirt. He wore a faded black and white chequered keffiyeh wrapped tightly around his head. The man was carrying a long package of soiled, rolled canvas or cloth that looked like his bedding.

As the taxi turned the corner and moved off, he walked slowly, slightly favouring one leg, across the street and into the dark site of an unfinished apartment building. He settled himself in the deep shadows of bare concrete pillars and piles of building materials, looking like a worker on the building site. He unwrapped the roll, taking out a well-oiled AK-47 automatic weapon. Setting it carefully on the cloth, he sat on a broken cement block.

Beside the construction site was an ochre apartment building with large, red-tiled balconies on the south side, looking toward the Mediterranean. Its green canvas awnings were designed to keep out the worst of the direct rays of the sun. Hani, the concierge, padded in his carpet slippers from the two small rooms he and his family lived in, behind the stone wall of the lobby, to check the lock on the front door. Then he turned away, ready for his day to begin again barely six hours later.

The night became increasingly quiet, save for a speaker on the fourth floor of the building across the street that was blaring out the songs of the ageless Lebanese diva Fairouz, some of them soft and compelling, others accompanied by the clanging and banging of Arabic instruments. As the music was first turned down, then off, the sounds of sporadic gunfire could be heard coming from the south and east. Heavy old women in the kitchens washed up the last of the dishes while men smoked and talked in low tones to friends on the balconies. One by one, the lights gradually flickered out. The man in the construction site alternately sat or crouched on his haunches, guarding the touches of light from his Cedar brand cigarettes with cupped hands. He watched vigilantly as the occasional vehicle approached from one end of the street or another and drove by.

CHAPTER SEVEN

BAABDA

Late in the night, at the presidential palace in Baabda, representatives of the president's office and parliament, plus half a dozen Palestinian representatives, walked down the largely darkened marble corridors from their meeting room. Wearing a well-tailored tan silk suit, the woman on the Palestinian delegation walked smartly. The click of her heels resounded through the otherwise sleeping office corridors.

Through the traditional Islamic arches that fronted the low-slung building, the delegates left the building and went into the humid night. They were struck by the strong scent of the pink oleander flowers in the garden. An exhausting night of negotiation had resulted in a fragile consensus to a ceasefire, even though the fundamental issues separating the parties remained unresolved and promised to remain that way. Several cars parked in the circular drive around the fountain and gardens had started up and moved to the front to pick up their charges.

Amina al Omeri sat down heavily in the back seat as Mahmoud, her driver, held the door for her. Looking in the rear-view mirror as they drove off, Mahmoud saw the strain on her face from the frustrating and largely ineffectual discussions, as well as from the late hour. She longed only to get home to rest and to see her beloved son, Salim. He was being cared for by her maid, and she hoped, would long since have been in bed asleep.

Her late husband, Suleiman, had been born in the late 1930s in Akka, Palestine. He'd been the scion of a well-to-do family closely associated with an important Sufi Islamic sect long established in the ancient city. With mentions in history for some four thousand years, Akka was proud of its past. It is said it is a city that the Canaanites held against the Israelites when they came from Egypt. Since that time, Phoenicians, Greeks, Romans, Islamic Caliphs, Christian Crusaders, Ottomans, and others had tramped through the city leaving boot tracks, cultural influences, and progeny.

Through education and a habit of learned family discussions, Suleiman had come to appreciate the continuum of history as well as the cultural influences brought by invaders over thousands of years. This background had led him to develop a tempered approach to the issues of his region. As a boy, he'd shared his community's stress from the influx of European Jews, supported in the region by the militant group Irgun. Their leaders had maintained that every Jew had a right to immigrate to Palestine, and furthermore, that they had a right to retaliate with arms when the overwhelmingly numerous native Arab population resisted.

The ancient city was populated by Muslims, Druze, Jews, Christians, and Baha'i. A walk through the narrow and often dark stone passageways, mosques, bustling markets, and a mosaic of back lanes was periodically broken by sporadic views of the sparkling blue Mediterranean. This proved to be a metaphor for Suleiman's unusually broad perspective and understanding of the prospect for the native Palestinian people. As a young man, he'd been drawn by his family's cultural attachment to the emerging activist Palestinian cause. He'd studied engineering at the American University of Beirut, where his respected family credentials, upbringing, and intelligence made him stand out amongst fellow students. As a father, he'd loved to talk to his son and instill a respect for that history into him.

"Well, Mahmoud," Amina said from the back seat, "I'm sorry to keep you from your family so late, but the situation is very difficult. Recent events need to be dealt with. I'm sure you're as tired as I am. I really want to get home to Salim."

Mahmoud could tell from her voice how exhausted she was. "Madame, I am here for you any time. You will soon be home and can rest."

"That is certainly something I could use." She sighed.

CHAPTER EIGHT

BEIRUT

The gunman tensed as the lights from a new black Mercedes turned into the street from a block away. As the purring car slowed in front of the ochre building beside where he was skulking in the shadows, he raised his weapon. Quickly and silently, he stepped through the dust to the corner of the construction site closest to the lobby of the neighbouring building. *I will be well paid for this, and my family will eat*, he thought.

"Thank you, Mahmoud," he heard the woman say as the driver held the car door open for her. "Please pick me up at eight o'clock in the morning."

Mahmoud turned and reached out to open the building door for her.

The gunman spat, stepped forward and began firing. One long burst from the AK-47 tore into Amina just as she entered the apartment building. She pitched forward, blood spurting from head wounds and her torn chest. He continued firing, hitting Mahmoud several times as the driver reached to help the woman to whom he had been so loyal. He fell over her into the lobby, screaming. All the glass in the lobby was shattered, and pieces fell from the rock wall behind. The aluminum posts holding the sheets of glass twisted, and several clattered onto the marble floor.

The gunman retreated to the shadows. Seconds later, his taxi came silently around the corner. He walked calmly to the car and got in. It then drove away at normal speed. The street was deathly quiet.

Mahmoud crawled to Amina, who was soaked in blood. The side of her head was blown away. He couldn't believe the amount of blood that was splattered throughout the foyer. Cautiously, he slithered through the slimy wreckage toward the protection of a corner. Bracing himself against the wall, he reached for the elevator door.

CHAPTER NINE

The Matheson family was sleeping fitfully after the events of the day when a drawn-out burst of automatic weapons fire—seemingly within the building—woke them abruptly. Alex jumped up and looked out the window. The street was empty, and all was apparently quiet. Elizabeth, her nerves already on edge during the late stages of her pregnancy, sat bolt upright, flushed, wide-eyed, and fearful.

"I don't see anyone or anything outside," Alex said.

They heard the *thump, thump, thump* of Sarah's little bare feet running down the marble-floored hall toward their bedroom. She leapt into bed and nestled into her mother's arms, whimpering. Alex realized that there had been no further shooting in the seconds since the gunfire. He looked out the side window again to see an old grey and red Mercedes taxi pull away from the building and then turn, one street away.

In shock, they sat quietly in bed, trying to process what might have happened. The stifling silence was broken as they heard the elevator cables start to move. Elizabeth gasped for breath. The sound of the moving elevator crept closer and stopped with a familiar *clunk* at their sixth floor. The elevator door opened, giving its usual sharp, metallic complaint. A heartbeat later, there was heavy hammering on the front door. Hair rising on the nape of his neck and cold shock sweeping through his body, Alex jumped for the phone. He hastily dialled the security brigade from a list of emergency numbers beside the bed. Hurriedly explaining who he was, he gabbled the address and recounted what had happened. Elizabeth gripped Sarah tightly and slid further under the covers.

Seconds later, with no further knock on the door and no more shooting, Alex crept cautiously into the front hall to look through the peephole. As he leaned in toward the door, the hammering resumed right at his ear, which seemed to vibrate with the blows. His heart leapt to his mouth. He heard Elizabeth give a brief cry of shock from the bedroom. Trying to lean over as much as possible so as not to expose himself to the door in case of more shooting, Alex looked through the opening. He saw the vague outline of a man standing back from the door. He was only just visible in the half light from a glass block window in the side of the staircase. Alex couldn't tell if the figure was carrying a weapon.

A shaking voice said, "Telephone."

"*La*, no, not here," Alex stammered.

The man outside the door hesitated and then turned and lurched down the stairs, shuffling on the steps. Alex heard brief shouting from a lower floor; then all went quiet. He returned to the bedroom, where his wife and daughter were just beginning to breathe normally again.

"Oh Alex, what's happening?" said Elizabeth, shaking and white with fear, holding Sarah closely. Sarah's eyes were wide open, and she seemed shocked into silence.

"Thank goodness there's been no more shooting," said Alex, trying to reassure them. "This must have been a family dispute, and it's now over. This is Lebanon, after all. Don't worry; it must have been a domestic incident, not an expansion of the fighting to this area."

As they anxiously awaited the arrival of the security forces, Alex called the night duty officer at the embassy and explained what had happened. The DO undertook to call the police and follow up with the security brigade. Fumbling in the dark, Alex pulled on some jeans and a sweater and sat back down on the bed. The three of them stayed huddled close together, talking quietly to calm each other. An interminable twenty minutes later, the wail of a siren approached. By that time, Sarah had drifted back to sleep and was put back in bed.

Alex and Elizabeth went out on the balcony, an arm around each other, and saw a lone ambulance and a police car stopped in front of the building, lights flashing. In the sweep of the emergency lights, people in night clothes watched from the six storeys of balconies across the street. Three or four men from other buildings walked in the street, peering at what was going on. Two ambulance attendants went into the apartment building where the Mathesons lived, emerging a few minutes later, bringing first one and then a second person out on stretchers. They loaded them into the ambulance and drove away with the siren wailing. The police vehicle followed. No security brigade forces or police ever came or called back.

In the caretaker's rooms, Hani and his wife, Zeina, had been awakened by the gunfire as they slept in their tiny bedroom. They rushed into their living and kitchen area, where Ali slept on a cot pulled out at night from behind an old, heavy couch. Ali was standing on the cot, holding onto the bars on the small, dirty side window looking out into the street. His mother rushed to him, enveloped him in her arms, and wailed with distress at the events.

An hour later, a well-dressed, elderly man arrived in a large, black Mercedes, followed by a dark blue GMC van. Four hard, armed men got out of the vehicles. The grey-haired man and two of the other men entered the building. After a few minutes, they left in the limo, taking away Amina's son, Salim, and her maid.

The next morning, after a restless night and an always-early start by their daughter, Elizabeth and Alex pulled themselves together. They made their morning tea and talked through the events of the past night while Sarah ate porridge. Warmed and rejuvenated by the hot liquid, Alex went to the door, where he expected Hani would have brought up the morning paper. Turning the lock and opening the door, he cried out in alarm. The carpet was darkly stained, and the door smeared, with what looked like drying blood. The air smelled vaguely like the sweet, metallic odour of a butcher shop. He turned on the landing light. Bloody handprints marred the yellowish paint in a chain going down the stairs, and smears of blood covered the elevator door.

"Whoever was at the door must have been badly wounded," he called from the hall to Elizabeth. "There's blood all over the landing. Don't come out here. I'm going downstairs to find out what happened."

"Be careful, Alex!" Elizabeth cautioned.

Alex stepped around the drying, dark stains, their sharp smell reaching his nostrils. He called the elevator and stepped into it carefully, avoiding the large splotch of blood on the carpet inside. After descending in the elevator, he found the small lobby of the apartment destroyed. Blood was sprayed everywhere, the three walls of glass were shattered, aluminum supports were twisted or broken, and pieces of rockface had fallen from the back wall. Bits of hair and teeth could be seen in pools of blood on the floor.

Hani was busy sweeping up the wreckage as if it were a normal morning. "Oh sir, you and Madame are well, and your little one? I am so sorry for these happenings. I will have it cleaned very soon."

"Yes, Hani, thank you. But what happened?"

"Madame from the top floor was killed last night, and her driver, Mahmoud, badly injured. He may not live. It is his blood on the elevator. After the attack, he went up to Madame Amina's apartment and then to the floor below you where her brother lives. Her brother could do little for them. You know she worked for the PLO and was attacked when she came home late last night. No one saw any shooters, and they must have left quickly."

"This is dreadful, Hani. Do you know why it might have happened? Have the police been here?"

"No, sir, no police. I will finish this cleaning now, sir." Hani turned his back and resumed his mopping and sweeping, clearly wanting to get the job done, his report having been delivered.

Alex returned to the apartment and called the embassy to report on the night's developments. He asked that Lebanese intelligence be contacted to see if they had any information, as even in Lebanon, this was clearly not just a domestic dispute. They had nothing to add yet regarding the events.

THE STRUGGLE CONTINUES

A crowd gathered outside the building, shouting and jostling with the excitement of the scene in front of them. They pushed and gaped at the carnage and blood stains, seemingly hoping to see cadavers.

Ali came out from behind the rock wall and tiptoed around the debris to join his father, who was going outside to respond to the demands for an explanation from the onlookers. The boy looked drawn and shaken.

Hani spoke to the anxious crowd. He identified the victims as Amina Omeri from the seventh floor and her driver, Mahmoud, who was badly wounded and likely now dead. A wave of reaction and speculation washed over the crowd. The usual frantic exchange of assumptions and fabricated details of the incident carried on. Arguments began about what had happened and why. Hani assured the gathering that he had seen nothing, and that there was no further information about the murder.

On turning to go back into the building, Ali whispered to his father, "As I said in the night, Father, I saw someone from the side window after the shooting. A man walked out quickly from in front of our building and got into a taxi. He had a small limp. I saw him in the street once in the past few days when I was coming home from school, and another time, around dark when I took out the garbage."

"Quiet!" said Hani sharply, turning to his son. "You did not see anything and will not talk about this. There is no way to tell who is on which side and why Madame was killed. Life can be brutal. Your wellbeing is important to me and your mother. Take care, Ali. Stay away from these troubles."

The street gradually returned to normal in the early morning as the heat rose and people got on with their daily activities. Men occupied their usual places on the benches in front of the drycleaners across the street, smoking and drinking coffee. Many lounged in their flannel pyjama pants and scratched themselves through their undershirts. Periodically, they looked up from the endless games of backgammon they called "tric trac." The men sat impassively as they watched Hani clear away the shattered glass and wash away the blood in the entrance foyer of the apartment building. They talked interminably. By the end of the day, the events had been grossly exaggerated, and many claimed to be the only witnesses. One police car came by briefly in the late afternoon and paused outside, but there was no apparent investigation into the previous evening's attack.

CHAPTER TEN

DAMOUR 1974

The teenaged boy took a shot with his soccer ball at a small net propped against a stone wall and missed wide. He stumbled on the rough ground as he chased his ball into a large patch of pink oleanders. He slipped on the gravel once more, scuffing the seat of his old denim pants as he hit the ground. Months earlier, Ali Hassan and his family had moved some twenty kilometres south of Beirut to the town of Damour, on the coastal road.

Concerned someone would hear that Ali might be able to identify the killer, Ali's parents had made the decision to leave Beirut. Before they could put a plan into effect, the murdered woman's father-in-law, who owned the apartment building, had sold it. On notice of only two days, as could so easily happen to Palestinian workers, Hani had been relieved of his job by the new owner and left to find somewhere else to live and work.

They moved into a three-room cinder-block house with Dalia, her husband, Sami Hadawi, and their daughter, Fatima. Dalia had been a friend of Zeina's since they were small children, and the couples had become close over the years. Dalia, who was short and heavy-set, sold vegetables from a small, wooden cart that she pushed through the town for an owner whose only thought was that all the vegetables must be sold. This was his view regardless of their condition, or else Dalia would have to pay for them. Sami collected used and scrap items and had built a small business with contacts throughout the area. Hani rode with him in his dented and scraped old van, which no one could imagine would run, and helped load materials, metals, and other scrap items that Sami felt could be sold or traded.

"*Yellah*[2] Ali, let's go," cried Fatima as she pulled him up, raced him around the corner of the house, and headed inside. "It's time to eat."

Ali felt close to Fatima, a girl just a year older than him. She was just over five feet tall and had lustrous dark hair and sparkling eyes. She was a clever and active girl, always ready to kick the ball and spend time with her friend. Ali had settled into Damour and his new school over the past months. Being the newcomer, he had been subjected to some teasing and bullying, but it was going all right.

It was Fatima who encouraged him in his schoolwork, played with him, and showed him she was his best friend in times of loneliness and stress. He needed that comfort when he had to deal with the rough boys at his small school. The area where they lived was populated mainly by Christian families who looked down on their few (and usually poorer) Palestinian neighbours. Ali missed the life he had left behind in Beirut, but he soon made friends with Marwan, a boy from school who lived very close by. Marwan's house was little more than a shed and not well suited for a family of parents and four children, yet they had been there for some years and seemed content.

Marwan's young uncle, Aduan, who often came around, was a fighter with the Palestine Liberation Army (PLA). He was only ten years older than the boys, and they looked up to him as a hero. Tall and very fit, he had an open and friendly personality. Whenever he visited, he spent time with Ali and Marwan. They hung on his every word about the training he was receiving as a fighter in Palestinian camps, and Marwan talked about how they would fight together in years to come.

Ali was a good student and helpful in the house to Dalia and his mother, who ran it together and expected the children to do their

---

2   Come on, or hurry up.

share. His quiet, thoughtful manner set him apart from much of the rough and tumble of the playground. He had actually seen real violence, and the bloodletting it brought, so he rejected it. Ali disliked the constant schoolyard and street talk of fighting and retribution. It didn't matter to him if it was against the Israelis. He knew they had driven his family from their village in Palestine years earlier to settle Eastern European Jews, but he felt much the same about the Christians who ran Beirut and treated his people worse than feral animals. *There must be a better way than fighting,* he thought.

Ali and Marwan liked to walk up the hills to the Delhamyeh golf club where Christian boys could earn a few *livres* caddying for golfers. The two of them scoured the thorny bushes for errant golf balls and made a few *piasters* when they turned them over to the Christian boys, who would sell them to golfers. Ali was coming to realize that he and the other Muslim boys would always be left on the fringes and never allowed to move up the food chain.

The boys would also run through the hills above the banana plantations on the coast, where they heard that a militia supporting a former president and Christian political leader, Camille Chamoun, had a militia training camp. As they climbed through the dry scrub and stunted pines, the boys could sometimes hear the sound of automatic weapons fire over the hills. With teenage bravado, they told each other that one day they would go farther and find the camp. Ali knew, however, that his parents would be extremely angry if he were to do that, and he would pay a price, at least in extra duties around the house.

One day, as the boys walked, they heard the piercing scream of military jets and watched as a MIG with Syrian markings thundered close by over their heads. It barely scraped over the scrub pines on the hilltop, chased by an Israeli Air Force jet. A stream of gunfire from the Israeli plane sprayed out as the Syrian shot ahead and pulled up to avoid the deadly fire. Ali and Marwan ducked behind some large rocks. They could actually feel the heat of the exhaust and were struck by the pungent odour of jet fuel burning as the pilot climbed rapidly. As the Israeli swept up and fired again, the Syrian plane paused, tumbled, and plunged straight down over a hilltop. Seconds later, the boys heard an explosion and saw a huge plume of smoke and fire burst into the sky. The Israeli plane climbed, circled, and flew off over the sea.

That night, Ali animatedly told his story to the family over dinner. His father and Sami explained that a war had just begun between the Israelis and the Syrians. This was a conflict that, in a few days' time, would see much of President Assad's armed forces decimated. Large parts of southern Syria were invaded by the Israelis. Populations were driven out of farms, villages, and towns.

"Be careful, Ali," said his father. "It may be exciting to see this action, but there is nothing positive about this fighting, and it will do nothing for the Palestinians. Although the Israelis have been our enemies since they drove us from our land in Palestine, we have no friends of any nationality or denomination here."

"But, Father," said Ali, "we have no reason not to have a good life here if we try to fit into the community."

"No, Ali, it's not that easy. Remember that we are only reluctantly received as guests in this country and are barely tolerated by any of the political parties or the Lebanese people. You must not take the side of anyone in these conflicts, for you do not always know where others stand."

At Marwan's house, the tone was different. Marwan encountered bitterness and invective from his father, Fouad, who blamed almost everyone for their sorry state. His mother, Mona, had heard the story many times. The family had been driven out of their village on the outskirts of Suhmata in 1948, when Fouad was a boy. The ancient town, which contained buildings from the Crusader times, was destroyed by Israeli forces, and the population dispersed. When the invading forces had come to move them out, Fouad's father and mother were killed defending the farmhouse where their family had lived and worked for generations. Fouad often reminded his wife and children of the trials of his family and how he had spent years scraping by and being abused by settlers, and later, by the Lebanese. Since then, he had never worked as more than a day labourer. He always said that it was Marwan's responsibility to struggle to regain the property that had been stolen from them and the self-respect that had been wrenched out of them. It was this atmosphere that encouraged Marwan to think that violence had its place.

CHAPTER ELEVEN

LEBANESE MOUNTAINS, JUNE 1974

Salim Omeri was a student at a long-established private school, where his parents expected he would be exposed to a broad perspective on the world and meet a wide variety of fellow students, admittedly wealthy but with diverse backgrounds. His paternal grandfather, Yazid, who had arrived to take him away from the horror of the night his mother was murdered, and with whom he now lived, was a distinguished professor of classical history. Yazid had a close relationship with Salim. He tried to balance the pressures of modern life on the boy with quiet evenings talking about the past, recounting stories from their rich family history and his own experiences when he was a boy in their houses in the mountains. Yazid had respected his late daughter-in-law, Amina, and her success in taking over the role his son had played within the Palestinian community.

Yazid was esteemed for the depth of his knowledge and traditional ways. He was a person with gravitas and had extensive contacts throughout the Lebanese and Palestinian communities of many denominations throughout the region. Political, media, academic, and religious figures in these communities often consulted him. He well knew how to deal with people—a trait he saw in his grandson and tried to nurture.

Salim woke up and stretched in the great, soft bed in his grandfather's house where he had often stayed on weekends but now lived permanently. His sadness over the death of his mother, Amina, was with him always. In the more than a year since that had happened, he was coming to cope with his loss and was looking ahead. He walked out onto the sunny stone patio off his room and looked down the valley toward the sea. The sun came up every day, bringing a new perspective, he was told. His grandfather encouraged him to recognize things in life that should not be and to look to the future and how those things might be rectified.

Salim, like many an only child, tended to have an easy relationship with adults and to be content with his own company. He had matured to the point where he'd realized that some thoughtful work and extra effort in his studies and writing brought good returns in school. His academic record and positive attitude had allowed him to stay in the mountains for the months until the end of the school year after his mother's death. The following year, he became a boarding student and on holidays, returned to his grandfather's house in the mountains.

That night, his grandfather planned to host a small gathering of prominent Palestinian leaders, and as he had once before, suggested to Salim that he be present. The conflict between the Lebanese government, private militias, and the Palestinians continued, albeit at a less frenzied pace. Fatah,[3] taking the political leadership of the Palestinians, had asked Yazid and other respected advisors to meet to discuss the situation and future political actions.

Late in the afternoon, a van carrying half a dozen armed men in fatigues arrived at the villa. After a brief discussion with Yazid, they toured the house, inside and out, and positioned themselves to secure access to the property. In the kitchen, maids were preparing food and the coffee, tea, and endless rounds of fruit juices that would be served later. The smell from the food—including a selection of katoufi pastries, hummus, nuts, dolmas, and yogurt with mint and garlic—filled the air. Salim loved the grilled and buttered

---

[3] Originally formed as a Palestinian political party in the 1950s by Yasser Arafat.

pita breads covered with za'atar, his favourite spice mixture made from thyme, sumac, and roasted sesame seeds.

The large living room had highly polished flagstone floors, heavy leather couches, and velvet drapes with the colour and sheen of polished chestnuts. These were tied back by vibrant sashes in rich golden and electric green threads with heavy, woven knots and fringes at the end. In the centre of the room, a glowing charcoal burner was tended to by the maids, who periodically sprinkled small pieces of frankincense resin on the coals, bringing an alluring and restful scent to the room. In one corner of the room was a highly polished table with bottles of soft drinks, whisky, arak, and glasses.

The visitors arrived after dark—some old, others younger. One arrived anonymously, driving his own old Peugeot. Another came in the usual local grey taxi, but with a driver and another fit, hard man in the front seat, both wearing fatigues. Others came in new Land Rovers or other fancy European cars, accompanied by their own bodyguards in a van or pickup truck. Yazid greeted them all at the door. He embraced them warmly and kissed them on both cheeks. Nonetheless, he and Salim could sense tensions as the guests shook hands or embraced the others in the room.

Throughout the evening, Salim sat at the back, listening to his grandfather guide the discussion on political and military developments in Lebanon and Syria and recounting stories and opinions forwarded from colleagues in Israel and the West Bank. The conversation stressed the political elements, and participants added their own perspectives. Led by Yazid, they moved to discuss the needs of the huge populations in the refugee communities that were coming under increasing pressure in South Lebanon from the Lebanese military and private militias. There were few allusions to the often-trying relationships between various Palestinian groups that were vying for power and influence, or to the military planning that was dealt with elsewhere.

Late in the evening, Yazid rose to thank the participants and to suggest that they would meet in perhaps a month, at a time to be determined. They moved toward the door talking, embracing, and performing the rituals of leaving as their drivers and guards brought the vehicles to the front of the house. Naef al Wazir, a senior Fatah representative, stood back, waiting for most to leave and calling to Salim to join him. They sat beside a large window looking over the garden.

Moments later, Yazid joined them and expressed satisfaction that the discussions that night had been useful and cooperative. "I was pleased with how the discussions went tonight. Everyone held their tongues and most of their usual biases," he said with a chuckle.

"This is a valuable group for all of us, but it does change with time. Not all the members are as young as our Salim," Naef said with a chuckle, clasping him on the shoulder. The three of them laughed. It was clear that Naef wanted to say more.

"I enjoy hearing the exchanges of views," said Salim, "and can see that it's not always easy for so many strong-minded men to contain their opinions of each other."

"How true, Salim. Thankfully, the respect they have for your grandfather helps keep the discussion in check. Chairman Arafat is aware of the dedication of your family to the Palestinian cause over many years. He had a particularly admiring and warm relationship with your mother, Amina. We all regret that she was killed and reflect with bitterness that no official investigation seems to have taken place to identify those responsible."

"I know this isn't easy, Salim, but the plight of our people is such that there are more things happening behind closed doors or in the darkness of our lives than we can always determine," said Yazid.

"We have looked very closely at the incident ourselves, without being able to determine who are the real culprits," Wazir continued. "From our inquiries, we can see that one possibility is that the responsible party may be the government of Lebanon itself. They would have been feeling intense pressure from the Phalangist Christian forces to continue the fighting. Their forces claim that they would have ultimately destroyed the Palestinian forces in this country. The instigator could also have been the Israelis, as they too would clearly like to see the fighting continue. Finally, we cannot rule out that the murder could have been committed by some of our Palestinian brothers, as your mother was seeking a ceasefire when she was killed. Some could have seen the path to greater power in continuing, even if it meant a Palestinian defeat."

"It's difficult to imagine all the different forces at play," said Salim.

"Salim," said Yazid, "you are growing up in a difficult neighbourhood, and not all of the neighbours are friendly. In fact, it could have been any combination of these parties that was responsible."

"Those are all credible possibilities for the instigation of the attack on your mother, Salim. We may never know who actually ordered it, but that is unfortunately part of our lives," said Wazir.

"I can hardly bear the pain of the loss, Grandfather," said Salim, "but I so appreciate the care you are providing to me." Then he turned his head back toward the Fatah official. "I know that I must do my best to learn the challenges of the neighbourhood, as you put it, *Sayed*[4] Naef."

"Looking ahead, Salim," said Wazir, "I am pleased to bring the news that Chairman Arafat wants to help you grow into the family responsibilities. Accordingly, he would like to see you go abroad for your schooling. He's prepared to pay all your school-related and travel expenses and will provide a monthly stipend for living."

"That is wonderful, Salim," said Yazid. "This will better ensure your safety and allow you to broaden your international view as your parents would have wanted. I was aware that this offer was to be made and am fully supportive. However, I will so miss having you in the house and our evening discussions."

"In return," said Wazir, "the chairman will look to you to mature and be the kind of man who can contribute to our cause. He sends his warmest greetings and would hope to see you periodically when you return to this region on school holidays."

---

4   An honorific or title of respect, "sir."

"Salim," said Yazid, "I see this as a generous offer and a great opportunity indeed. You need to have broader experiences and to spend time with others of your own age, not spend so many evenings playing chess with an old man."

"*Alhamdulillah,*[5] *Sayed* Naef," said Salim. "I am honoured to be so recognized. My parents and grandfather have instilled in me a responsibility to stand for our people. I look forward to the opportunities that this gift will bring me to do that. I am so grateful and will do everything I can to show my appreciation for this honour."

***

Late that summer, Salim and his grandfather were driven to the Beirut airport. They boarded an Air France business-class flight to Paris and spent four nights in a small hotel just off Rue de Passy, close to the Eiffel Tower, getting used to the time change. They found the area elegant and with a rich cultural history.

"Salim," said Yazid as they walked the beautiful streets and boulevards, "this area was home to Benjamin Franklin while he was American Ambassador to France. It was also home to a host of composers and artists, such as Camille Pissarro, the author Honoré de Balzac, and politicians such as Clemenceau. Centuries ago, even scientists were installed in the nearby Château de la Muette by Louis XV. It's an elegant building that was once a royal hunting lodge and is now the headquarters of perhaps the best-regarded economic policy organization in the world: the Organization for Economic Cooperation and Development. The whole of Paris is built on a splendid past, and that is woven into the present."

"Grandfather, you are clearly so enjoying strolling through Paris, pointing out historic sights, and telling me of the culture of France. I really appreciate that. I must say, however, that no part is more enticing than the cream and Nutella crêpes from that outdoor stand

---

5   Thanks be to God.

at Place de la Muette!" Salim said, grabbing at his grandfather's sleeve and pulling him in that direction.

Yazid smiled. "Salim, a city such as this is a reflection of the depth and wealth of their fine culture. You must see what a civilization can do if it appreciates its history and builds on it."

"I can only agree, Grandfather. It is magnificent, but let's get another crêpe!" Salim's eyes gleamed with anticipation.

"Salim," Yazid laughed as they made their way to the Place de la Muette, "we will get another crêpe, but you must remember these sights and the stories I have told you. You have to appreciate that they are reflections of the grandeur of the civilization around us." He stepped around the steaming faeces that a tiny dog had left on the pavement moments before, its elegantly coiffed and dressed owner walking ahead and paying no attention whatsoever, aside from a brief pause while the animal did its business.

"Palestinians have had limited opportunity to build on our history and develop a distinctive society. This society shows what can be done over time. The future Palestine will not look like this, of course, as it must reflect our own culture and history. But for that, we need our land, and we need peace. Remember that. The land issue is very important. We must look back to our cultural beginnings and ahead to the centuries in which it can be nourished and grow. *Insh'allah,* it will happen in time."

CHAPTER TWELVE

NEW YORK, SEPTEMBER 1974

On arrival at JFK airport in New York, Yazid and Salim were met by a young man from the Palestinian Observer Mission to the United Nations. He introduced himself as Ghassan al Hanoud. He was dressed in a dark-grey suit, a light-blue shirt with a button-down collar, and a red tie, all of which made him fit into city life. His hair was slicked back with Brylcreem.

"Welcome to New York, Professor and Master Salim." He declined his head in deference to Yazid as he spoke. "His Excellency Nabil Obeidi has sent me to greet you and take you directly to the school in Connecticut. The ambassador is unfortunately out of town for a few days but has ensured that all of your arrangements are in place."

"Thank you, Ghassan," said Yazid, his eyes conveying his gratitude as much as his words. "I appreciate your kindness and offer my thanks to my old friend Nabil for his attention to our arrival."

"Salim, perhaps you would like to sit in front with the driver so you can see better, and I will sit in the rear with your grandfather," said Ghassan. They climbed into the gleaming, black Lincoln Continental. It drew away smoothly from the terminal and settled into a steady speed along the Van Wyck Expressway, turning onto Interstate 678 through the northern section of the Borough of Queens. They soon crossed the East River on the huge spans of the Whitestone Bridge. Salim, whose eyes could hardly take it all in, marvelled at the giant suspension bridge, a structure many times higher than any he had ever seen.

Ghassan, who had been talking quietly with Yazid in the back seat, leaned ahead and put his arm over the front seat. "Salim, this bridge, and many of those around New York, were designed by an engineer named Othmar Ammann. He almost sounds as if he could be a countryman, but he was born in German Switzerland." He laughed.

They passed through the toll station and onto the leafy Hutchison Parkway, providing some shade on the hot, late summer day. Winding north through Westchester County, they crossed into Connecticut just after the town of Rye. Turning onto a winding secondary road, they drove through an entrance, where there was an ornate, carved, gilded sign marking that they were entering the Stuyvesant School for Boys. Later, Salim was to learn that the school was named after Peter Stuyvesant, the Director-General of the Colony of New Amsterdam in the mid-seventeenth century when the area was first settled by the Dutch.

Yazid and Salim looked ahead to see a cluster of imposing, four-storey limestone buildings on a hillside, arranged around a great lawn. Farther back were a number of more-modern buildings, housing classrooms and laboratories. Several playing fields, a field-house and track, and a large indoor swimming pool were to the left of the central buildings. Four three-storey residence buildings were situated on the right, backed by a dense forest of oaks, sycamore, and maple trees quivering in the light breeze.

"This looks wonderful, Salim," said Yazid. "What a pleasant atmosphere, and the facilities look amazing. This isn't like driving through the dense, diesel-exhaust-spewing traffic in the centre of Beirut to your school, wedged between apartments and illegal factories. This should be very enjoyable. I would like to stay myself!"

Salim laughed at the thought and replied to his grandfather, "Yes, we could compete for grades. This is very exciting, and the school looks wonderful!"

Leaning forward, his grandfather affectionately squeezed Salim's shoulder.

"We only have time to drive through the grounds today," said Ghassan. "Now I will take you into the town of Greenwich and to your hotel." After ensuring they were settled in a small suite in the local Marriott Hotel, Ghassan bade them farewell. "I will return tomorrow morning just before nine o'clock and take you to the school for your scheduled meeting with the headmaster."

"Thank you, Ghassan," said Yazid. "Again, my thanks to the ambassador for being so helpful." He and Salim looked at each other, scarcely believing what they had seen during the day.

CHAPTER THIRTEEN

DAMOUR, 1975

By the mid 1970s, the Palestinians in Lebanon had become increasingly active, and attacks against Israeli border villages multiplied. In retaliation, the Israelis rained artillery fire on the border area, driving the population into the hills and enraging the Palestinian fighters—known as the fedayeen—when they found the Israeli fire following them into their hideouts and sanctuaries. The pattern of their rocket fire into Israeli settlements and retaliatory Israeli air and ground incursions into the region were repeated over and over.

At the same time, tensions between the Palestinians and the Lebanese government grew. Much of the native population, notably the right-wing Christian politicians and their fighters, reacted against the growing Palestinian movement within Lebanon. Rumours circulated that the Christian militias were financed by the Israelis to counter the growing Palestinian threat, and most believed it. In the streets, tension grew, and the ominous mood deepened.

One late afternoon, as Ali and Marwan made their way home from school, a group of some half-dozen older teenagers who lived in the area suddenly emerged from the shadows.

A tall, heavy boy with a crooked sneer and bad skin stepped in front. "You filthy Palestinian dogs must leave Lebanon and take your whores with you," he spat at them. "You are the people who are ruining our country, and you're not welcome in Damour."

One of the others pushed Marwan, and a husky boy moved swiftly to kick his feet out from under him. Ali leapt forward to help his friend but got smashed on the head with a solid stick and fell to the ground. The others moved in quickly, kicking and punching as Ali and Marwan writhed on the street, trying to avoid their blows. The thugs finally backed off, leaving the boys gasping for breath on the ground, blood running from their noses and red welts and ugly black bruises quickly forming on their arms and legs.

"Remember what we said. Next time, your friend Fatima will get to talk to us," the tall leader growled. The attackers laughed and moved off up the road, jostling each other victoriously and feeling pride in their demonstration of manhood.

Ali and Marwan lay still until the gang had moved away. Ali could hear his blood rushing in his ears. Marwan lay on the ground, moaning and clutching his stomach, where he had been kicked. Ali gingerly helped him stand, seeing also that his friend's left wrist was swollen and badly turned. Both had lacerations on their faces. They limped together down the street and into the alley leading to Ali's house.

Almost falling through the door, Ali was caught by Dalia, who screamed at the sight of the blood. His mother, Zeina, turned quickly from the washing dish, throwing her hands in the air and running to hold him. Marwan slumped against the wall. Dalia bolted out the door and returned in minutes with Marwan's mother, Mona, who screamed, wrapped her son in her arms, and sobbed into his neck. After coming into the kitchen to investigate the commotion, Fatima threw her arms around Ali, hugged him, and caressed his bloody, tear-stained cheeks. The mothers tenderly cleaned and treated the boys' cuts and bound Marwan's wrist in a tight bandage.

The boys began to calm down, and soon, Marwan was taken home. He knew that his father would have a great deal to say about the brawl that night. Fatima spent the rest of the afternoon sitting quietly with Ali, chatting and helping him overcome the anguish he felt from the event. Both boys felt humiliated and were determined to never be pushed around like that again. The next afternoon, with Marwan's wrist having been iced overnight and then tightly wrapped, they went to a construction site behind the house, where they found a few cement blocks and some weighty pieces of sandstone.

"Okay, Ali," said Marwan as he scuffed a line in the dirt with his sandal. "Let's see how far we can throw these blocks."

"I bet I can throw it farther than you can, Marwan."

Ali grabbed a concrete building block and raised it to his chest. He heaved it with all his might, watching as it fell only two metres away. Marwan did the same, besting his friend's effort by a small margin. Hands in the air and whooping, but feeling his wrist throbbing, Marwan did a small jig around a circle, as if he had won the bet. They continued with the game, sometimes going for distance and other times trying to land in a drawn circle. The boys left the lot after some time, sweating heavily but vowing to return.

The next day, they did so, and on the third day, both rose from their beds complaining of sore shoulders. With stiff muscles, they found themselves less able to exercise but persisted, slowly feeling they were able to throw the blocks a little farther. Over the following weeks, they added straight lifts over their heads and other exercises using bricks, concrete blocks, and limestone.

One day, they scavenged an iron bar and mounted it over the right angle of a stone wall to practise pullups. Ali and Marwan gradually developed greater strength, balance, and endurance. Combined with natural growth spurts, they soon looked and felt leaner, stronger, and harder.

Aduan came around the back of the house one day, eating an orange. "Here, boys. I've brought some for you as well," he said, smiling and holding out the fruit. The boys sat on a bench, drinking their fill of water and sweating from their workout. "So, you two, growing bigger and more fierce, are you?" Aduan laughed at his own comment. "Soon I might ask you to come to our camp and see what training is all about. The men there could show you what building yourselves up really means."

"Yes, yes," said Marwan excitedly. Then he stopped and looked tentative, lowering his eyes. "My father would strongly approve, but you know my mother wouldn't like it."

"We only want to be able to defend ourselves, not go after others," said Ali.

Aduan laughed again as he punched Ali lightly on the shoulder. "We will see how long you keep that attitude as you get older, Ali. There are others to defend besides yourselves."

CHAPTER FOURTEEN

KARANTINA, JANUARY 1976

Sami and Hani threw some tools in the back and piled into the old truck one cool January morning. They were headed for East Beirut. Karantina was an impoverished slum—largely made up of crumbling buildings and makeshift shelters—that was controlled by PLO forces. Sami said he had been in touch with a friend who had copper piping to sell, which he had scavenged from a ruined building. "Let's just hope we get there before Jamal's neighbours steal it all from him, Hani," he said with a smile.

"*Insh'allah*, but maybe Jamal already stole it from them," Hani said, laughing, as they turned off the rutted track in front of the house and started for the highway into Beirut.

After driving for twenty minutes, they bumped over broken asphalt into the main road of the Karantina area. The streets were noisily crowded with carts and people hawking all manner of garden produce and cheap household goods. The stench of decaying litter and sewage hung heavily in the air as the men searched for a small cross street.

"Even if we're in the small number of Muslims in Damour living with all those Christian Maronites, life here looks more difficult," said Hani.

"Yes, the community looks so poor. Everyone here seems to be wanting to sell something, and there are more sellers than buyers."

"Just look how impoverished these people are, Sami. Their clothes are so ragged."

They pulled around a tumble-down building at a corner, stopping a few feet ahead at a comparably well-maintained house, and then got out to see Sami's friend standing at the open door.

"*Salaam aleikum, habibi,*[6]" said Jamal.

"*Wa aleikum a salaam,*[7] Jamal," said Sami as each embraced the other and kissed both cheeks.

"Jamal, please meet my friend, Hani."

"*Marhaba*, welcome, Hani. Please come in," Jamal said, pumping his hand and gesturing to the two visitors to enter his house. The tea kettle was already on the gas ring. Jamal sat while it boiled and then poured the tea, asking about their families, life in Damour, the health of his visitors, and the price of fruit in the markets.

After half an hour of conversation, several cups of tea, dates, and pieces of fruit, there had been no mention of the pipe. Jamal, content that the pleasantries had been observed, rose and beckoned Sami and Hani into a shed in an adjoining lot. They opened the old wooden gate and walked into the dark shed, which smelled strongly of the old, bony horse standing in a small stall.

Jamal patted the thin, brown animal and lifted some sacking in the two-wheeled cart beside it. "You will see that this is the best copper piping, my friend."

"Let me see. How much is there, Jamal? And what are you asking for it?" Sami looked at the seemingly ancient, green, broken, and twisted pieces of piping that, indeed, were copper. "How much do you want for these disintegrating pieces, Jamal?"

"I will ask the lowest price I can, Sami, but you know my family has to live on what I can make from these sales."

"And I will pay you a special price, my friend, but you know I have family members, and I must pay Hani for his help as well. What do you—"

---

6   Hello, and peace be upon you, my friend.

7   And peace unto you.

They were interrupted by a huge blast. The door to the shed blew open and banged. The three men coughed as a hot gust of wind, carrying thick dust, burst through the doorway. The horse whinnied, snorted, and stamped in his traces, his eyes rolling back and bulging with fear. The men ran into the house, slamming and bolting the door to a backdrop of rapid, repeated, popping gunfire. Women and children were screaming from the back room as the men secured the wooden shutters and called to each other to dive under the tables and beds.

Shouting filled the street as a pair of Toyota pickup trucks with automatic weapons mounted in the back careened around the corner into the main road. As the three men peeked from the front window, the smell of scorched tires filled their noses. As the second truck passed the house, they saw a patterned line of bullet holes bloom in the side wall of the house across the way. Fire suddenly burst from those windows, possibly from a punctured gas cylinder, and one long, chilling, agonized, barely human scream briefly drowned out the other commotion.

"Those men look like Phalangist militia!" shouted Sami. "Come, Hani, we've got to get out of here! *Ma'a salama,*[8] Jamal." Sami threw open the door and rushed out with Hani close behind, and they leapt into their truck.

They jerked and bumped forward, the engine complaining and roaring as Sami pushed the truck into gear and squealed away in the direction the pickups had come from. He turned sharply left two streets later, then again left, and roared down the street until they came to the main road.

They barely slowed at the intersection, looking in both directions. Seeing no immediate danger but hearing it in the background, Sami floored the gas pedal. They turned into the main road and accelerated as fast as they could. People were running in all directions, panicked by the continuing explosions and gunfire. At

---

8 Goodbye. Go in peace.

the next intersection, Sami saw a pile of concrete building blocks being erected by armed men in fatigues. He pressed the gas pedal to the floor, veering to the right to swing around the blockade. Several fighters opened fire on the van. Sami slumped forward, bleeding profusely from the head as he wrenched the wheel and crashed into the nearside building. Steam rose from the engine, and the horn blared, the noise bouncing off the buildings.

Gunmen from the blockade ran up, firing repeatedly into the air as they approached the vehicle. Hani, who had hit his head on the dashboard in the crash and was bleeding heavily, threw up his hands in terror. "Sami! Sami!" he screamed as he was dragged from the van onto the ground at the feet of several militia members. He was struck in the head with a rifle butt and then grabbed by the collar and pulled away from the van. Others yelled at him and kicked as he was roughly pushed into a building. While being kicked from behind, Sami knocked his bloody forehead and painfully scraped his shoulder on the door jamb as he fell into the room. Inside were men of all ages on the floor, cowering under the shadow of hostile, armed militia fighters. Hani vomited as he slumped to the ground, massaging his head. His hand came away slick with blood.

CHAPTER FIFTEEN

DAMOUR

After dark, Aduan arrived quietly at Sami's small house in Damour with two armed companions. "Dalia," he said, "you must all leave at once. Take only one small bag each and leave immediately. There have been tragic events in East Beirut, and there is imminent danger."

"Oh Aduan, Sami and Hani went to Beirut today and haven't returned. Zeina, come here," Dalia called to her friend who was in the back room. "There have been terrible events in Beirut. Aduan says we must leave."

Dalia and Zeina both talked without stopping for breath, wanting to know what had happened and telling Aduan over and over that Sami and Hani had not returned.

Aduan and his men bundled a trembling Zeina and Ali, plus Fatima and Dalia, into his open-back army truck. Marwan and his family and others were already there.

"Ali," said Marwan, pushing through the others sitting on the bed of the truck. He sat next to his friend. "The Maronites have killed many in Beirut."

"I know, Marwan. Aduan has told us too. *Insh'allah* it is not in Karantina because my father and Sami are there today," Ali said.

They rolled from side to side as the truck roared up the street and around a corner. They crossed the eerily quiet main highway, winding into the hills on gravel roads. Finally, the vehicle turned down what was little more than a cart path through some pines. They slowed and stopped at a dark, crumbling, old concrete-block farmhouse with a few outbuildings. Two donkeys and a few chickens were loose in the yard.

Everyone in the truck was urged to go into the main house, where Aduan called out for the attention of the twenty or so people in the room. "There has been a major attack on Palestinian forces in Karantina by right-wing Christian forces," he said. "Hundreds have been killed and much of the area destroyed."

Zeina and Dalia sank to the floor and began sobbing and wailing, as did many of the others. Fatima and Ali joined them, offering words of comfort they didn't believe in.

"Many are streaming out of the area," said Aduan. "Some will be here before long and will bring more news. For the moment, you will be safe here."

Within an hour the rooms were filling with refugees from Karantina. The smell of unwashed bodies and fear made the inside of the house unbearable. The new arrivals told horrific stories of men and teenage boys being herded through the streets by dozens of militia members while others were driven in large trucks and pushed out in the main square. A woman's voice frantically called out from across the room. "The men were forced to stand in lines if they could, but many were injured and lying on the ground. Militia members opened fire with their automatic weapons, killing many hundreds."

At that moment, a distraught old friend of Dalia's fell on her, sobbing that she had seen Sami's van, with his body inside, pushed across the main street in Karantina to be added to a barrier. She said she had not seen anyone else she knew.

Dalia wailed at the thought that Sami was dead and sank into a dark corner with Zeina's arms around her, sobbing and shaking. Fatima sat in stunned silence with the boys, who trembled at the news.

More refugees from Karantina arrived with unspeakable stories, including another old friend of Hani and Zeina's, who claimed she had seen Hani in a crowd of Palestinian men and boys, stumbling along and being pushed and shoved down the street to the killing ground of the square. "There can be no doubt that he has been killed. There is no security. Our fighters have been overwhelmed," she said.

Sobbing and shaking, Fatima tried to pull herself together and took Ali's hand. "Come, Ali. I can barely breathe. We need some quiet." Fatima led him out into the courtyard, through scores of women and children wailing and keening in the yard. They left the compound by a break in the back wall and walked a little into the pines, where they could find a quiet place to sit.

Fatima and Ali hugged each other as they shared their grief.

"Our fathers are dead. How can such evil things happen, Fatima? What kind of people can carry out such atrocities? We are all just people who want to live our lives in peace."

"Ali, this is such a tragedy," said Fatima. "My father never hurt his neighbours or tried to put his religion in the way of anyone else. His religion was the desire to protect our family and lead a good life. I need my family around me."

"Oh Fatima, my father has always been the same. There's no real reason for this killing. The hatred some men carry in their hearts is the real evil. He always said that the leaders bring that evil and play on it for their own reasons, not for the benefit of their people."

The two sat leaning against a tree, holding each other tightly while waves of sorrow passed over them. After a while, they just sat and wept quietly. The cold filtered into their bodies as a low fog settled onto the hill.

"I must go back to my mother," said Fatima. "She needs me with her."

"Me too," said Ali. "Our mothers are so upset. We must step forward and care for our families now. But we must also care for each other, Fatima. You and I are so close, and we must remain that way."

Fatima put her arms around Ali's neck and kissed him gently on the cheek, holding him tightly. They both could feel their hearts beating.

They returned to the house, where Aduan had gathered the women and was sitting with Marwan's family. "Ali," said Marwan,

"Aduan has told me about the killings of your father and Sami. I can't believe they're dead. I am so sorry for you and the family. You must be feeling so badly."

Ali was subdued, his eyes full of tears. "Thank you, Marwan. I can hardly believe it. I can't bear the thought that my father and Sami are no longer with us. This means that I have the responsibility of leading and caring for my family."

"My own father has left here with some fighters, Ali. You know he always takes a strong position on these things. He is devastated at the loss of good people in Karantina and your father. We cannot go back to live in Damour. It's a Christian town. We must forever stay with our own people."

Aduan moved from group to group in the rooms of the farmhouse. He came to the boys to say that dawn was coming, and they must leave the farm. "Ali, Marwan, I have arranged a large truck to take people to another Palestinian refugee camp. There are fighters there who will protect them, and the UN will feed them. They must move quickly and drive in the dark. Help me get your families and the others onto the transport."

"I will not go to the camp," said Marwan. "I am now old enough to stand and defend our people. I want to join with you at your training camp, Aduan."

"So do I," said Ali. "We can have no peace or security for our families without being strong. Mother," he said, turning to her, "I will go to the camp with Aduan to join with the fighters. I am now the head of this family, and I want you, Dalia, and Fatima to go to the refugee camp for your safety."

The mothers wailed and sobbed, saying that the boys, at sixteen, were too young and in danger. But time was running out. Aduan insisted that, while the women should leave, he would look after Ali and Marwan.

Fatima rushed to Ali. "I beg you to take care, Ali," she said as she threw her arms around him, sobbing. "We will always be together, Ali. My heart goes with you." She pressed her face into his neck and kissed his cheek. "We will forever stay close."

"And my thoughts go with you, Fatima. I'll join you when I can." Ali's face showed a determination that he wasn't sure he felt.

The cold, predawn sea fog hung in the pine forest as women and children climbed into the back of trucks and vans. They left the farm, standing as the trucks lurched up the dusty and rough track, headed for Tel al Zaatar to the east of Beirut. Tens of thousands of Palestinians already lived there, but the pressure to take in more refugees was immense. Babies cried, and mothers called to their little ones to stay close, offering little comfort in the dense atmosphere of tension and the smell of fear. Their men were either left behind dead in the remains of Karantina or about to enter new fighting. Many would never be seen again. A growing number of armed Palestinian fighters were gathering as the trucks left the courtyard.

CHAPTER SIXTEEN

Ali and Marwan gasped for breath as they followed Aduan and some forty armed fedayeen as they moved quickly along the dark, rocky, dusty trails. A quick stop at a well for water was interrupted by guarded, whispered commands to move along. The boys panted, and their muscles screamed. They realized that they weren't in as good shape as they had thought. Aduan periodically stopped the group and looked up into the dark sky when they heard helicopters overhead or the wind brought the sounds of gunfire from a distance. For more than an hour, they scrambled until he called a halt. The men dropped to the ground to catch their breath at last and took a drink from their bottles.

Marwan and Ali fell over each other as they slumped to the ground and lay panting in the pine needles. They waited in the darkness for another hour until they heard the noise of men approaching through the bush. They felt anxious, not knowing if whoever was out there in the dark were government or militia troops. This thought faded as Aduan stood and spoke up. "I'm in contact with other groups of our forces on my radio. The men arriving are PLA and followers."

As the men came into the small clearing, Aduan stepped forward and hugged two or three of the newcomers, exchanging welcomes and good wishes.

The group, now a force of one hundred, were led by PLA officers, who called to the men to move on. Leading them through the pine woods at a rapid pace for another half hour, they came to a stone farmhouse and animal shelters. More fighters had gathered there, and a dozen vehicles were parked nearby. Fires were blazing. Food and water were being distributed to the hungry men. A sense of camaraderie and purpose was clear in the friendly exchanges between the fighters.

By the time the first streaks of light began to touch the sky, hundreds of fighters had gathered. Abu Ahmed, a grey-haired, senior PLA officer with a full-brush moustache, strode to the centre of the yard and spoke to the group leaders. He surveyed the fighters before him: members of the Popular Front for the Liberation of Palestine, Fatah supporters, and PLA men, working together, united by the horror of Karantina.

"My brothers, the Christian Phalange militias have devastated Karantina. Many of our families and friends have been murdered mercilessly. We know that the government of Lebanon and their Israeli allies support this massacre. We must repay them. You will be divided into three groups and led down the hills to attack the Phalangist military base in Damour. Chairman Arafat and Georges Habash send their blessings to you brave fighters. They know you will fight with the spirit of your dead family members and friends alongside. Commanders, gather your fighters."

Aduan turned to Ali and Marwan. "You will stay here, my sons, and help others guard these trucks when we depart. Your mothers have paid a huge price today, and I will not be responsible for making them pay more."

Marwan cried out, "No, Aduan! We must fight! That's our town. That's where we've been bullied and laughed at. We deserve to make the bullies feel the strength of our reply."

Ali yelled, "Yes! We can't stay behind!"

Aduan placed his hands heavily on their shoulders. "No. Your time will come. This is not the end, just one of many attacks to avenge our losses. I will not be disobeyed in this."

Within a few minutes, several hundred Palestinian fighters left, forming three columns and moving quickly down the winding trails to the south, north, and directly into the town. In a short time, Ali and Marwan heard shouting and gunfire, followed by RPG explosions and the bloodthirsty cries of the fighters sweeping into the darkened town.

The majority of fighters converged on the small Phalangist military base in Damour as the Christian militia were sleeping soundly, exhausted from their part in the day's attack on Karantina. Surprise gave the Palestinians a huge advantage, and the attack was devastatingly effective. Two or three dozen militia were killed quickly, defending their base. The barracks and administration buildings blazed ferociously as Palestinians poured gasoline on the stairs and doors and set them on fire. The screaming from inside, and the smoke and crackling of the fires, promised more fatalities. Fighters charged into a storeroom and seized weaponry and supplies, commandeering pickup trucks and loading them with whatever they could. Other fedayeen charged through the main streets, shouting and firing their weapons at any signs of life.

Screaming, "Karantina! Karantina!" the fighters terrorized the town. They dragged men and older boys out of their houses to the Damour town square, where they were herded to the centre and fired on mercilessly. Wailing and shrieking women ran to the square to save their husbands and brothers, sons and friends. Many of them faced the same end. Within a short period, more than five hundred civilians had been killed. Much of the town was razed by fire as seemingly crazed fedayeen ran from street to street, targeting Christian houses and businesses.

Radio calls later brought the trucks down from the hills to pick up the fighters. Ali and Marwan jumped into one of them and rode down the hills into Damour. They sped through the littered streets and the waves of dark smoke from fires, excitedly pointing out to each other the houses of those who had tormented them, seeing burning buildings and even bodies on the doorsteps. "Karantina! Karantina!" they shouted, as did the others. A massacre for a massacre.

CHAPTER SEVENTEEN

TEL AL ZAATAR

Fatima, wearing a worn and faded dress—too long for her and badly stained with sweat—carried a large, blue and red striped sack through the winding, pounded dirt streets and broken pavements of the Tel al Zaatar camp along the Beirut River. Much of the camp was comprised of three- or four-storey yellowish stone or concrete buildings, many of them showing the scars of battle. These were interspersed with low stores and houses. Open lots were covered in tents and shacks housing thousands of Palestinians seeking refuge. The oppressive heat and humidity had drained her of strength, as she had spent two hours at her afternoon job of cleaning up at the vegetable market. Today had been a good one, as she had collected several kilos of fruit and vegetables. These had been put aside by the vendors as no longer suitable for selling. It was cheaper for them to offer her payment in kind rather than pay her even a few *piasters* for her work. Her red plastic sandals slapped on the dusty roadway as she hefted the bag higher and continued.

She moved quickly as she came to a crossroads a short distance up from where she lived. Palestinian fighters were manning a concrete-block installation. There were always two or three unshaven and dirty-looking fighters sitting up on the sandbags at the top, smoking, calling out rude remarks, and making any girls going by feel uncomfortable.

Her mother, Dalia, and Ali's mother, Zeina, had made a two-room concrete cellar a seemingly safe and quite comfortable place to live since they'd had to leave Damour. After the massacre at Karantina, the subsequent reprisal raid, and the occupation of Damour by Palestinian forces, Tel al Zaatar had become a larger and more militarized encampment. The women had chosen to stay in the camp, as they had no way to return and nothing to return to. After months of having little to do, Ali had talked his mother into allowing him to go to Aduan's camp for training. Marwan had gone first, as his father was anxious for him to join the military. Dalia had found a job as a cleaner at a military barracks, and after months of finding no work, Zeina had set up a small loom and was making washcloths and sewing children's clothing, which she sold from a basket as she walked the streets and markets.

Fatima walked down the outside concrete stairs to the basement and into what had been a storeroom for the shops above. She put down her bag. The kitchen area held a small, two-burner propane cook top and a heavily scratched and rusty metal sink with a warped wooden counter beside it. There was a large, blue plastic container of water on the floor. A rickety wooden table with ancient green paint and three faded, plastic garden chairs provided a place to work and eat. Six wooden boxes, stacked and tied together in two columns of three, were nailed to the wall to make cupboards. The concrete floor was covered with fraying, raffia-style plastic mats. The walls had some colourful materials hanging to soften the harshness of the concrete. Three wooden-frame chairs, with jute ties on leather seats and backs, were at the other end of the room, as well as a large, heavy wooden box upended to serve as a table. In the corner, half folded, was a foam mattress and several throws of colourful material that made a bed for Zeina. The second room was little more than a large closet, and the foam mattresses and lengths of material where Fatima and Dalia slept largely filled the space.

Food was hard to find and expensive. Jobs were even more scarce amongst the twenty thousand Palestinians living in the camp. The United Nations Relief Works Agency (UNRWA) distributed supplies to the camp regularly, but Fatima saw that the often-arrogant PLA fighters housed throughout the camp were always there to take the first food and medical supplies. No one thought of challenging them as they said (and she knew) that they were there to protect the population from the threats of attack by the Lebanese Christians.

Fatima was aware, however, from the endless conversations throughout the camp, that it worked both ways. Since the Palestinian forces had virtually taken control of the entire southern half of Lebanon, pressures were rising amongst the Lebanese, notably the Christian population and militias, to contain these intruders and take back their country.

Fatima was happy, as Ali had come to visit the family in Tel al Zaatar. He was bigger and stronger, she was sure. He seemed older, and physically more adult, having spent months in a PLA training camp in the south. He had arrived the day before on a truck bringing sacks of flour to the camp. They had held each other, and Ali felt a warmth and compassion that he'd almost forgotten, just knowing that Fatima was there and cared so much for him. His mother and Dalia had made a great fuss and even acquired a rare piece of lamb for his dinner to mark his return, even if it was only for a couple of days.

Zeina had been in a state of profound melancholy since her husband, Hani, had been killed. Previously a quiet, pleasant, and caring person, she had always gotten along well with her neighbours in the Raouché district of Beirut, of whatever religion or nationality, and she had friends in Damour. Her tone now took on real bitterness, however, as she denounced the increasing pressures on the Palestinians by the government of Lebanon and the Christian militias.

"Ali, everyone in the streets knows the militias are on the verge of attacking this camp to kill or drive out the Palestinians. I can only praise and pray for those who are ready to take the fight to the streets and sacrifice their lives for the cause."

Ali was stunned to hear his gentle mother talk that way. Zeina had received with enthusiasm the news from Ali that his friend, Marwan, had been selected for a bomb-making course. She said he was now the natural warrior he'd always hoped to be. Ali thought back to the days when he and Marwan had wrestled and played and run through the streets of Damour and Marwan was just one of the other kids. It seemed so long ago.

"Ali, remember that your gentle and loving father was killed by these animals. You must stand up for your family and the Palestinian people," she said, "even if that means putting your life on the line." This is not what he expected from his mother, any mother, but she was not prepared to relent. She turned away, leaving Ali stunned.

Ali tried to speak quietly to her about her attitude several times. "Mother, I realize we are in danger from the Lebanese militias, but that's not our only problem. You know that we're all in danger from the Israelis in the south. Our own Palestinian community is being torn apart by political divisions. It's difficult to know who to look to for the safety of our families. Is it not also important to seek ways to better the lives of the population, even if it means some accommodation with others?" he asked her, throwing up his hands, a questioning look on his face.

"Ali, we cannot talk to or give in to our enemies. The only way to protect ourselves is to take up arms and resist. I want you to do the same. Be a man. There can be no agreement with our oppressors. Our people can only flourish when we all return to Palestine."

"Mother, this doesn't sound like you. You need to take it easy." Ali sat back in his chair and rubbed his hands through his hair in distress. He knew her dream was unlikely to be realized.

Dalia later told Ali that she could no longer talk to her friend about these things. "Zeina has become hardened with grief and won't entertain any of what she calls weakness. I know that Zeina has never been like this before, Ali. She always brought you up to be gentle and avoid conflict. To her these days, military solutions are the only way."

Ali and Fatima later went for a walk to avoid Zeina's anger and the sullenness that lay like a miasma over the room. Fatima told Ali that, indeed, Zeina had adopted a different manner completely in the past months and that the atmosphere at home was often tense and unpleasant. They walked for a while, and then she noticed that Ali was favouring one leg.

"Ali, what have you done to injure your leg?"

"It's nothing, Fatima. I received a nasty cut during training. It was seen to in a rough manner, and a week later, it was festering. It will be better with time," Ali said, trying to reassure her.

"I'll take you to the medical station where I volunteer, to dress the wound. We at least have some antiseptic." What she really wanted to do was show him off to the others working there, as she had often talked of her brave Ali.

Fatima and Ali walked past a grizzled old man in a well-worn PLA uniform, smelling strongly of urine, slouched in an old chair outside the entrance to the Red Cross clinic and cradling a rifle. Taking Ali's hand, she skipped into the clinic.

The lights were very bright, and the white walls and light grey, painted floorboards shone like nothing else in the camp. The sharp smell of an acerbic cleaning solution permeated the air. An unattended reception desk was on one side with a couple of well-worn and partially broken plastic chairs, one blue and one red, beside it. Behind the counter were glass-fronted cupboards of medications with heavy locks on them. White curtains, hanging on metal tubular frames two-thirds of the way to the ceiling, divided the entranceway from the treatment area that might have had half a dozen cubicles. In a corner was an old woman with grey hair gathered in a bun and tied with a piece of green cloth. She bent over a large sink, washing small, enamelled dishes and metal instruments and then dropping them into a bucket of Dettol or some other amber-coloured disinfectant to soak. Behind the curtains, they could hear muted conversations as others attended to patients.

An attractive, tall, blonde woman in her late twenties, with her hair tied back, walked into the front area with a smile, greeting Fatima. She wore a grey-blue, tailored dress with half sleeves and a long, starched white pinafore.

Fatima blushed and smiled. "Hello, Lara. This is my friend Ali. He has come from the south and has an injury to his leg that needs some attention."

"Of course, Fatima," Lara replied with her surprisingly soft and charming Swiss-German accent. "It's a quiet time for a change, and seeing that you're our favourite volunteer, we'd be pleased to help. Follow me, Ali," she said, flashing Fatima a smile and opening her eyes widely as she led Ali into a cubicle, while Fatima sat, blushing again, on one of the chairs.

Unwrapping the dirty bandage on his leg and seeing an abscess over a raw cut, Lara said, "This isn't too bad, Ali, but it's better to attend to it before it gets worse." She pierced the inflamed and partially healed cut and pushed at the sides to drain the pus. She wiped the area with a disinfectant pad and looked closely at the cut. Ali sat straight and tried not to react to the pain of her touch.

"How did this happen, Ali?" Lara asked.

"I was at a training camp and cut my leg during an exercise. I lost my footing while I was running and fell, landing on the edge of some broken concrete. This happened a week ago, and I thought it would soon heal. Thanks for dealing with this. I'm sure it will soon be better." Ali's tone was formal, as he was embarrassed, recognizing that he was known to Lara and others in the clinic from Fatima.

"I'll wash it thoroughly for you. I don't think there's any need for an antibiotic, and our supplies are always limited anyway. It should heal in a few days if you can keep it dry and clean." When she was done cleaning it, Lara crossed the cut with some butterfly bandages to keep it tightly together. She finished wrapping the affected area of the leg with a clean outer bandage and then gathered the soiled ones and her supplies.

"Ali, I've heard quite a bit about you and your family from Fatima in the six months I've been here. She's very concerned that you take care, as you're clearly very important to her," Lara said with a smile.

Ali was deeply embarrassed by Lara's comments and shifted on his chair uneasily. *Please don't talk about these things*, Ali thought. *It sounds as if Fatima has been too chatty.*

"It can't be easy for you having your mother living in this camp since your father was killed. Fatima is stressed at having both her mother and yours to look after. This kind of responsibility should not be on the shoulders of someone her age. What worries her the most, and I can appreciate that, is concern that you could become involved in the fighting."

Ali was disconcerted again. *What can I say*? he thought. "You are right, Lara. She doesn't want me to get involved in actual fighting. Fatima seems to be the only one who really knows me because I don't want to fight either."

"I know there's not much other work to do, Ali, but the military usually isn't a very good option for a teenager."

"Even though Fatima hates the military," said Ali, opening up, "she appreciates why I'm now also involved with them, although in a supportive role. I do the standard physical training, but mostly, I order and carry supplies and keep track of what we need to help in our unit. Seeing how our people are treated in Lebanon, I must play a part." Ali balked a little as he reflected to himself that this would be too little for his mother.

"Well, you must take care of yourself, Ali. I've seen so much devastation of people and societies in the past. With the Red Cross, I was in Biafra, in Eastern Nigeria, for eighteen months. More than a million people were killed in the conflict, and the impact on young people who lived through it will last their entire lives."

"Thank you for your concern about me, Lara. You have seen some awful situations, and I understand how terrible that would be. I agree that wars are horrible. Why can't people get along?" said Ali with a sigh and a shrug.

"It's not just war, Ali. Societies get torn apart. I then went to the Sahel during a major drought, and people were dying by the hundreds of thousands without a major conflict. But the deprivation will lead to more conflicts, and men will die." *Why is it that women seem to be the only ones who worry about these things?* thought Lara.

It's not just the men who suffer, Ali thought. "My mother hasn't gotten over the death of my father and sees me in the training camp as if I should be preparing to avenge my father's murder. My mother's bitterness doesn't allow her to understand the conflict I feel at wanting to have good relationships and work together with people, not fight them." Ali was surprised at himself, telling a complete stranger all of this.

"I understand your position, Ali. It's not easy to live in the climate of violence and hatred that surrounds people here."

Lara led Ali back to the entrance, where Fatima waited anxiously. "He will survive, Fatima, and his leg isn't badly hurt. It's been very nice to meet you, Ali. We've heard so much about you. See you soon, Fatima, and take care of yourself, Ali," Lara said, turning to go back to her patients.

"Thank you so much, Lara," said Fatima. "I'll take good care of him."

Lara nodded and smiled before disappearing back into the clinic. "Bye, Ali, take care," she said over her shoulder.

Fatima and Ali walked home through the failing summer light. The stones of the buildings still had a yellowish glow, and the community seemed quiet and peaceful.

"Fatima, I have to return to my unit tomorrow," Ali said. "I'll leave about six in the morning, catching a ride going south. It's been so important to me to spend a few hours with you. I so miss you when we're not together. I'm really concerned at my mother's attitude but don't know what I can do about it. Hopefully, with time, the bitterness and anger she's carrying inside will fade. She's not the same person who brought me up."

"Ali, I understand why you're concerned. Her anxiety isn't easy to deal with in the house. You can't imagine how close we come to arguing with each other daily. The tensions in the community as a whole are ever increasing and are a worry to us all. I'll do what I can to take care of her as well as my mother, but you can imagine that life is demanding. We feel fairly secure in the camp, and our house suits our needs. We can only hope that better times are ahead."

They held hands tightly as they approached the house.

CHAPTER EIGHTEEN

SOUTH LEBANON

The rough barracks where Ali had his cot slept some thirty men and had been an animal shed in a past life. The greyed, weathered roof angled down to the ground from a twisted, old, discoloured beam. The long main wall had been constructed from used lumber of varying dimensions, some painted, some not. The dirt floor was tamped down and hardened by years of use. Others at the training camp were in tents of varying resistance to the weather.

The PLA recruits were awakened at dawn by the shouting of an officer from the end of the building. The young men in the barracks groaned and complained to no one in particular, reaching up to stretch their muscles, stiff from the exertions of the previous day. They slept on narrow, metal cots with whatever they might have found as a mattress. Some had foam pieces, covered in usually garish, flowered cotton; others had only straw that was some comfort but attracted insects. Others had an old sleeping bag, but most slept under coarse, grey blankets that had never seen a washtub.

They stumbled outside toward the latrines and then washed under a cold-water hosepipe before joining the disorderly queue at a green, open-sided, canvas food tent. Several old women stood behind the long wooden serving table, pulling small portions of sticky dough they had prepared the night before out of huge, cracked pottery bowls.

The first woman rolled dough with a few drops of olive oil and then passed the ball to the next, who was standing over a small, three-sided brick pit, glowing with fiery charcoal. Resting on the bricks was a bread pillow, or *saj*, an inverted metal bowl searingly hot from the fire. With a backhanded wave she dusted the pillow with a little flour and stretched the dough to make a paper-thin covering. She left it to blister and brown for a few seconds before turning the bread, lifting it with her seemingly asbestos hands and placing it on a platter on the serving table. This hot **marouk** bread lasted only seconds as the men greedily grabbed two or three pieces and put them on their tin plates for their breakfast. A third crone slopped a ladle of *ful madamas*—boiled and mashed fava beans with spices—onto the plate. The final hand reached out with a smaller spoonful of thick Lebanese yogurt and spices, called **labneh**. The men moved away to find a place to sit, enjoying what was likely the best part of the day, and they ate their meal accompanied by mugs of strong, very sweet tea.

Ali jumped as a hand slapped him on the back. He swiveled around. "Marwan! It's so good to see you back. You've been on that bomb-making course for weeks. Now you look very dangerous," he said with a laugh. Others nearby joined in.

"Some bomb-making course," said Marwan with a hoot. "I had to drive the old truck that went to the market for food every day, and when I returned, I had to dig latrines and carry the garbage. The closest I got to bomb making was hearing them fire off from a distance. Maybe that was just as well, as several people on the course managed to lose fingers or feet trying to build and set off the devices. I think I'll look for other opportunities to attack our enemies."

Ali and Marwan were so delighted to see each other that they wrestled to the ground, enjoying the sense of playfulness from the days of their youth that increasingly seemed far in the past.

"*Yellah*, come on, follow me," hollered their platoon commander, charging at full speed past them and up the dry and stony hill toward the workout area. The following four hours were spent crawling under barbed wire in a muddy track, running and stepping at high speed through tires set at a good lunge on one side or another, and scaling eight-foot walls with the help of their colleagues pushing, pulling, and sweating profusely, all to the din of shouts from the trainers and arguing amongst the trainees. The trainees later collapsed under the shade of some bushes and ate their rations of bread, hummus, and oranges.

"All right, back to the barracks. On the double!" the commander shouted about fifteen minutes later.

Panting again, the trainees scrambled down the hill, slipping on the sandy soil and stones, until they entered the gate and headed straight for the hosepipes for a drink and the chance to slop the cool water over their heads.

CHAPTER NINETEEN

TEL AL ZAATAR

Several weeks later, Ali returned to Tel al Zaatar with about twenty others in the back of an open truck. Reports of heavily increased pressure from the Christian militias had made life much more difficult. Trucks carrying supplies were only periodically allowed in and out after they were searched for weapons. Even UN drivers, bringing food and medicines in their white trucks with UN decals, were being hassled.

The Palestinians in Ali's truck had been sent to the camp to bolster the defences of the area and join the forces who had been digging tunnels in the hillsides to hide military equipment and ammunition. His group was put to work around the perimeter of the camp, building berms and constructing gun emplacements with small tunnels for ammunition and cover. They also poured concrete bases where heavier guns could be set. Ali toiled in the high humidity, with heat in the mid-thirties. Exhausted after hours of work, the men collapsed and slept on the hard floor of an old factory that served as their barracks after a meagre meal of poor food and brackish water.

Lying in the dark on the hard flooring, wrapped in an old jute bag, Ali thought of Fatima and his mother and Dalia, who were so close but out of his reach. He lay there, listening to the periodic bursts from mortar shells that were sent randomly into the camp, seemingly only to keep everyone on edge. He couldn't help but be concerned that, before long, a concentrated effort would be made to drive the Palestinians out of Tel al Zaatar.

After ten days, he was given leave to visit his family. Walking through the narrow streets and alleys of the camp, he could sense the increase in tensions and fear. The streets were more crowded, everyone was in a hurry, and civility had diminished. He pushed open the door to his mother's basement rooms and saw her sitting at her loom, sour and slumped in tiredness. "Mother, I am back," he called as he pushed open the front door.

Zeina lurched backwards in her plastic chair and unsteadily stood to welcome him. Ali was struck by how much older she looked. "Ali, *al hamdulilla*," she blurted out. "We need your help. We have almost no food, and I cannot help. I can no longer bring myself to sell the goods I make in the streets for fear we are to be invaded. Ali, are you fighting? Can you drive these Lebanese devils away from our camp? We have nowhere to go. There is very little food, and the water is brown and smells rank."

"Wait, Mother, calm down. Let me speak," said Ali. He walked over to her and put his arms around her gently. He could feel how thin and frail she had become. Her body trembled against him.

"Ali, I can take no more." Zeina sounded weak and defeated. "Since they started shooting flares over the camp every night, my eyes are full of light. Then they shoot smoke cylinders to frighten us and choke us. There are mortars falling, and shooting, and I am very afraid. At night, I can hear the Lebanese fighters laughing outside the camp as they pressure us. No, Ali, the Lebanese militias are trying to drive us out. I am very frightened, and there's nowhere to go. You must kill them. Dalia doesn't understand. She is too calm and quiet. She goes about her days as if all of this is only an inconvenience. I cannot make her realize the danger we're in. We must leave. Your father would have found a way." Zeina slumped down into her plastic chair and turned her back on Ali, covering her face with her dry, cracked hands.

"Mother, you must not get so distressed. Much of the noise is probably from the work we're doing on defences for the camp. Many of the explosions are from us digging tunnels to protect everyone. There are many of us here, building defences. It's not easy to leave,

Mother. You know that the militias have all but encircled Tel al Zaatar, and only one road is left open. Our leaders are saying we must stay. They say our cause demands that we stand together. And where else would we go?" Ali took her worn hands in his. He looked at her prematurely ageing face and saw the sorrow in her eyes.

"I cannot take this any longer, my son," Zeina said softly. "Help me."

"Mother, I can't stand seeing you like this. Your sorrow and fear are overwhelming you. I want the joyful and positive mother I've always had," he said, slipping his arms around her neck and holding her close. "I wish I could do something for you and will try my best. I heard we are about to return to my unit in the south, and I really want to see Fatima before I go," said Ali. "Where is she, Mother?"

"She can no longer work at the market, Ali, as the vendors now keep even the rotting produce for their families. Dalia is carrying supplies around for the fighters, and they talk about it but do not pay her. We need *your* help." Zeina emphasized and looked up, appealing to Ali with watery eyes.

"But Mother, where is she?"

"Fatima now spends all her time at the clinic, as there are many injuries from the shelling. She's there now and will be until late." Zeina was not giving up. "Ali, conditions are very bad, and we cannot survive. You must try to take us out of the camp."

Ali sighed and stood up. "We'll talk about this again later, Mother. I'm going to the clinic to find Fatima."

Ali left the basement, catching his breath from the tension of the exchange with his mother. He walked up the street to the clinic. Since his last visit only weeks earlier, the clinic had expanded into a neighbouring building, and a long line was waiting outside. He passed men with bloody bandages and women with small children. Many looked undernourished and stressed. He talked his way past the two armed men at the door and walked into the reception room to find it filled with individuals and families. Crying children and injured workers sat on the floor, many moaning with their discomfort.

"Could I speak to Fatima Hadawi, please?" said Ali, addressing a harried-looking older woman at the reception desk.

"Look at this clinic! Does it look as if we have time to talk?" she said harshly and turned away immediately to bark at a woman standing beside her and repeatedly asking for attention.

"But I only need to see her for a moment," Ali insisted.

"Go into the far room," she said, dismissing him with a wave of her arm. "I think she's at the back, but don't keep her from work."

Ali went past several of the curtained but mostly open and busy cubicles. He could see that the level of cleanliness that had so struck him on his earlier visit was no longer in evidence. He saw the Swiss nurse, Lara, bent over a young man and dealing with a rusty piece of wire that was around his bloody lower arm. There were rings of sweat around her armpits, staining the cloth dark. At the back of the room was a short hallway leading to an inner room, where he saw Fatima straining to lift an old woman onto a commode. The woman's garments were already soiled, and the rank smell permeated the small room.

"Hello, Fatima."

Ali's voice broke through Fatima's concentration. She looked up, startled. Ali could see it was all she could do to hold back a sob, and she barely managed to keep hold of the woman.

"Oh, my Ali. **Mashallah.**[9] It is so good to see you. I've been here since early morning and was supposed to leave an hour ago, but there is so much to do. Please wait for me outside, and I will come." Fatima turned back to the grunting old woman, dismissing him.

Almost two hours later, Fatima awakened Ali. He had fallen dead asleep on the floor of the reception area, leaning against a corner of the wall.

They walked together through darkening and dusty alleyways. Fatima told Ali about recent incidents, all of which showed that Zeina had deteriorated mentally and was increasingly negative and anxious.

---

9   Thanks to God.

"It's becoming increasingly difficult to live with Zeina and care for her, Ali. All night she mutters and cries, often leaping up if there is shell fire, even if it's from our side. We are becoming more and more exhausted from disturbed sleep but don't know what we can do." Fatima fell silent after this explanation, as if the effort had drained her physically.

"I'm so sorry, Fatima. I was really struck on my last visit by how much she had changed and how stressed she is. It must be very difficult for you, but I have no idea what else we can do. Since the Syrian Army has now sent forces to support the Lebanese government, I know that our fighters have been very stretched. In our camp, the Fatah officers tell us every day that we must fight harder and resist the militias. I have to tell you that, when I return to my camp, I'll be put into daily physical and more intense weapons training, as there is a sense of more and more fighting to come soon." Ali felt guilty at his inability to ease the strain for Fatima.

"Fatima, you know that there has been huge pressure for Palestinians to come to Tel al Zaatar to be together for defence. People are being urged to come, even though we know that some groups of new arrivals have been shot at by militias. Our leaders, including Arafat, are telling our fighters that we must stand together in Tel al Zaatar, no matter what."

Fatima looked disgusted. "That can't be, Ali. Are we just pawns in a military game?"

"The chairman continues to say that we must stay in Tel al Zaatar, even if life is becoming much more difficult. He says we need to fight through this sense of hopelessness, but he isn't here to experience it. The leader's view is that if many people were to leave and the camp closed, it would be a huge political victory for the Christian militias. Farouk Khaddoumi of the PLO political office has called for volunteers to save the Palestinian revolution. By that he means for them come here and defend Tel al Zaatar, no matter what the cost."

Fatima looked both frightened and disbelieving. "Ali, that would mean staying in Tel al Zaatar to be overwhelmed by the militias, so the PLO can say we are all martyrs to the cause."

"That is the message, Fatima. But that will not happen. There will be a way to save our people. I have no intention of becoming a martyr, and I do not want that to happen to you and our mothers either," Ali said firmly.

"But Ali, we're just people who are trying to live and care for each other. I don't want any more politics or fighting. I want peace, and so do we all. Think of the thousands in this camp who are children and family members, not fedayeen fighters."

***

Over the following weeks, the Lebanese militias constructed concrete outposts in the hilly areas around Tel al Zaatar. A line of them could be seen across the Beirut River, where bulldozers pushed up sandy berms. Workmen set concrete blocks into the top, providing viewing places and firing positions. These positions were continued in a line across the river and around the camp in a horseshoe shape. The militia forces continued building, gradually bringing the outposts close to merging, virtually surrounding the camp save for one principal road that led down to Highway 30, the Damascus Road. The constant drone of heavy machinery, the pervasive dust, and the smell of diesel from the engines heightened the frustrations and tensions in the camp under what had become a siege.

The several different PLO factions within the camp had been regularly smuggling in arms. Areas near the river were fortified with artillery. Mortars, surface to surface missiles, and anti-aircraft guns were put in place. The bunkers and the tunnel system within the camp were enlarged and strengthened, and safe-haven shelters were hastily built for the population. The Palestinian leadership called for more and more sacrifices from their people, most of whom were simply trying to live through the day. Nights became ever more tense with heightened exchanges of fire from artillery and mortars. Pressures built and continued for weeks. The International Red Cross and Red Crescent dealt with both sides, seeking truces that would not be observed. Plans were developed by them for an evacuation, so that civilians and fighters alike, with international observers, could leave the camp under escort.

Ali and his crew eventually left the camp, returning to their bases in the south. As is always the case between conflicting parties, secret contacts between the Palestinian leadership and that of the militias took place periodically. The Lebanese government and militia leaders called for an end to the fighting and for the Palestinians to leave Tel al Zaatar.

But the Palestinians refused, saying they had nowhere to go. Eventually, they agreed to reduce the number of people in the camp. This would take some pressure off the challenge of accommodating so many thousands of displaced people in a relatively small area. While the numbers in the camp were mostly Palestinians, there were also Syrians, Kurds, and even some Turks, who felt they could not return to their countries because of political activities, conflict with neighbours or other religious or ethnic communities, or simply a criminal record or outstanding charges.

CHAPTER TWENTY

A tall and fit soldier in his mid-thirties, accompanied by two aides in unusually clean and trim uniforms, approached the Palestinian forces command centre in the Tel al Zaatar camp and was admitted to the main office.

"I am Major Fadi Mughani from PLO headquarters," he said to the officer at the reception, who was standing to salute his superior. "I have an important message to be delivered only to Colonel Abu Jayash."

"Major, please take a seat," said the officer. "I am First Lieutenant Elias al Shafi. You are expected, sir. Please wait one moment while I see if the colonel is available."

The smart staff officers contrasted with the shabby office. The dirty piece of carpeting covering the old, scraped, tiled floor was threadbare. Green paint was peeling from the walls, revealing an ancient layer of cream below. The only decoration was a small, framed photo of Yasser Arafat, tilted in its place high on a wall stained with brownish water from an old leak. Three uniformed men, heavy and unfit, slumped on a folding metal chair and a plastic-covered couch that was split and dirty. Two of them appeared to be asleep. A boy in dark pants and wearing a stained white smock appeared instantly, carrying a tray with cups of ginger tea and glasses of Turkish coffee. He offered them to the officers silently.

"*Naam, shoukran,*"[10] Mughani replied. His aides also each took a glass, one holding it to the light and looking at it closely to see how clean it was. They stood together and looked around, not at all surprised at the state of the office. Moments later, Shafi reappeared and invited the major into the office.

"*A salaam aleikum,* Major."

"*Wa aleikum a salaam,* Colonel," he replied, delivering a crisp salute.

Handing the superior officer an envelope, Mughani said, "I have been asked to provide you with signed orders, arising from the discussion you participated in at our headquarters recently. This confirms the decisions that were made. I gather that you understand the rationale behind them. I should add that, when you have read these orders, the letter should be destroyed, but the orders remain valid."

"Of course, Major." Colonel Abu Jayash waved his hand impatiently. "Let me read the letter right now." He did so, mumbling the words to himself and moving his lips as he read. "That is consistent with the discussions at the meeting." He then reached for his cigarette lighter, setting it to the paper and dropping it in a metal waste basket that, thankfully, was empty.

"Thank you, Colonel. I will report that I have delivered the letter," said Mughani.

"And I will confirm to your headquarters by telephone when the orders have been carried out, Major."

"*Ma'a salama,* Colonel," the major said, turning with a smart salute and leaving the office.

"Lieutenant Elias, come in here," called the colonel. "You have seen the major, who has instructions for us. Gather the group leaders. I want a meeting here in half an hour."

***

---

10 Yes, thank you.

Several days of particularly heavy firing from all directions had assaulted the camp. The relentless detonation of mortars, intense firing of flares, and flashes from gunfire throughout the nights exhausted the population. More than ever, the tense atmosphere felt like one of futility and exasperation. People either hid in their houses or aimlessly wandered the streets, looking wan and increasingly feeble. Zeina and Dalia bickered endlessly. The only relief came when one of them found a reason to leave the house.

CHAPTER TWENTY-ONE

"Dalia! Dalia!" Zeina shouted, running back to their rooms with a bucket of water. "I have just been near the main gates, and many are preparing to leave the camp!"

"Zeina, this cannot be." Dalia gave a heavy sigh, shrugged her shoulders, and didn't look up from the wrinkled vegetables she was peeling.

"Yes, yes," Zeina persisted, waving her arms wildly. "They are letting us leave safely. Everyone says we'll be taken to a new place away from the fighting." Her tone was urgent, almost frantic, as she grabbed at Dalia's green shawl. "We must go now. Get our things together. We must tell Fatima at the clinic. *Alhamdulillah*, we can leave this place before we are overwhelmed by the militias."

"Zeina, if we are to leave, where would we go? We have nowhere," Dalia said, scraping the cuttings from her vegetables into a pot, where she would later boil them for soup.

"No. No. People say there will be trucks to take us away, and we will go to a safe place," said Zeina, who was already stuffing a few clothes and personal things into a canvas sack. "I will go myself to get Fatima and bring her back if you want to stay in this hell, Dalia."

Dalia threw up her hands and lumbered over to the door to watch as Zeina ran out of the house and up the street toward the clinic.

Zeina paused at its entrance, panting for breath, beads of perspiration running down her face and neck. She then burst in, bypassing a line of patients who complained at the disturbance. She rushed into the crowded reception room, calling loudly for Fatima.

"Fatima is not here, Zeina," said Nadia, the heavy-set woman with a whiskery upper lip, sitting at the desk. She has gone with some others to meet a truck bringing medical supplies. They will unpack them and bring them back here later today."

"Tell her to come home immediately or to meet me at the main gate. We are leaving the camp today. Now!" Zeina barked. She then rushed out of the clinic and continued up the street, pushing her way desperately through the milling crowd and dragging her sack. In a few minutes, she arrived at the gate. An anxious crowd was gathering, and a hubbub of chatter all about leaving the camp rumbled like thunder. Soldiers struggled to keep the thrusting crowd from opening the gates.

"This is not safe! There are militias outside, and they could fire on you!" the soldiers roared at the crowd. "Stay back! Stay back!" they shouted, brandishing their AK-47s.

"Do not go out," said a soldier who appeared to be in charge, his authoritative voice briefly catching the attention of the throng. They checked and then surged forward again. The noise level rose to deafening levels.

In the command centre, Colonel Abu Jayash put down the phone and called to Lieutenant al Safi. "Come with me," he said, walking toward the door. "We must take charge of the situation at the gate." He walked quickly through the blazing heat across the crowded square to the guardhouse at the side of the gate. A dozen fighters were gathered uneasily, watching the growing confusion outside with increasing unease.

Taking the squad leader in the guardhouse aside, the colonel leaned into him and quietly said, "We spoke yesterday about our orders. We will now open the gates and carry them out to the letter. You have the necessary men advised and prepared?"

The squad leader confirmed his answer with a nod. "Yes, Colonel. They are ready. I will order them to take their place on the gate houses on either side immediately."

"Good. I must first address the crowd," said the colonel, moving quickly out of the guardhouse.

Standing on the steps to the guardhouse, the colonel motioned to the squad leader standing immediately in front of the main gate. The soldier fired several shots into the air to draw the attention of the crowd.

The colonel took advantage of the shock-induced silence. "Brothers and sisters of Tel al Zaatar." His voice was calm and commanding. "Your leadership bleeds for your anguish and pain. After months of discussion and argument with the government of Lebanon and militia leaders, an agreement has been reached by the Palestinian leadership that will ease the pressures on our people. I have been instructed to tell you that a ceasefire has been arranged with the militias, and some people will be allowed to leave the camp."

The frantic crowd roared with approval.

Colonel Abu Jayash raised his arms to quiet them. "Transportation has been provided that will take many of you to a new camp in the south. In thirty minutes, we will open the gate, and you may leave safely. Tell your families, gather your things, and for those who wish to go, prepare to leave this camp within the hour."

The crowd burst into a rippling shock wave of shouting and shrieks of joy. From the back of the crowd, Zeina joined in the high-pitched ululating of tongues as the women in the crowd expressed their deep emotional reaction to this statement. Arguments broke out as some questioned whether this could be true, while others threw arms in the air in joyful acceptance. Men and women alike pushed and shoved their neighbours as they scrambled through the streets to spread the news.

Zeina ran home, her plastic slippers slapping on the street. As she lurched down the steps and entered their rooms, she crashed headlong into Dalia, who was at the door. Zeina was half weeping, half shouting as she blurted out the news and repeatedly wiped her flushed face on her rough shawl.

"But Zeina, can this really be true?" said Dalia in a skeptical tone. "I can't imagine that we are allowed to leave. The Lebanese and militias want only to regain their territory and drive us out. They would never allow our fighters to spread out into the country."

Zeina's widening eyes burned with excitement. "Dalia, this is our only chance to escape death."

"No, Zeina, it isn't. Listen to me." Dalia was calm and quiet in contrast to Zeina. "The militias fear that an exodus of civilians, as well as many of our fighting forces, would lead to more organized fighting. Surely, they would rather have our fighters penned into a camp. Besides, I saw Fatima moments ago, and she says she will not abandon her responsibilities at the clinic. They have so many people who depend on them and cannot leave."

"I will then go by myself, Dalia." Zeina's face was set into a determined grimace. "You may stay here to be killed, but I will move to a new place. This could be our only chance. I can no longer stand it here."

An hour later, hundreds of people had gathered their things in boxes and sheets, filled and knotted. They packed the square in front of the main gate, jostling and pushing to get to the front. The shouting and crying rose to a crescendo. Some called to others standing on the side to come with them. In turn, many of those were crying and urging their relatives and friends not to go. The frenzy of the crowd threatened to explode as the colonel again stood before them. A hush settled over the crowd. "Open the gate," he ordered.

The metal bar was lifted, and the heavy wooden gate pulled back with a complaining screech. Those at the front who had pressed against it shuffled back to allow the gate to open. The crowd remained largely silent as they absorbed the scene. The chirp of a single bird flying overhead could be heard. The heat of the day became palpable. The road outside the camp was open and empty for perhaps one hundred metres. Beyond that, three people in Lebanese and militia officers' uniforms started walking toward the camp gate. Behind them, several dozen armed men in military dress stood in place. A line of perhaps a dozen large trucks covered with green canvas tops promised a means of escape. Two or three Palestinian youths broke ranks at the front and cautiously stepped forward. As if by a pre-arranged signal, others pushed through the opening gate and started running for the vehicles.

The Lebanese officer at the trucks outside raised his arm and waved to those leaving the camp, urging them to come forward to him and directing them to the transport.

"Now," said the colonel, quietly.

The squad leader put his arm straight up then pulled it down quickly. Shots rang out from behind the camp wall, directed just over the heads of the soldiers near the vehicles outside. Several threw themselves onto the ground. The Lebanese officers in front scattered. The soldiers behind them began firing towards the camp gate and into the crowd. People were instantly hit, screaming, writhing, and falling in front of their friends and relatives, who were pushed forward by the momentum of the crowd. Those in front tripped and fell over their fellow Palestinians who had been mowed down by the gunfire. Those who could do so struggled to return to the protection of the camp, while others sat or lay bleeding in the road. Some pushed their way through the melee, grabbing those in their way by the arm, shoulder, or clothes, or shoving them aside.

"Close the gate," shouted the squad leader. Several soldiers inside the camp beat their way against the tide of the now returning crowd to push the gate closed against the press of people. Other fighters had rushed out and were dragging bodies and the injured into the camp. When the soldiers reached the gate, they crammed the last few people, squalling and crying, through the opening. The gate was pushed closed with a thump, and the bars were slammed shut against it.

"The gate is closed, Colonel," said Lieutenant Safi.

"We have fulfilled our orders," said Colonel Abu Jayash.

CHAPTER TWENTY-TWO

SOUTH LEBANON

"Ali, you must come to the camp immediately. Your mother has been badly injured. Please come."

Ali read the note from Fatima again, dated four days earlier. He crumpled the paper that had been given to him by the truck driver who had been delivering food from the World Food Program to Tel al Zaatar. Ali ran across the field and entered the main building, panting as he approached his section commander. He saluted and leaned over the desk, smoothing out the note he had received. "Sir, I seek permission for leave to go to Tel al Zaatar. I have just received news that my mother has been badly hurt."

"Yes, Ali. There is nothing more important than family, and most of all your mother. You have my permission to go, but you must return in the morning." His commander signed a blue pass and pushed it across the desk.

"Thank you, sir. I am so concerned about her."

In the late afternoon, a truck with markings on the sides from a local food distributor left for Tel al Zaatar, taking munitions to the fighters. Ali's concern grew as the driver talked incessantly about the horrors of recent events when several Palestinians had been killed and wounded at the gate of the camp. Ali was sick with worry by the time the truck turned into a closely guarded back gate and entered the camp.

He walked quickly through the narrow streets to the rooms where his mother, Dalia, and Fatima lived. As he neared the building, his apprehension swelled inside.

Fatima emerged from the doorway and threw her arms around him. "Ali, it's too late," she said, sobbing. "Your mother has died. We did everything we could for her at the clinic, but she had been shot in the stomach and lost a great deal of blood." She clung to Ali, and they hugged each other tightly.

Ali gulped for a breath and shouted into the heavy night sky. Consumed by grief, he fell to his knees. He felt anchorless and bereft of life. Fatima knelt beside him, crying softly. After a time, she helped him to his feet, and they went into the house. Dalia emerged from the shadows, hugged him, and offered comfort. She then put a coffee pot on the propane ring. The three of them sank onto the cushions and leaned against the wall, united in their grief.

"Ali," said Fatima, "your mother so suffered from her worsening anxiety and growing feeling of desperation. She was focused only on leaving the camp. We didn't believe the story that flooded through the camp that we would be allowed to leave under a truce, but we couldn't make her understand."

"Fatima, I had told her that our leadership didn't want our people to leave Tel al Zaatar. It would expose our fighters and weaken the Palestinian position by moving us all out," replied Ali. "Besides, where would all these people go? Abandoning this camp can't happen unless we are defeated. How could she think that way?"

"I remember you saying that, Ali," said Dalia, "but she was only concerned for her life."

"When the colonel made his statement about leaving, it swept through the camp like a violent windstorm," said Fatima. "No one was thinking, and few questioned it. There are many in the same frightened state of mind as your mother, Ali. You should have seen the people near the gate. People were crying and shouting. Many were begging their relatives not to go, and others were urging them on. It was mass emotional confusion."

"I understand that there was nothing you two could do," said Ali.

"Regretfully, that is too true, Ali," Fatima said with compassion. "The final chapter was the confusion over the alleged agreement for a ceasefire and who fired first at the gate. Then we had the horror of finding her there, covered in blood and suffering badly from her wounds."

"There is great controversy in the camp, Ali," said Dalia. "Most say that the Lebanese militias fired into the crowd. Some say the Palestinian guards at the gate first shot at those who were outside to move people to the trucks. But it doesn't matter who opened fire first when your mother's life was taken. We were with her before she died, so she was well aware of our love, Ali."

"But Fatima, this is so tragic. Will she even go to paradise?" Ali was aghast at the possibility that she would not.

"Don't worry," Fatima reassured him. "Before she died, she said her *shahada*.[11] We then washed her body and wrapped her in a white shroud. Everyone knows that she has been a good person and a marvellous wife and mother. She will experience peace and contentment having risen into the arms of Allah. Of course, she was buried before the sun set that day."

Ali let out an agonized moan and wept. "Fatima, I can't believe that I have now lost both parents. I have lost my real family, and there is no community I belong to. Only you and Dalia remain. How can I live without my parents? I belong to no one."

"Oh, don't say that," said Dalia. "The love of your parents stays with you and will guide you throughout your life. We are now your close family, and the three of us must care for each other."

Fatima took Ali in her arms, crying for his pain and loss. "Wherever you go, never think that we are not together. You are in my thoughts every moment, and I hope that you feel the same way."

"Yes, Fatima. While my immediate family has left us, we are always together in our hearts, and may it remain that way."

---

11 The Muslim profession of faith ("There is no god but Allah, and Muhammad is his messenger).

CHAPTER TWENTY-THREE

TEL AL ZAATAR

The situation in the camp remained extremely tense for months. The attacks from the militias outside intensified, and the rage of battle never relented. Living conditions were more difficult, and the mood in the camp became more frenzied.

"Fatima," said Dalia, "if you go back to the clinic tonight, you will collapse. You must have some rest and care for that terrible cough you have developed."

Fatima turned her tired eyes to her mother and coughed as she said, "I cannot, Mother; we must all do what we can. Through all these months, I have learned how to do so much of the nursing. I am needed there."

"You cannot help if you're very sick yourself. You must take care."

Night was falling as Fatima left their rooms to walk to the clinic. More and more houses and buildings in the camp had been hit lately by incoming artillery fire, knocking stones and blocks into the street. Fatima stepped around the rubble and coughed from the acrid smoke wafting through the night. She looked across the camp toward the main part of Beirut, where the Lebanese's own civil war continued. She could even see the smoke and the flare of shells falling amongst the buildings. Fatima knew the horror of the conflict for families under that random fire as they tried to protect their loved ones. *It's no different or better here,* she thought. *Who does a war serve? It's only the leadership that begins and maintains the fighting in these conflicts.*

The clinic had expanded again to occupy adjoining buildings as demand for medical care increased. Fortunately, the International Red Cross had been able to bring in supplies periodically, although the threat of them stopping altogether was real. A haggard Lara, now the head nurse of four, stood beside a heavy, exhausted, and perspiring elderly Egyptian doctor, Dr. Moussa Tarek. He had dried blood smeared down his once white coat and was stooped from tiredness. Two guards put up their hands and stopped a pair of young men who had knocked into Fatima as they rushed through the clinic's doorway, carrying a completely still body on a stretcher.

The sweating doctor bent over and peered into the face of the gaunt woman on the stretcher as it was lowered to the floor. The deep lines on the pallid face of the woman betrayed age, hardship, and the pain of years spent attempting to keep her family alive. Her clothes were old and faded, her feet bare and heavily calloused. Her worn and stained clothing reflected the hardships of her life.

Reaching out and taking her head in his hands, Dr. Tarek turned her slightly to expose a wide, ugly opening where the back of her head had collapsed from a severe blow. "There is no life here. I am sorry," he said. "You will have to take her across the street where we keep the dead."

"My grandmother, my heart mother," sobbed the young man at her head, collapsing onto the floor. He fell on her body, shaking and crying.

"We have been close friends from the same village for years," said the second man to the doctor, sorrowfully. "This woman lost her own two sons and their wives long ago and has cared for this boy, her grandson, for more than five years, moving from village to camp to camp. The only member of that family remaining is my friend. Now alone."

Suddenly, shouting and crying rose in a swell outside. "The safety bunker has collapsed!" shouted a voice in the crowd.

"Stones are falling on the people!" screamed another.

Lara, Fatima, and two other aides from the clinic pushed through the melee. They headed for the nearby underground shelter that had been dug out and covered with a concrete roof for the protection of the civilian population. Men and women milled around the entrance as clouds of dust swirled out of the hall. A few people, most covered in a soft, grey powder, ran or stumbled out of the shelter, choking for breath. Sirens wailed in the background. Lara and Fatima covered their mouths with their aprons and entered the large room. Ahead, they could see a beam from a streetlight through part of the roof that had collapsed, the light disappearing into a thick cloud of dust.

"This is unbelievable! Fatima, there are two or three people over there on the ground by that concrete slab!" screamed Lara, waving her arm in their direction. "At least they are moving. Take a look at them. There are children's voices calling from farther back. I'll go there."

Half a dozen men rushed in behind them. Some were in military fatigues. Others came from the market across the street. They called for everyone to get out immediately. It was apparent that there had been scores of people, mainly women and children, in the shelter at the time. Many had been preparing an evening meal, and the floor was dotted with coals from charcoal braziers, forbidden inside because of the fumes but still often used. People rushed in through the clouds of dust to help, and family members arrived, calling out for loved ones. They pushed and jostled each other and often blocked the way as victims tried to make their way out, coughing, choking, and gasping for breath, some bleeding heavily, though many were just dazed.

"I'm from the clinic; let me look at these people," said Fatima as she was jostled aside.

"Yes," said a soldier, "come with me." He led Fatima down a partially caved-in corridor and waved his arm at a dazed young woman in a shawl and brown dress covered with dust, who was lying awkwardly on the floor. "That woman has a leg trapped. We will try to lift the block of concrete off her leg."

Three men heaved on a large piece of concrete, just tipping it enough that the woman was no longer trapped by the foot, while others took her shoulders and pulled her back.

As Fatima reached for the woman to help her with her injury, a loud crack and grinding sounds were heard. Small pieces of the roofing rained down on the rescuers in a cloud of dust. A large chunk of concrete, partially supported by rebar, swung toward the floor. Fatima shouted in pain as it hit her upper left arm, practically tearing it from the socket. She scraped and twisted her ankle as she fell backward onto the floor and passed out, lying in her own blood. The trapped woman disappeared under the rubble.

Fatima awoke hours later. She was on an operating table in the clinic. Looking up and trying to raise her head, she saw the unsmiling but kindly face of Dr. Tarek looking down at her. *"Alhamdulillah,* our Fatima. You are not looking as bright and active as usual, though I can assure you that you will recover. But you won't be working hard for us for some time."

Fatima burst into tears and sobbed. "That cannot be. I must."

Dr. Tarek spoke to her softly in the matter-of-fact tone of a doctor used to delivering bad news. "I'm sorry to say that your upper shoulder has been torn from the socket and broken. The muscles in your arm have been badly stripped and damaged. I've done what the conditions allow and, *insh'allah,* all will be well. You have received gas to keep you sedated while I worked on your arm. The effects of that will take some time to clear. Also, I'll give you some painkillers that are quite strong."

"I feel as if my head is weaving back and forth. I can hardly think," said Fatima, falling back in exhaustion.

"If you feel shaky and numb and can't clearly see or think, that is all it is. Your ankle has been badly sprained as well, but that will be better in a few days. Stay off it and sit with it raised if you can. Your mother has been here most of the night watching over you, but she went back to your house a little while ago to sleep. You should do the same. We'll try to keep you quiet in a back room, as you deserve special treatment for all you've done for us in this clinic."

Lara appeared from behind Dr. Tarek and hovered anxiously. "Fatima," she said, "we all feel so badly that you've been injured, but you've received the best medical care we can offer. Go to sleep now, and I'll watch over you."

CHAPTER TWENTY-FOUR

The following days saw renewed heavy shelling from both sides. After months of siege, a sense of looming defeat permeated the streets. The people were in a mental pressure cooker. Fears that the situation would worsen were fed by exaggerated stories of those who had been trapped in the shelter. Heavy smoke from fires sparked by incoming shells and Palestinian artillery firing alike made for a dome of dense, oppressive smog over the camp with the smell of black powder. In the early mornings, the firing faded, and residents put it down to exhaustion on the part of the forces. Rumours started to circulate that there would be another attempt to allow some people to leave the camp.

Several days later, fighters manning the guard posts could see lines of Red Cross marked vehicles stopped just beyond the militia outposts where the trucks had been earlier. Civilians walked back and forth between groups of Lebanese uniformed men talking and those in militia uniforms. Red Cross workers finally moved toward the gates and spoke to a small group of military guards and then returned to the militias. Neither group showed any level of trust in the other. Talks had brought a truce close to agreement once again. The militias resisted and charged that Palestinian forces and weapons would be brought out of the camp only to harass them elsewhere. The Palestinians feared that militia forces would use the trucks like a Trojan horse to bring fighters into Tel al Zaatar. A fragile cessation of hostilities was eventually agreed on to allow injured civilians to leave the camp. After hours of delay, men in the guard posts stood back as cars and trucks decorated with Red Cross/Red Crescent insignia entered the camp unhindered.

Several hundred of the wounded, including civilians injured in the underground shelter, were prepared to be taken out, as well as many elderly residents. From her bed in the back room of the clinic, Fatima, in constant pain and lethargic from the medications for her shoulder injury, heard a commotion in the clinic itself.

Lara appeared at her bedside. "There is news," she said. "Our director told us just now that an agreement has really been reached this time. Many of our patients will be allowed to leave the camp, and I insist that you are to be among them."

"I will not leave, Lara; my mother needs me, as does this clinic," Fatima said stubbornly. "I'll be able to resume some kind of work before long and must be here."

"No, Fatima, you need more attention than we can give you and a quieter place to rest. Dalia will be allowed to accompany you, and you'll be moved later today." Lara's gentle voice was firm and brooked no argument.

"But where will we go?" Fatima asked.

"It does seem ironic, but it seems that those leaving the camp will be taken to Damour! It is now controlled by the Palestinians again. I know you had to escape from there after the events in Karantina. Arafat has said that they are establishing what he calls a 'martyrs' village' to shelter those injured in the siege here." Lara laid a cool hand on Fatima's forehead, sweeping back strands of her dark hair. "I will return when we know more about the move. Stay quiet, Fatima." Then she left her to digest this news.

An hour later, Lara came back into the room with Dalia, who set down a large bundle wrapped in a brown shawl. Dalia looked excited at the prospect of leaving the camp, but concern lurked behind her dark-brown eyes. "The time for us to leave has come," she said. "What would Zeina say if she were here? God bless her soul. We will go back to Damour, but I don't expect it will be to our old house. I have as many of our things as I can carry, and we must go now."

"Fatima," said Lara, "you have worked very hard here. We don't want to lose your smile, and you have contributed a great deal to the work of the clinic. I will miss you terribly. But I know you will have better medical care and be safer out of Tel al Zaatar. Go now while you can, as this truce is only to last a short time."

"I hate to leave, Lara," Fatima said. "You do so much for our people, and the pressures are ever increasing. Thank you so much for your caring and attention to me and to everyone."

Lara helped ease Fatima into the only wheelchair in the clinic. Fatima winced, gasped, and almost passed out as she felt her arm had been wrenched, when in reality there was only a slight movement. She sat awkwardly in a contraption familiar to her—an old, upright, partially carpeted chair with wheels roughly hammered into the bottom. A male aide pushed the chair, with its screaming wheels swiveling from side to side, through the main room of the clinic. Fatima saw with surprise that it had been almost emptied of patients. Cleaners were industriously dumping a green antiseptic solution onto the floor from pails on one side of the room and whisking the liquid around with mops.

"We don't expect to be without patients for long, Fatima, so we're taking advantage of this quieter day to clean and prepare," said Lara.

At the door, a boy in fatigues took one side of the chair, and with the aide, lifted it and Fatima into the back of a large, grey van. She caught her breath and moaned in searing pain as she was eased onto a side bench. A soft bundle of straw was placed to cushion her injured foot. A harried woman in a nurse's uniform, who muttered something in words Fatima couldn't understand, though in soothing tones, strapped her in. Dalia climbed up into the van and took a place beside her daughter, gripping her hand. "Now we move to a new stage, Fatima. *Insh'allah,* life will be better."

As the door to the van closed, Fatima saw a haggard Lara waving goodbye.

While the truce held, the Red Cross evacuated more and more civilians, who could see that many fedayeen were being true to their orders to keep up the fight. In tattered clothes, carrying or dragging whatever they could, civilians were rushing to leave the camp, scrambling over the rubble in the streets and throwing their bundles into the trucks. At the same time, every weapon and instrument of battle was being mobilized for what all were convinced would be the final assault on the camp.

The ceasefire broke as the sky darkened. Heavy firing resounded through the camp. Residents who had been left behind surged out, finding themselves in the chaos of the field of fire between the forces. Many were killed by whichever side was firing and fell in the dirt to be overrun by their neighbours, whose only focus was to leave. The barrage of heavy artillery by the attackers turned the night into a thundering hell, with shells falling throughout the camp. The air became so poisoned with the smoke and the smell of cordite that many people in the streets covered their mouths with cloths. Palestinian fighters were trapped in their tunnels, which had collapsed under the barrage. Many were suffocated as the sand and clay fell on them from the artillery barrage. Others crawled over the bodies of their fellow fedayeen, choking and gasping for air, clawing with their bloody hands in largely vain attempts to escape the graves they had dug for themselves.

As the Lebanese and militia forces drew their noose around the camp, the artillery bombardment changed to mortars and then flame throwers. Lebanese Christian forces poured through the gates and rampaged through the streets of the camp. The stench of gasoline and burning buildings, possessions, and flesh sucked the oxygen out of the area. Many Palestinians who tried to surrender were cut down with their hands in the air. Some bodies were tied behind cars by whooping Christian militia members. They drove off in victory with their horns honking, even dragging their prey behind them through the crowded streets of nearby Christian areas of Beirut.

With the complete collapse of the defending forces and appeals from the Red Cross, orders went out for the militias to stand back. Their trucks returned and took away dead and wounded as quickly as possible. Within hours, the camp that had held tens of thousands of refugees for years, and had been under UN administration, was bulldozed. No one could think that the Palestinians could ever return.

CHAPTER TWENTY-FIVE

CAIRO, 1977

Having been through a rigorous search by guards at the gate and confirmation of his identity, and appointment from an unseen party inside the house, Salim was pronounced fit to enter the gate. He walked through the lush gardens and up the marble stairs to the grand mansion in the upscale Zamalek district of Gezira Island in the Nile, in central Cairo. At the massive, carved door, he was met by a tall and powerfully muscled security guard, wearing slim khaki pants and a tight, olive-green t-shirt, who escorted him in. Two other men in army fatigues stood down the hall, their AK-47s at rest but close beside them. Salim marvelled at the high ceilings and wide, curved staircase in front of him and was escorted into a small side reception room where he was to meet the PLO Chairman, Yasser Arafat.

Salim stood for a few moments, looking at the beautiful silk and wool Nain Persian carpet in ivory, blues, and reds, feeling guilty that he was standing on it. A side door opened, and he looked up to see Arafat enter. Arafat was a short man in his early fifties, of medium build, and in need of physical activity. He walked forward with a beaming smile, wearing a khaki military uniform of indeterminate origin. On his head was a traditional black and white chequered keffiyeh, held in place by a black agal, or cord. Most distinctively, Arafat bore his trademark one-week beard, clearly greying.

"Salim, *habibi*," said the PLO chairman as he wrapped his arms around the young man and kissed him on both cheeks. "It has been some time since I have seen you. Please sit here." He motioned with his hand toward two brightly upholstered armchairs separated by a small, wooden table. A servant in white pants and shirt and a red sash appeared as if by magic and set out dates, olives, nuts, and glasses of mint tea.

"*Shoukran,*" said Arafat. The server backed away silently and left the two of them in the room.

"I do appreciate that you have kept in touch with me with reports on your progress at the school in America, Salim. You will recall that I had hoped to see you periodically in New York, but contrary to the terms of their agreement with the UN to host its headquarters, the Americans kept denying me a visa. The years have gone by."

"Chairman Arafat, or if I may use your honorific, Abu Ammar, I cannot offer too many thanks for your support."

Arafat beamed and inclined his head to one side in acknowledgment of Salim's show of respect.

Salim was awed at being in the presence of his revered leader, and the words came out in a rush. "The funds you have generously provided allowed me to attend the school in Connecticut, and now I will soon finish my undergraduate work at New York University. It has been a marvellous experience. I also extend my thanks to Ambassador Obeidi in New York for his kind attention. I am also fortunate that my grandfather continues to play such an important role in my life."

"Salim, your grandfather Yazid has always been very generous in providing advice to us. His views are always well thought out and valuable. He is so proud of the work you have done at your school and the excellent results you have obtained. I am sure you will have earned a place at your choice of universities for further studies." Arafat looked at Salim with a pride close to paternal.

"It has been a special opportunity that has laid out a path for my future," Salim said humbly. "I am pleased to say that my choice is to enter the school of law at the University of Cairo."

"Wonderful, Salim!" said Arafat, clearly delighted and raising his arms in celebration. "This is the university I attended myself, where I studied for my degree in civil engineering. The law school has an excellent reputation and has been in operation for over a hundred years. It will provide a very strong basis for your future interests. In fact, I was once the president of the General Union of Palestinian Students, the kind of activity I can recommend to you."

"Joining the General Union will be one of my first activities," Salim assured him.

"Salim," Arafat continued, obviously pleased, "there will be a meeting between some of my closest advisors and the Egyptians. I suggest that you join in to further your experience. There is talk that the Egyptians and the Israelis are making some progress on an agreement to settle their land claims in the Sinai and design a framework to improve their relations. We are apprehensive that this could mean the Egyptians will sell us out."

"Can that be?" Salim was shocked that the Egyptians would deal so openly with the Israelis at the expense of the Palestinians.

Arafat waved his hand in a dismissive gesture. "The Americans have made some proposals. President Carter has expressed a desire to see the principles of UN Security Council resolutions 242 and 338 form the basis of the agreement."

"Yes, sir," said Salim. "We read those in school, and there was some discussion."

"Well, there could be a better place to begin, as that would not recognize our claims to the lands that we lost in 1948 when the international community gave them to the European Jews. Nor do they acknowledge our right of return to those lands, where we have lived for centuries. Unfortunately, Salim, we are not included in any of these talks about our land and future." Arafat leaned back in his chair and stared moodily into the middle distance.

Salim leaned forward, eager to show his interest. "Chairman, Ambassador Obeidi in New York has been discussing these matters as well and has told me of the American proposals."

"As I'm sure you know, Salim, Resolution 242 was adopted after the war the Israelis started in 1967. It calls on Israel to withdraw from 'territories' occupied during that conflict. This is a dangerous vagueness. Of course, they only use the English version of the resolution in these discussions. The French version of the resolution, which is equally legal and authentic at the UN, says that Israel should retreat from *'les territoires'* occupied during the conflict. That would imply 'all' the territories occupied, not just some of them. Too bad we don't conduct our discussions in French!" Abu Ammar added with a rueful laugh.

Dommage, too bad, thought Salim, remembering a phrase from French class at his high school.

Arafat continued earnestly. "Resolution 242 calls on all parties to cease acts of belligerence and for them to recognize the territorial integrity of all states in the region. It then calls for a settlement of the refugee problem, never directly mentioning the Palestinian people and our rights."

"I have been raised to appreciate the importance of Palestinians regaining their traditional lands as the basis for the development of our society, Abu Ammar," said Salim. "If we are treated only as a refugee issue, and the UN recognizes no claim on our part to any of our traditional lands, what is our future?"

Arafat seemed defeated. "President Carter, who is behind the scenes in the planning of Sadat's position, also seems to be unwilling to recognize the people of Palestine and their rights. Then it gets more difficult. Resolution 338, as I'm sure you know, was adopted after the Ramadan War of 1973 and calls for the implementation of the terms of Resolution 242. Thanks to the pressure by the Americans and their Israeli friends on the Egyptians, we will be the losers. If President Sadat agrees to recognize Israel in return for an Israeli withdrawal from the Sinai Peninsula, the basis for discussion of regional matters has changed forever. It has become land for peace without including the Palestinians."

Salim was appalled. "That would mean giving up East Jerusalem, the Old City that we all cherish as the heart of our country! My grandfather has always taught me that our society cannot grow and mature without our land. Surely, we can't agree to any settlement that allows the Israelis to profit from their aggressive military action that captured and holds Old Jerusalem!"

"You are right. My concern is that President Sadat anxiously wants to follow up his visit to Jerusalem last year by coming to some agreement with Begin and Israel. That will mean mutual recognition by those two states and will further prejudice our interests. Again, we are being left out completely." Arafat stood up suddenly and went to the window, standing with crossed arms and looking out as if he could see the region changing before him.

"Abu Ammar, I so appreciate learning from you how you see the situation. It's a very sorrowful prospect for our people. I see my future as playing a role in helping to resolve such problems." Salim joined Arafat at the window, and the chairman put an arm around the young man's shoulders as they stood side by side, looking at the peaceful scene of the gardens.

"Yes, Salim, that is what I would like to see also. Accordingly, I would like you to sit in on the discussions with our Egyptian contacts to see how such talks go. It will provide you with a perspective that will be valuable to you in the future."

"Oh, many thanks, Chairman. I would be honoured to participate," said Salim, beaming.

CHAPTER TWENTY-SIX

Three days later, having received a message that the meeting with the Egyptians would take place that day, Salim dressed in a pair of black pants and a well-ironed blue dress shirt and donned a black blazer. He was ready early and sat looking out the front window of the villa where he was staying with family friends. A car came up the street. Naef al Wazir stepped out and walked up the path to the house.

"Salim, it's good to see you," he said, first extending a hand and then embracing the young man. "It has been years since we met at your grandfather's house in Lebanon and talked about the arrangements for your school in the United States. I know that your time there was a success." He stood back and looked at Salim admiringly. "You were a young student then and are now a full adult. You will soon be ready to go to the law school at the university, I understand."

Salim was delighted to see the older man. *"Sayed* Naef, I am very pleased to see you. Yes, my experience at school in the United States has been excellent. I've also had opportunities to meet our delegation to the UN and to work there during the summers. I'm honoured that Abu Ammar asked if I'd like to sit in on these discussions with Egyptian officials."

"We'll meet them in one hour at a villa in the southern part of the city. There we will join some friends who will be in the meeting with us. Come now. The traffic in Cairo is so terrible that you can never tell how long a trip from one point to another will take."

Wazir extended his hand toward the door, and together they went out to the waiting car.

The old Mercedes, an indistinct, sandy-grey colour from the bleaching of the sun, noisily started down the street to a main intersection, followed by a thick trail of blue smoke. After crawling through traffic, avoiding drivers in their well-banged-up vehicles, motorbikes, and even loaded donkey carts on the main road, Wazir's driver turned off into an equally crowded side street, dodging handcarts, more animals, and people. A few buildings along, they saw a fit young man in loose-fitting beige pants and a white shirt. To Salim, he was indistinguishable from others at the stalls, but he waved them into a side alley. The driver turned and stopped the car in front of a set of stairs in front of a shabby, tan plastered building.

Salim and Wazir got out as the hot engine pinged and smelled of burning rubber. Two others appeared from the building and greeted Wazir. As he turned to go up the stone stairs, Salim noticed that the alley entrance behind them was now blocked by a pickup truck. He looked ahead and saw that the other end of the alley had a truck across the opening, and several armed men were standing around.

"Come with me, Salim," said Wazir, walking across a surprisingly large, cool, marbled hallway into a receiving room. Inside was a grouping of six chairs upholstered in a heavy brocade. Between the chairs were small, low tables with bowls and trays of dates, pastries, and fruit. A large, carved wooden table with a huge floral arrangement on it was against the wall. Along the side walls were several hard chairs.

"Come and meet Farouk Abu Abbas, Salim," Wazir said. "He is the Director of Political Affairs of the PLO."

A tall, well-groomed man in a pair of slim-fitting slacks, a blue sports jacket, and a pale blue shirt, and wearing a pair of Ray-Ban sunglasses, was sitting in one of the large, upholstered chairs.

"Farouk, I'd like to introduce Salim al Omeri, who is with us today at the request of Chairman Arafat."

The man laughed and smiled warmly. "Indeed, I know that Salim is to sit in with us today, Naef. Salim, I am pleased to meet you, having known your grandfather and family for many years. I understand that you're here in training for my job," he said with a large smile.

"It is my pleasure and honour to meet you, sir, "said Salim. "I owe a great deal to our chairman and am privileged to be able to sit in today."

"Having this exposure and experience can be very helpful to you, Salim. As you become more involved in the diplomatic efforts behind our cause, you'll need a good deal of exposure to such meetings."

"Salim, just sit there on one of these chairs," said Wazir, pointing at the hard chairs at the side. "Listen and be invisible. The Egyptians should be here shortly."

Salim did as he was told. In the hot and stuffy room, he was grateful for the one clanking air conditioner at the window. After about an hour, a young man came out of a back room with some papers tucked under one arm and sat on the next chair. He also carried a full briefcase. He looked down as he spread out the papers on his lap and started to organize them.

"*Marhaba*, I am Salim Omeri," Salim said, extending his hand to shake his neighbour's. "I am here with Naef al Wazir."

"Nice to meet you, Salim. I am Ahmed Hamad, an assistant to Abu Abbas. I don't believe we've met before."

"No," said Salim, "although I've had some experience as a summer intern with the delegation to the UN in New York, this is the first time I've been to such a meeting. I'm sure it will be very interesting."

Hamad was open and friendly, and the two young men chatted quietly about Salim's background. Hamad told him the names and positions of several people as they entered the room and waited for the Egyptians to arrive.

A flurry of activity at the door indicated that their contacts had arrived. Khufu El Masri, from the office of President Sadat, entered the room, wiping his brow. He was a heavy, middle-aged man in a rumpled grey suit, wearing a white shirt with no tie, and showing the usual several days' growth of beard. He was greeted by Abu Abbas with an embrace and was introduced to the other Palestinians in the main grouping of chairs. The Egyptian's two colleagues similarly did the rounds of greeting, clearly familiar with some, not others. Four other Egyptians, the heavy protection, entered the room and stood along the sides.

Through a small side door, two servants in white pants, shirts, and turbans appeared quickly with trays of juice and tea. The principals sat, making small talk and drinking their tea. The servants hovered close by, constantly refilling the glasses and offering trays of pastries.

After some time, Abu Abbas set aside his glass and welcomed his guests more formally. "Chairman Arafat is pleased that this opportunity is available to bring his people up to date on the discussions between Egypt and Israel under the auspices of the Americans. We would appreciate it, **Sayed** Khufu, if you would wish to make some remarks about the state of the negotiations and how they might affect the Palestinian people."

"You will appreciate, my friend, that the discussions are not at all finalized, so I can offer only so much. The interests of the people of Palestine are, of course, very important to President Sadat and always factor into his positions," said El Masri.

The conversation went back and forth, but Salim couldn't hear all of it. Abu Abbas became agitated and increasingly frustrated. The Egyptians mentioned co-existence, and the Palestinians countered that this meant capitulation and emphasized recognition of the Palestinian people and their rights. There was a lengthy exchange on what each side wanted in any agreement and whether an end to the enduring conflict in the region was something that could realistically be imagined.

After an hour of intense exchanges, Abu Abbas leaned forward and spoke, spreading his hands before him and leaving no doubt that the Egyptians were to remember his words as the basis of the Palestinian position. "I want you to take this message back to your negotiators. You must realize that Chairman Arafat will not be pleased to hear the direction that President Sadat's discussions with the Israelis is taking. He is aware of the pro-Israeli position that the American president will take because of the Jewish lobby in the United States. The chairman had hoped that Carter would have some personal values that would lead him to recognize the legitimate rights of the Palestinians. This does not seem to be the case. The chairman expects President Sadat to uphold the interests of our people. That is a duty of the Arab nation. You will be aware that the PLO must support the Palestinian people and will not accept any agreement by other parties that denies the rights of our people."

"My friend, President Sadat appreciates the position that the chairman is in, but he has his own political interests to consider. We will be glad to keep you informed as discussions ensue," said El Masri. The Egyptian's dismissal of the Palestinian position was clear.

As the Egyptians left the room, the other Palestinian delegates were also clearly displeased by the conversation. They huddled at the sitting area, commenting on the meeting and the unsatisfactory information offered by the Egyptians. As they started to leave, Abu Abbas came over and said, "Well, Salim, what did you think of that?"

Salim had been watching and listening intently to the conversation. "It was fascinating to see a group sitting like this to talk through issues of such importance to our people. It's quite extraordinary to see that the futures of all the people involved can be determined by discussions such as these. Everyone in the group was respectful to the others. They clearly understand where the others are coming from, even if their positions are far apart. I don't see that the discussions with the Israelis and Americans will be of any benefit to us."

"Salim," said Abu Abbas, "there has probably been no conflict in history in which the parties do not somehow meet secretly with their enemies or emissaries to exchange views or threats. The same thing happens with those who are mostly on the same side, as we saw today. All the parties involved in a dispute need to set out their positions and the basis for them. Knowledge of each party's positions and the rationale for them are essential to working out how they can come together. History, however, shows that it's not always possible."

"Indeed," Naef said, smiling, "as Abu Abbas said earlier, maybe you'll want to take his job one day! Learn well, **habibi!**"

As they walked out, Salim shook hands with Ahmed Hamad. "Thanks for your helpful comments on the people and discussion, Ahmed. I hope we'll have the opportunity to meet again."

"Oh, I expect we will, Salim. This has been interesting indeed, and it was nice to meet you."

CHAPTER TWENTY-SEVEN

NEW YORK, 1978

The sun was shining brightly as Alex Matheson walked out of the apartment hotel into a cool December morning in New York. Even at 8:00 a.m., there were sirens in the distance, a sound that didn't seem to have stopped all night. Matheson had slept fitfully in the excitement of a new foreign assignment to the Permanent Delegation of Canada to the United Nations. The street was bustling with people on their way to work. First Avenue was crowded with honking yellow taxis. Women in smart business suits clicked along the sidewalk in their high heels, sharing space obliviously with homeless men in rough clothes, rummaging into bins for bottles and cans. Men in grey or blue Barney's or Brooks Brothers suits swung their leather briefcases and marched with confidence into the week as one of the greatest cities of the world shook off the briefly quieter and less busy rest period of the night, and flexed its muscles to run the world for another day.

Matheson had arrived in New York over the weekend in mid-month. His family was to join him after the Christmas break. This allowed Alex time to familiarize himself with the office and his work before going back to Ottawa for the holidays to move the family. He and Elizabeth had visited New York several times over the years when he had been at various UN meetings, and they had found the city stimulating and challenging. They were both so looking forward to living there. Taking on his new position in the delegation's political section was, however, an entirely new matter. The multilateral negotiating environment was immensely appealing, and the political subject matter of his brief—a good part of which was the Middle East—was challenging and endlessly alluring.

He started toward the offices of the delegation, located just off First Avenue near 49th Street. Moments later, he automatically apologized, saying, "Sorry," as a ragged pile of smelly clothes pushing a shopping cart came around a corner and walked straight at him. He almost backed into two men who veered around him and didn't miss a beat in their conversation, let alone see him. *Big city smarts to learn,* he thought.

Matheson walked into the building and took the elevator to the third floor. He noted, with pride, the large Canadian coat of arms on the wall behind the reception area.

"Good morning, I'm Alex Matheson, and I've just been posted to the delegation," he said to the stylishly dressed, thirtyish woman behind the thick security glass.

"Yes, welcome. We are expecting you," she said with a slight French-Canadian accent. Her voice was crisp and professional. "My name is Monique. Please come in, and I'll call Mr. Davis, the Deputy Permanent Representative."

Moments later, a slim and well-dressed man wearing a grey suit and highly polished brown brogues, in his forties with thinning hair, opened the door into the lobby and shook Alex's hand warmly. Rob Davis had been at the delegation for two years and was a very capable and thoughtful officer with an excellent reputation for working well with his colleagues.

"We're so glad you were able to arrive before the holidays, Alex. Great to see you again. We still have a few days of the General Assembly session to complete, and as you know, your predecessor had to leave quickly for family reasons. Come with me, and we'll do the tour." Davis ushered Alex into the inner sanctum beyond the security airlock.

The first stop was a brief meeting with Ambassador Sylvie Tremblay. Madame Tremblay, who carried herself elegantly, was a well-toned woman of about sixty. She had thick, dark hair naturally streaked with grey and worn in a short, crisp cut. Alex noticed she was wearing a sleek, seafoam-green silk suit with a Hermes scarf around her neck. The ambassador had a career alternating between public service and academia and was well known and regarded in Canada and New York. Mme. Tremblay was articulate and well versed in UN matters. This earned her the respect of other ambassadors and delegates and gave her considerable influence in the deliberations of the institution.

"Welcome to the delegation, Alex. Please have a seat," she said. "Rob, please stay; coffee will be here in a moment. I, of course, received the usual background notes when Ottawa proposed you for the position, and they do say good things about you. Your experience on posting in Beirut and in the Middle East Division at headquarters will be valuable to us. Rob tells me that you've also been here a number of times for meetings, so the transition shouldn't be difficult."

"Thank you, Ambassador, I was very pleased when personnel approached me for this assignment. As Rob knows, I've really enjoyed my time here and particularly like the multilateral environment," said Alex.

Mme. Tremblay's assistant brought in the coffee and poured it into mugs with maple leaves on them. The conversation covered the current activities of the delegation as well as travel plans for Alex's family.

"Alex, I realize the difficulty for your family of changing countries and schools in the middle of the academic year, but I can assure you that the administrative side of the move will be well handled by Teresa Hamilton, our administration officer," said Mme. Tremblay.

"Yes, thank you, things seem to be in good hands," Alex said. "She was in touch with me before I left Ottawa. From the photographs Teresa sent, we'll be assigned a lovely, fully furnished apartment on East 64th. In addition, the children have been registered at the Lycée Français on 72nd Street just off Fifth Avenue. That transition is expected to be an easy one for them, as the children are in a bilingual program in Ottawa. However, my wife, Elizabeth, and I know we must face the always difficult 'We have no friends' issue that arises with the kids. We can deal with that."

Following that discussion, they went down the hall and into the conference room, where the delegation was assembling for the weekly staff meeting around a huge oval table finished in polished teak, with bucket chairs upholstered in red leatherette.

Rob presided, and first of all, welcomed Alex to the delegation, introducing him as the replacement for David MacDonald, who had been responsible for Middle East, East Asian, and African issues in the General Assembly and Security Council.

"Alex, whom some of you know, has been Deputy Director of the Middle East Division at headquarters. He was earlier posted to Beirut, so he brings with him lots of experience in perhaps the most intractable issue that comes before the UN. We fully expect him to untangle that region's problems during his posting here."

The assembled delegates burst into derisive laughter.

When the mild amusement had died down, Rob went around the table, asking the half-dozen officers on the delegation to introduce themselves and identify the area of their responsibilities: human rights, legal, disarmament and other political issues, military and peacekeeping matters, development and economic issues, and UN finance and institutional issues.

In chairs behind sat half a dozen fresh-faced new officers, whose first foreign assignment, a few months after joining the Department of Foreign Affairs, was to spend four months in New York during the annual General Assembly. They wrote several reports a day on major speakers and issues that were of particular interest to Canada and sent them back to Ottawa. They also served to fill the Canadian seat in the GA or committees when some minor speaker was at the podium, thus observing the diplomatic niceties of Canadian interest in them and their views by being present.

After a precise run-through of the agenda and events of the day, as well as a round of comments by officers on emerging issues in their areas, the meeting ended. Everyone gathered their papers and rose to go to morning meetings and committees. Rob suggested to Alex that the two of them walk over to the UN building to collect his security pass and then see what was going on in the General Assembly.

As they left the office and walked up the short hill on First Avenue, past the park at the end of the UN, Rob said, "You have a pretty good idea of how we work and the UN environment, Alex. We have a good group of officers, and they work well together."

"I'm really pleased to be here, Rob. I appreciate your confidence in my abilities to solve the problems of the Middle East, although I suspect that line has been used before," Alex said with a chuckle. "I don't have any great expectations. To paraphrase Churchill describing Russia, 'The Middle East is a riddle, wrapped in a mystery, inside an enigma.'"

"If only it was that clear," said Rob. They both laughed.

They walked through the main gates and up the curved driveway, then passed through the wide, glass doors into the vast, marbled lobby of the UN building itself. Rob showed his pass, vouched for Alex, and said they were going to security to pick up a new pass. Although Rob was well known to the guards, they were escorted downstairs to security where—after a not very flattering photo was taken—the pass was issued. Following the required scowl and squinting of eyes by the self-important clerk to ensure he was giving the pass to the right person; Alex was identified as a real member of the Canadian delegation and left feeling quite pleased with himself.

As they walked through the halls, Alex was introduced enroute to other delegates and UN staff as a new member of the delegation. Finally, they entered the massive hall of the General Assembly. It was the first time Alex had been to the UN when the General Assembly was in session, and he was struck by the sense of place that this hall held. He thought of the views and opinions that had been exchanged there and the host of famous speakers who had taken the podium over the years. The height of the ceiling and the grandeur of the fixtures, including the high, green marbled podium where the UN Secretary General and the elected president of that year's General Assembly sat, were truly impressive.

So familiar from television news reports, the sight of close to two hundred desks rising in a half moon of tiers, where national delegates sat behind their country's name plate, was striking. Alex and Rob walked up the stairs about two-thirds of the way, where the delegation of Canada was seated between those of Cameroon and Cape Verde. The closest seats to the front were based on the annual drawing of one country to sit in the first row and were allocated thereafter by alphabetical order. Ambassador Tremblay was at the Canada desk with one of the junior officers. Alex caught his breath at the scene as they sat behind to listen to the next speaker. He was the eloquent foreign minister of Italy, a distinguished, well-tanned man with dark hair and silver sides, wearing a perfectly tailored suit, the quality and styling of which stood out.

I am really here, thought Alex with satisfaction.

CHAPTER TWENTY-EIGHT

That evening, Alex called home from his hotel to report on his first day with the delegation. "Elizabeth, it was quite a day. It was amazing to be in the GA to see it actually at work before me, and realizing that just being there means I've been recognized as a representative of Canada. Certainly a different feeling from just attending a committee meeting"

"Wonderful, but start at the beginning, Alex. Tell me all about your whole day." Elizabeth could hear the clink of ice falling into a glass and smiled to herself. She knew he was pouring a glass of scotch for himself.

Alex filled her in on his day, starting with the walk to the office, his meeting with Rob and the ambassador, the staff meeting, and going to the UN building. "Sitting in the GA behind the 'Canada' name plate was quite exciting. Even more so than I expected," he enthused. "About fifteen minutes after Rob and I arrived in the hall, the speaker finished, and there was a five-minute break. I just sat there at the desk, looking around to take in the sight. Then Rob and the ambassador and the other officer got up to leave. Rob said they had other things to do and would leave me there to vote. He handed me a paper with some twenty resolutions attached and told me the position we wanted to take on each resolution. All I had to do, he said, was press the green button to support, the red to oppose, and the yellow one to abstain and no explanations of vote were necessary on this batch.

"I was feeling very uncertain and asked, 'What if I press the wrong button?' but he told me all I had to do in that case was to press the correct one and it would be changed on the large electronic boards on each side of the podium in front. Then he told me I couldn't go wrong and said, 'See you later.'"

"Wow!" Elizabeth exclaimed. "So, no pressure then?"

Alex continued, "The agenda then turned to the voting on those resolutions that had been proposed by various delegations and had been thoroughly talked through in the corridors. When enough delegations commit to them by co-sponsoring, they're presented to the General Assembly."

"I see. I didn't really know how they got to that stage," said Elizabeth.

"Anyway, Elizabeth, I have to admit I was quite nervous, but I voted on all twenty-three without a mistake." Elizabeth heard him take a swallow of his whisky. "I can tell you I was pretty relieved when it was over."

Elizabeth laughed her beautiful laugh. "Thank goodness, Alex. A story to remember, but I have news as well. I had a call this morning from the consulate in New York, offering me that position I'd applied for in the public affairs section, so our concern about a job for me is settled."

"That's wonderful! Congratulations." Alex was delighted, not just at the prospect of more family income but that Elizabeth had secured a position in her field. "Things are falling into place, Elizabeth. We should so enjoy this posting, and the kids will love their school."

***

That Friday, Alex was invited to a business lunch to mark the coming Christmas season with what was called a "likeminded" group of delegates, one of several that Canada participated in on a variety of issues. Just after 1:00 p.m., he walked up 49th Street in drizzling rain and entered the Bistro Chagall. It was a very smart restaurant on a corner with black, wooden-framed glass windows across the front and one side, and a row of miniature Italian cypresses in pots across the front. At the door, he handed his coat to an attractive, smiling, dark-haired hostess in a slim-fitting black dress, and the maître d' led him into a main dining room that was bright and welcoming. Complementing the winter season and the blowing rain was a low fire burning. The tinkling of glassware and cutlery sounded almost musical as he was escorted toward a private room at the back.

Arne Sorenson, the Counsellor on the Swedish delegation, and host for that month, rose and welcomed him. Arne wore a mid-blue suit with a dark tie. His thick, blond hair almost covered his eyes on the right side. He introduced representatives from Finland, Norway, Denmark, and the Netherlands, who were the members of the unofficial group, noting that Alex was David MacDonald's replacement. Everyone smiled and reached out to shake Alex's hand, welcoming him to New York.

Arne continued, "David has told us something of your background, Alex. We're pleased to have someone join us with your Middle East experience. Because of our countries' participation in peacekeeping missions and our donations to humanitarian aid in the region, we like to share our thoughts on these issues. This isn't a problem that will be going away soon. Having you on the issue and working together on draft resolutions will be very helpful. In fact, our Norwegian colleague, Jorn, will be returning to Oslo over Christmas and will be replaced by Martin Fredriksen, who has been counsellor at their embassy in Tehran. That will also help broaden our understanding of the issues of the larger region."

"Thank you, Arne, I'm really pleased to be here and hope I can make a useful contribution to the discussions." Alex felt as if he had truly arrived. With his new colleagues, he raised the glass of red wine that had appeared beside him in a cordial salute to the season.

CHAPTER TWENTY-NINE

SOUTH LEBANON, 1978

Ali was still profoundly troubled by the conflict and the impact it had on his family. He often sat on his bunk morosely, feeling deeply tired and alone. Both of his parents were now dead. He rarely saw Fatima, and he felt he had little to look forward to. The door to his barracks creaked open, and he looked up to see that Marwan's uncle Aduan had come by to talk to him. His friend's concern was etched in his face.

"Ali," Aduan began tentatively, sitting on the edge of the bed and putting a brotherly arm around Ali's shoulders. "You know that I am deeply sorry at the loss of your mother. This is a great loss, but time and life go on. You must look ahead at how your life can be fulfilling. There are many who love you and can give you the closeness of a family."

Ali's expression didn't change, and Aduan could feel the tension in his shoulders.

"This isn't an easy time, Aduan. I am depressed at the loss of both my father and my mother, and I so miss Fatima. Often, I want to pull away from everyone and sit by myself with my sadness. I can't seem to overcome that. Other times, I feel I must reach out and seek retribution for these deaths and the conditions our people live in."

Aduan's tone was firm and purposeful. "Ali, you must recognize that your life is being part of the brotherhood of our Palestinian cause, and close to our fellow fighters. We will act against the enemy, within Lebanon and in Israeli occupied lands. Look ahead at the effort to regain our lands occupied by Israel. There is a part for you to play. You are a clever young man and have much to offer. You will have opportunities to put yourself forward, to achieve recognition and a reputation that others will admire." Aduan turned Ali's shoulders to face him and forced the young man to look into his eyes.

Ali held his gaze for a few moments, then moodily cast them down again. "Aduan, I realize that I am responsible for my own future path. I must try to overcome this sadness, but that's not easy to do. I know my friends in the movement are supportive and realize they are what remains of my family. You and others have said that working with them is a way I can deal with the many negative influences on my life. I can see that would help, but I can't get myself up to do it. I know I must put in every effort to rise to these challenges. I will try."

"That sounds positive, Ali. It does take time. I can help you move in the direction that will allow you to deal with your aims. Your future will be bright. But for now, let's get Marwan and kick the soccer ball around!" Aduan stood and put out his hand to Ali.

Ali scowled but pushed himself to his feet with both arms like an old man. He shuffled after him as they turned and went outside. As he left the barracks, Ali covered his eyes from the bright sun but followed Aduan to the pitch.

In the following months, Ali's mental state improved, but he was often sullen and uncommunicative with his fellow fighters. Gradually, he pushed himself harder and harder in training exercises. He didn't hold back and seemed to carry the hand-to-hand combat drills to a point of frenzy, always one step further than his compatriots.

"Ali," said Marwan, taking him aside after a particularly vigorous physical session, "in the quiet of the night, some of the others have been saying that they are becoming reluctant to train with you. They think you should save your real fighting for the enemy, not for your friends."

Ali's eyes blazed at his friend's words. "Marwan, I love my fellow fighters and feel strongly that I am a part of this campaign and cause. I am becoming driven to follow my mother's wishes and become a real fighter. I know I didn't used to see any benefit in physical aggression, but that's changing. This is how I am rising out of my depression."

"I can see that you have become more aggressive than you used to be. I fully understand why. You do show that it's working and making you a better fighter!"

"Yes, Marwan, you should understand that. We will do this together, my warrior friend. I can hardly wait for a real opportunity."

"Our leaders say we will have opportunities soon to show what we can do against our enemies."

"And as I said, we will do this together, my friend," said Ali. "This is our community, and it's important that we work and fight together and protect each other as well. I will remember what you said, Marwan, but it might serve the others well to have experience wrestling with someone determined to take them out!"

CHAPTER THIRTY

In the late 1970s, chaos reigned throughout Lebanon as the civil war carried on. Major Saad Haddad commanded a battalion in South Lebanon, where they fought against PLO forces with materiel and other support from the Israelis. Haddad broke from the Lebanese army and formed his own Army of Free Lebanon, and his militia, later named the South Lebanon Army (the SLA), fought through much of the area south of the Litani River. This region was home to thousands of PLO fighters and more than 100,000 Palestinian civilians, amongst others.

Mustapha, one of the three men in the small guard post at the entrance to the PLA camp, stretched, scratched himself, and leaned to one side, loudly passing gas as he looked down the narrow valley road in the gloom of the predawn light. "Two more hours, Mohammed, and we will be relieved. It's so quiet and still, I can barely keep awake." Ahmed, the third man, had already dozed off in the back.

They shared the last of the strong coffee from the flask and rubbed their eyes to stay awake. It was too early even for the first birdsong, and the fighters slowly felt, rather than heard, a low trembling far in the distance.

"Is there something out there, Mustapha?" said Mohammed, suddenly coming wide awake. "Look," he said, pointing down the road. "I saw a tiny flash of light!" He jumped forward, grabbing the metal bar on the sill of the open front of the outpost. "Quiet. Listen. Do you hear vehicles?"

Ahmed heard this exchange and shook himself awake. The three of them stood side by side, peering down the road. Their eyes strained to focus through the darkness. An impression of movement suddenly turned into the shape of a Giat AMX-13 75-mm light tank. It bumped up over a hill on the road, followed closely by an FV4101 Charioteer and three Panhard AML 90 armoured vehicles, all former Lebanese army equipment. Even at a distance, the men could identify the equipment through the gloom.

"Call the commander!" shouted Mohammed.

Ahmed took off running up the hill toward the camp to spread the word. Within seconds, the intruders opened fire, with a burst of shells landing near the guard post and a rain of machine-gun fire sweeping the roadside. Ahmed raced onto the parade square, shouting, "Attack! Attack!"

Ali and Marwan scrambled into pants and shirts, and with their comrades, grabbed weapons as they raced for the barracks door.

"We have nothing that we can defend ourselves with in the face of such equipment. Into the hills," the officers shouted, looking at the approaching vehicles.

The fighters scrambled across the rocks and through dry brush to gain higher ground and find places where they could set up defences. Moments later, the armed vehicles passed the flaming guardhouse and roared into the open ground in front of the camp. Soldiers wearing the uniform and badges of the South Lebanon Army jumped down from the personnel carriers and torched the sheds and other temporary buildings. An officer on the top of the Charioteer opened fire with the heavy machine gun and sprayed the surrounding hills at random with gunfire.

Ali plunged ahead, running wildly as a bullet whined by his ear. The fighter a few feet in front of him suddenly bent backwards as a bullet hit him in the middle of his back. Ali was so close to him that he tripped over the slumping body and fell beside him, seeing the horror on the face of his colleague as he died. Ali covered his own head with his arms and felt other rounds slam into the ground close to him. After a few minutes, the firing ceased and an SLA officer in the square took out a loud hailer.

"This area has been declared the property of the South Lebanon Army." The loud hailer crackled and emitted squealing, high notes as the officer spat out his message. "We will not chase the few of you into the hills, but you will leave tonight. There are more important targets to deal with. We will not waste our resources on a few scared vermin. Any evidence of continued activity here will be seen from the air, and the Israeli Air Force will take joy in eliminating you for practice. God praise and keep Lebanon free."

The Palestinians slowly emerged from behind the rocks and bushes on the hill as the vehicles disappeared down the valley road. Four of their number, including Mohammed and Mustapha at the guard post, had been killed, and another three had minor wounds.

"I've called for transport," said the commander. "Collect anything you find that might be useful, and we'll leave here shortly."

Ali and Marwan fell into step as they returned shakily to the camp, soaked with sweat from fear and running. "That was quite a wake-up, Marwan," said Ali.

"Yes. It's horrifying when we seem to have so few supplies and our forces are so poorly equipped compared to our opponents."

Within fifteen minutes, two trucks lumbered up the hill. The Palestinian fighters jumped into them, carrying their pitiful armoury of guns and supplies.

CHAPTER THIRTY-ONE

DAMOUR

Walking down the hill in the morning sunlight, Ali felt more relaxed than he had for a long time. *Getting away from the camp for a day or two is a good thing,* he thought. After weeks of ever more strenuous training and several small sorties against the South Lebanon Army, Ali was becoming hardened. He was still obsessed by the death of his mother and deeply felt the melancholy that was part of his life. *There is no one but Fatima to whom I can turn, who appreciates my feelings and understands me,* he thought.

Fatima had also become a source of anxiety since her move back to Damour after leaving Tel al Zaatar. It would still be a long while before her injuries would be fully healed. The muscles and tendons in her shoulder had been badly injured in the incident at Tel al Zaatar and prevented her from doing much.

Ali noticed how odd it seemed to see children at play and hear the call of little voices from the schoolyard across the way. For months, he had been immersed in his training program, and the only people he'd seen for weeks on end were his fellow fighters. Women on the street were beating colourful carpets, sweeping in front of their doors, and calling to their friends. He could smell ripening fruit and inhaled the succulent scent of baking bread from the houses and shacks along the roadside. He took in the atmosphere of a peaceful Damour, where he had lived before the massacre in Karantina and the counter operation against the Christian forces. He smiled to himself as he recalled playing with Marwan as boys, not all that long ago. His eyes narrowed as he recalled quarreling with their Christian neighbours and the fights that he and his friends had with them at times.

Ali remembered the great times he'd had with Marwan, roaming the hills together, throwing concrete blocks around to build up their strength, and imagining themselves as Palestinian fighters. *"Warrior" Marwan was always the one who had wanted to fight*, thought Ali. "Karantina, Karantina," he whispered to himself, remembering the two of them shouting it out like fedayeen when they had ridden down from the hills in the back of a truck after the Palestinian fighters had taken their revenge for the massacre that had killed his father, now years earlier.

Ali walked down a narrow path between two stone walls and entered a tidy yard with several decrepit concrete block houses facing on to it. Toward the back was a shack with a rough wooden frame and sheets of layered plastic over it. A tin roof looked ready to slide off. Half a dozen chickens clucked and scratched around the yard, looking for insects in the weeds.

"Fatima," he called out. "Fatima?"

"I'm here, Ali," he heard, coming from behind the shack. "I'm just getting water."

He ran around the corner of the hut, seeking the voice, and threw his arms around Fatima, holding her closely.

"It is so good to see you, my lovely Fatima. How are you?" he demanded, stepping back and holding her softly by the shoulders, appraising her with a frown on his face.

"Fine, fine, but be careful of my arm," she said, twisting away from him gingerly. "My injuries are still tender to the touch. It is so wonderful to see you. How do you look bigger and more handsome every time I see you?" she said, blushing and reaching out to touch his cheek.

"Oh Fatima, I think of you every day. You're as pretty as ever," he said, taking her gently in his arms.

"Come into the house, Ali, and we'll have some tea. Mother has another fruit cart to work from and will be away in the streets all day."

THE STRUGGLE CONTINUES

The two of them sat closely together against the wall, quietly looking at each other and smiling while leaning back on large pillows with covers made from old and faded, but still soft, blankets. Fatima got up and made a fuss of preparing and pouring glasses of rich and heavily sweet mint tea to mark the occasion. Then she said, "All right, Ali, tell me how you've been feeling and what you've been doing. What is life like these days in the camp? I worry about you all the time."

Ali leaned back and sipped his tea, careful not to spill it on the pillows or himself. "Don't worry about me, Fatima. I'm training hard and plans are coming for some major attacks. We will not allow Haddad and his filthy men to push us around."

"He has a bad reputation amongst the Lebanese. We see it in the newspapers from Beirut, and people are complaining that he's trying to break up the country."

"He's just a comical puppet of the Israelis and needs to be dealt with. I've come to realize that those who oppose us and treat the Palestinians like dogs understand only force. We will take the fight to them."

Fatima was shocked at his tone as well as his words. "Ali, that doesn't sound like you!"

"Yes, it is me. I have changed. How can I see my parents killed, you injured, and our people devastated without it arousing bitterness in my heart? I am burning with desire to strike back." Ali finished his tea and put the glass down beside him.

"Oh Ali, you must take care. Is this really what you think, or are you taking on the views of those fighters you spend all your time with?" Fatima's dark brown eyes looked searchingly into Ali's face.

He returned her gaze and then had to look away. Looking into the middle distance, he spoke. "Fatima, my brothers in the fedayeen have become close and reliable friends. We work together and take care of each other. Belonging to them and being active in the movement shows people who I am." He rose to his feet in one swift movement and held out his hand to help Fatima up. "Come, let us walk. I want to see what remains of the town."

The two of them walked the streets. They saw many houses that had been damaged in the fighting. Others were very neat and set in rows along the tree-lined streets, with geraniums in window boxes. Children played in the streets, and mothers—looking stressed from their endless work—chatted with their neighbours as they watched over the little ones. Life looked quite normal. Fatima told Ali of their hard, daily struggle for existence.

"It's not just our people who are suffering, Ali. One of my other friends at the clinic told me that Lara became so depressed after the destruction of Tel al Zaatar that she had a breakdown and can't work. She has gone back to Switzerland and will remain there for some time."

"You always seemed so connected to that clinic, Fatima, and loved the work. You felt you were doing something useful. We need medical workers badly. Are you working in a clinic or hospital here?"

"No. With my injured arm, they don't want me to help in the clinic here." Fatima's voice cracked a little, betraying her frustration. "Doctors and nurses have come to work here from Jordan and Egypt, even Libya, and they run everything. All they have for me is cleaning. I hope this arm gets better."

They returned to the shack late in the day and shared a meagre meal with Dalia, who brought some bruised fruit that she couldn't sell from her cart. Ali provided Dalia with a short form of the views he had given Fatima during the day. As the light began to fall, he left to pick up a ride that was going south toward his camp.

Fatima walked with him to the main road. "Ali, I'm concerned at your attitude. You have become hardened. This is not the Ali I have known. Remember the better times and your concern for others?"

"I understand, but I must be realistic. The situation of our people is desperate. Here comes the truck," he said, looking up toward a battered farm vehicle with an open back, clattering along the road toward them. "I must go. Take care."

After he had gone, Fatima returned home, feeling downhearted. Clearly troubled, Dalia spoke up as soon as she entered the room. "Fatima," she said, "Ali is not the same gentle person he was as a boy. He has never talked in such a hard manner. He sounds all too much like his mother as her anxieties took over her thinking."

Fatima let out a deep sigh. "I too am concerned, Mother. May Allah go with him and protect him."

CHAPTER THIRTY-TWO

SOUTH LEBANON

Marching across the square toward the assembled fighters, Company Commander Said al Musawi looked particularly determined. His posture was unusually upright, and the puffs of dust from where he walked seemed to rise higher than usual. His bronzed belt buckle shone in the afternoon sun, and his polished boots glistened, as if daring the dust to come anywhere near them.

He addressed his troops. "Men, we have an important mission to undertake. We have information from a loyal resident in a village across the border that the Israelis are assembling special electronic survey equipment. This would endanger our forces across southern Lebanon. We must take steps immediately to destroy this equipment. Your officers have determined that the Haytham platoon will undertake this mission. Platoon leader, take over. May Allah go with you."

Ali threw his shoulders back and stood straighter than ever, his face flushed with pride and his heart beating faster. *At last,* he thought, *a real operation against the Israelis!*

Ashraf, the platoon leader, started talking as the commander turned and walked away and the other platoons dispersed. "Men, there is more," he said. "For this mission, I will be replaced by a specially trained combat officer from another unit farther north who has knowledge of the equipment and goals of this action."

He swung his arm out to the left and waved his hand, beckoning a fighter standing at the side to come closer. "I introduce your leader for this mission, Abadiyah al Ghazzawi." A slim, well-tanned, and quite attractive woman of about twenty-five stepped forward.

Ali was not the only fighter to show surprise, but their disciplined training prevented even one of them from reacting verbally.

The woman spoke forcefully and directly. "Fellow fedayeen, tonight we will embark on a mission that our colleagues and the people of Palestine will long remember. Not only will we offer protection to our fighters in their camps but we will show the Israelis that they are not immune from attack, even as they occupy our land. Beyond that, the international community will see that dealing with Israel, whether selling them sensitive communications gear or even going to Israeli occupied areas as businessmen, tourists, or settlers, comes with a price to pay. You have thirty minutes. Go first to the food shelters and eat, and then bring your gear here. We leave shortly after."

Ali was elated. "Marwan, this is wonderful. Not only do we get to participate in our first venture into Israel, but we do it together," he said, gathering his gear in the barracks and looking over the grey-blanketed beds to his friend Marwan. "I am very excited."

"This will be our making as PLA fighters. We'll soon be veterans and able to tell stories to the recruits," replied Marwan. "Come on, let's be the first of our platoon back on the parade ground."

Light was falling as the dozen men gathered, sharing the excitement of the operation ahead. *"Yellah,* let's go," called Abadiyah as a battered, old, grey, diesel farm truck slowed to a stop on the ground. "Everyone in the back. Move."

They climbed to the deck of the truck, which had wooden slats along the sides and a wooden gate at the back. A fighter leaned over and pulled up the gate, securing it with a simple latch. Abadiyah jumped on the running board and got in the front cab. They drove south for forty-five minutes toward the coast. By then it was dark. The driver turned and bumped down onto a farm road, then drove into a banana plantation. The men felt the humidity and smelled the thick, musty scent of the vegetation. The tang of the sea rose to mingle with the dank air. The driver turned right onto an even narrower and little used track. The fighters in the back were standing, peering over the side with interest, trying to see ahead. The leaves of the banana plants swept over them. Marwan licked his lips and rubbed his face as the vegetation brushed his head.

After a hundred metres, Abadiyah jumped down and walked ahead, the truck creeping behind her through the tall plants. The driver had extinguished the headlights. "Stop," she said in a whisper, motioning to the driver. "Wait here." Her boots becoming soaked on the wet ground, she walked forward noiselessly and disappeared into the bushes. The platoon waited tensely, sensitive to every crack, or whine of insects, or rustling of reptiles in the undergrowth.

Fifteen minutes later, Abadiyah returned out of the gloom. She waved at the truck driver to follow her and then turned and walked back into the darkness. Only the faint sound of waves on the shore could be heard in the background. The truck moved forward slowly, swinging from side to side on the uneven ground. Fronds from the plants continued to sweep the top and sides of the vehicle, whipping at the men standing in the back. All at once, they parted the last of the plants and entered a small clearing beside the water. A dark blue, rusted van stood waiting. Two men in dark, loose clothes and knitted hats were leaning against the land side of the vehicle, smoking. Out in the water, perhaps a kilometre away, was a darkened fishing boat, just visible in the moonlight. A tall, bearded man stood in a five-metre inflatable Zodiac that bobbed at the shore.

"All right, everyone down from the truck. Keep quiet. You and you," Abadiyah said, pointing at Ali and Ahmad, another fighter, "take your rifles. Go along the sand for one hundred metres on either side and stand guard. Move just off the beach, so you can't be seen easily. The rest of you, we need to unload the gear from this van and put it in the boat over there." Abadiyah opened the back of the van. There were wooden boxes of automatic rifles, explosives, grenades, and clips of ammunition from floor to ceiling. The fighters quickly complied, and in a few minutes, half of the gear was loaded.

"That's enough for now. Six of you get in the boat. Take these boxes and guns to the trawler out there. They'll come back for us," she said to the others on the shore. She waved impatiently at the silent man from the trawler, who crouched by the outboard motor.

THE STRUGGLE CONTINUES

As the fighters tumbled in, he pulled the starter cord and the boat surged away from the shore. Those left behind brought the rest of the gear from the van to the shore, ready to load for the second trip.

The two men with the now empty van turned it around and left, disappearing smoothly into the gloom of the plantation. The fighters' own truck driver had made a tight turn in the small clearing and stood ready to leave when ordered.

After what seemed a long time, the Zodiac returned. The man at the tiller cut the engine and drifted up onto the shingle beach. "Load up quickly," Abadiyah said in a harsh whisper.

As the fighters handed the gear to others who had jumped into the boat to load, a signal flashed from the fishing boat. "Now. We go immediately," Abadiyah called. "Push out. Go. Go."

On guard down the beach, Ali and Ahmad heard her order and ran back toward the boat as the others scrambled in. Ali ran hard along the shore, pumping his arms, but stepped into an underwater hole. He fell headlong into the water and righted himself, gasping for breath from the cold water. His sodden clothes hampered him as he tried to run toward the boat, which was starting to move. "Wait! Wait!" he called out.

"Go! Go!" said Abadiyah, urging the boat forward.

Ahmad just managed to grab a hand hold and was hauled in bodily. Looking straight out to sea, Abadiyah screamed at the man on the engine to turn it to full throttle. As the boat leapt forward, Ali jumped too but collapsed into the water as the boat pulled away from the shore and sped out to sea.

He sat back in the water, waist deep, soaked, and forlorn. The operation had left him behind.

The truck driver called *"Yellah."*

Ali shuffled over to the truck in his soggy clothes. With great effort, he pulled himself up and collapsed onto the seat. He had a last look out to sea. They were not coming back for him. *This will not go well,* he thought as the truck driver engaged the gears and lurched along the track into the gloom. Ali stifled a sob as he felt his failure stain his soul.

CHAPTER THIRTY-THREE

COAST OF ISRAEL

It was quiet. Early morning. The trawler had moved ahead slowly through the night and was close to the coast. The sun was poised to rise in the sky to the east. High, pink clouds drifted across a deep-blue sky. The area looked empty with only a few low buildings in the distance and no people or animals visible. A light wind blew sand over the grassy top of the ridge at the back of the beach. Marwan, who had arrived on the shore from the trawler on the second trip, helped the others drag the Zodiac up the garbage-strewn sand toward a clump of tall, sugar-cane-like plants at the edge of the low bank. The faint stench of sewage fouled the air, and a trickle of polluted water seeped in a stinking pool around the base of the plants. After heaving the boat partially under the cover of the foliage, the fighters sat in the sand and looked back out to sea. A slight swell moved the water in lazy waves toward the shore. There was no sign of their fishing boat or other vessels.

"This doesn't look much like a village with electronic survey equipment," Marwan whispered to the man next to him.

"I heard that," said Abadiyah sharply. "Indeed, we are on a different mission. I couldn't say anything until we had left because of security. This operation has taken us to Israeli occupied Palestine as promised, but not for the reason you expect. This will allow you to show your devotion to Allah and to see his glory." She dramatically pulled a long knife from a scabbard on her waist and plunged it into the fabric of the boat several times. "We will not need this again," she said, ominously.

Shoving Ahmad and Mohammed, the two men beside her, she said, "I need to know exactly where we are. Go up the bank and see if you can identify any landmarks." The pair scampered up the low bank and paused, squatting at the crest to look over. To their left, some distance away, a lone jogger, a woman in her thirties, was coming their way in the morning gloom. They crouched below the grasses and waited. Two or three minutes passed until they could hear the slap of her shoes on the path. Just as she passed their hiding spot, they jumped up, startling her. The woman stumbled in surprise, and Ahmad and Mohammed grabbed her roughly by the arms. The jogger fell sideways heavily onto the grass beside the path. Ahmad leaned over her menacingly and peered into her face.

"Who are you? What is this village?" he demanded in Arabic, waving his arm toward the few buildings in the distance.

"No Arab," she said in an incomprehensible tongue. She mumbled "Rooshah" a couple of times, and shuddering with fear, burst into tears.

Abadiyah appeared and stood over them. "She must be Russian," she said. "I learned a little when I went to Moscow on combat courses. Who are you and where are we?" Abadiyah spat in broken Russian.

"This is my village where I have lived for my three months in Israel. Haifa is thirty kilometres that way," the woman said, shaking with fear and pointing a trembling finger across the fields.

"How many people are in the village?" Abadiyah demanded, slapping her across the face.

"About fifty," she said. "It is just a small farming village."

Abadiyah translated this information for her men. "We will go there and look for transport," she said. As she spoke, she reached under her jacket and pulled out a pistol that glistened metallic blue in the sun. "Welcome to Palestine, Jew," she said quietly as she shot the woman full in the face. The woman groaned and slumped to the grass. She convulsed for a second or two, then was deadly quiet.

The others standing close by on the beach were shocked. Marwan felt the bile rise in his throat, and he projectile vomited into the grass. Another joined him, and several others looked unsteady. "Roll her body over the bank, and let's move out," their leader said, striding toward the village that was perhaps a kilometre away.

"We're going to Tel Aviv," she told the men. "We need transport. There must be a truck in the village to take." She laughed. "We can't carry all these weapons and walk there."

They followed the path and turned on to a farm track into the village. Early in the morning, most people were already in the fields, but two women, a man, and two children were standing at a central crossroads. Abadiyah ordered half the men to stay behind and told the rest to walk together. They continued walking openly, up the track toward what was now clearly a bus stop, as if they were a normal group of fatigue-wearing military men on a training hike with nothing to hide.

"When I give the word, open fire on them," she said quietly to the men at the front. As the fighters drew closer, now fifty metres away, the people looked at them with interest but no alarm.

"Now!" she cried.

The group at the bus stop jumped and moved all at once as the automatic weapons fire slammed into them. One woman fell on her back, her hands grasping for her small child, who had been shot in the neck and whose bloody body fell on her dying torso. The man fell to his knees, clutching his stomach as the fighters closed in and fired multiple rounds into him. The second woman and her child already lay on the ground, bodies twisted and motionless. In moments, all were dead.

"Drag those bodies behind that equipment," said Abadiyah, pointing at a small harvester. The men in the second group, who had stayed back, ran to join the other fighters. "I can see dust in the air over there," she said. "It must be the bus they were waiting for. We'll take that. I want two men at the stop and the rest behind the building." She brushed back her hair with her hand and stood at the stop with two others. An old, faded blue and white bus, liberally dented and belching smoke, approached. The brakes shrieked as it drew to a halt, and a hiss of air announced the blue door opening.

Abadiyah jumped up on the step, raised her sub-machine gun, and fired into the roof of the bus. Two other fighters crowded in behind her. The quiet exploded into the sounds of screaming and the noise of baggage and packages falling. Passengers tripped and stumbled as they tried to get onto the floor.

"Be still and very quiet, everyone. We're going for a ride, but we have more passengers who want to board. Anyone who moves or makes noise will be shot." The rest of Abadiyah's crew jumped onto the bus, pushing the dozen or so passengers to the back. "Driver. Move!" Abadiyah shouted, and the old bus lurched into motion.

As the bus picked up speed, the mood became more relaxed amongst the fighters. "It's like going to a football match," one laughed. "Should we be singing a song?"

Most of the passengers cowered in their seats and tried not to be noticed. Two old women, sitting together, and a wrinkled, grey-haired man sat upright in their seats, staring at the Palestinians, memories of an earlier, dark time in Europe reflected in their faces.

"We will sing when we are welcomed by Allah," replied Abadiyah joyfully. Her plan and her ambitions were moving along.

Marwan stood toward the back of the bus with his rifle aimed at the terrified passengers. *This does not look like the operation I expected*, he thought. *I'm here to fight for our cause, not to kill innocent farm workers and children.*

Jacob, a gangly and pimpled teenager, slowly worked his arm around his shorter friend, Aron, and put his hand on the rear escape door behind them as he watched the Palestinians. He put a little pressure on the handle, and it moved ever so slightly. "If I were to open this door, we could escape," Jacob whispered to Aron. "The bus will slow on a hill and provide an opportunity. Even better, if we do so around a curve, those who get out will be out of the line of sight of the moving bus for a few moments."

The bus lumbered along the secondary road, spreading blue exhaust smoke through a hamlet where two people were waiting for it. It didn't slow down. One of the fighters opened fire at the people as the bus passed, and several others cheered as they saw the man and woman slump to the ground. "Well," the fighter said with a laugh, "we saved them the cost of a bus ticket."

The bus rattled on, belching diesel exhaust and causing animals to raise their heads as it passed. The driver, with Abadiyah's pistol at his head, slammed his foot to the floor and shifted the long, floor-mounted gear stick as he started up a winding hill.

Jacob glanced ahead and saw them approaching the hill just as the driver engaged a lower gear. The engine roared as it challenged the hill, and the bus strained to keep up the momentum. With a lunge, Jacob pushed down on the handle, and the rear escape door started to open. A sweep of air combined with dark exhaust rushed through the opening. Jacob fell forward out of the back of the bus, pulling Aron with him as he grabbed his arm. Cries erupted from the passengers as two small children also fell from the opening onto the road. Abadiyah did not immediately react, as she was at the front beside the driver, urging him on.

Hearing the commotion and turning to see the back door open, she shouted, "Throw a grenade! Throw a grenade! Marwan, throw it!" Marwan, the fighter closest to the door, quickly grabbed at his belt. As he did so, he lunged toward the opening. He looked out to see the four individuals twisted together on the road and slowly falling behind as the bus moved ahead. Marwan unhooked a grenade from his webbed belt, pulled the pin, and as he did so, tripped over a passenger on the floor. The grenade flew from his hand out the open door and onto the pavement, where it bounced. He watched as it rolled, seemingly in slow motion, the short distance down the hill toward the passengers on the road, scrambling to get up. It came to rest against Jacob's chest and exploded with a tremendous blast. Dust and red mist filled the air. The bus's brakes screamed and clanked as the driver slammed his feet to the floor. As the dust settled, Marwan could see that all four of the passengers had been obliterated, limbs severed and strewn across the road like debris after a tornado.

Abadiyah pushed her way to the back of the bus, cheering and slapping Marwan on the back for the "excellent work" he had done.

The passengers slumped into corners and lay on the floor, wailing and moaning. "You will all be quiet and stay on the floor," shouted Abadiyah, firing her pistol into the roof. One fighter leaned out and closed and secured the escape door and then stood by it.

"All right, we go on," Abadiyah said, walking back to the terrified and sweating driver. He put the bus in gear, and it lurched forward uncertainly.

Marwan leaned against the side of a seat and felt a sharp headache pound through his temples. He tried to clear his head with deep breathing. The tension in the muscles in his shoulders hardened like iron. *How could this happen?* he thought. *How did I get involved in this kind of operation?*

The bus carried on toward Tel Aviv at speed. The fighters were both enervated and frightened as they came to realize this could only end in their deaths. There was no more humorous banter. After a while, the road led between two small hills. The sides had been carved back to make way for the roadway and then were graveled and topped with grass. Goats were grazing lazily on the hilltops in the sun. As the bus emerged from the cut, a heavy armoured car swung out from each side, trying to block the road. The dumbfounded bus driver stepped on the gas, then the brakes, and swung the wheel. He looked up to see that he was careening into an intersection where other, and larger, military vehicles were halted to block the road. Heavily armed soldiers crouched and leaned against them. They opened fire from both sides on the front of the bus where Abadiyah stood.

Her body was shredded instantly by the impact of heavy bullets, and she collapsed on the driver in a shower of glass and blood. The fighters leaned out of the windows, firing their automatic rifles, and trying to throw grenades. One hit a window divider and bounced back into the bus, exploding and tearing into both Palestinian fighters and Israeli passengers. Suddenly, flames erupted and leapt to the roof, igniting the explosives the Palestinians were carrying. Dense, acrid smoke filled the bus. Fighters and passengers alike screamed with fear and pain as the bus was engulfed. Firing inside continued for a few moments, with no one really knowing who was firing at whom.

Shortly after, the army commander called to his men to cease fire, and they stood down. No more shooting or shouting came from the bus. The soldiers watched the horror of the inferno before them, realizing that the bus had contained many Israeli citizens.

CHAPTER THIRTY-FOUR

SOUTH LEBANON, 1978

Following the events on the Haifa to Tel Aviv Road, the Israelis swiftly launched an invasion of southern Lebanon. The region had seen years of attacks by Palestinians on civilian settlements in northern Israel and return raids by Israeli forces, some jointly with Haddad and his men. These intense conflicts made life all but unlivable on both sides of the border, and Israel was determined to bring that to an end. The military operation put additional pressure on the civilian population north of the border to move, and enormous numbers of Palestinians and Lebanese were displaced. This added to the tensions within Lebanon that had already intensified their civil war. One result was the expansion of the area controlled by Haddad, along with his extended cooperation with the Israelis.

The office of Israeli Prime Minister Menachem Begin issued a statement on an attack on the Haifa-Tel Aviv Road that had taken the lives of three dozen Israelis and wounded many more. Israeli security forces said that eleven Palestinian terrorists had been involved. Begin blamed the head of the military wing of Fatah, Abu Jihad, and laid final responsibility at the feet of PLO leader Yasser Arafat. Begin understood terrorism very well, having been the commander of Irgun for some years, an underground group that was regarded internationally as a terrorist organization and was then fighting to establish a Jewish state in the region. Irgun would later form the Likud Party.

A few days later, an aerial and artillery bombardment of South Lebanon preceded the invasion by 25,000 Israeli ground troops.

Most Palestinian and Lebanese residents fled to avoid the fighting, as did Palestinian forces. Some remained behind to fire artillery at advancing Israeli forces and the civilian settlements beyond them. The overwhelming power of the Israeli military made short work of their defences, and they quickly occupied the area up to the Litani River, except for the ancient Phoenician port of Tyre.

Ali and his platoon formed up with several others as they trudged north, seeking a safer place to establish a new base. After two exhausting days on the road with little food or water, they met with a transport truck and were driven several kilometres further north, and eventually, holed up in a school basement. The rooms were crowded with hundreds of exhausted, ready-to-drop Palestinian fighters. The smell of rank, unwashed bodies alone was enough to cause many fighters to sleep in the open. The outbuildings were full of weaponry, which was more important to the leaders than the manpower. The chaos caused by the Israeli invasion decimated the Palestinian military. The leadership was so widely dispersed that it took weeks to pull together. Villagers were forced to provide food and water for the fighters, imposing a burden on them, shared with family members who had also fled north. Haddad's radio station spoke of triumph over the Palestinians and the permanent nature of the secure zone across the south of Lebanon.

CHAPTER THIRTY-FIVE

"Ali," said Aduan, meeting him a week later in the school basement, "I have been looking for you in several temporary camps. Conditions are terrible, and no one knows what to do next. I'm sad to say that we can only assume that our Marwan was killed in the bus operation."

"I'm glad to see you," said Ali. "I feel so terrible about Marwan and full of shame that I failed to carry through with the operation."

"Ali, that is a tragedy, but the operation sent a strong signal to the Israelis that we will never let them keep our land. I understand that you feel ashamed that you failed to get into the boat, but your life has been spared. Your platoon leader, Ashraf, related what happened. The driver of the truck told him how hard you tried to make the departing boat. None of this is your fault."

"I feel wretched, Aduan. I haven't had any other friend as close as Marwan, and his life has now been lost. I know it was a brave mission for the cause, but I've lost a great deal. It's so depressing to lose first my family, now my best friend. I can only think of retribution, yet I can barely get up in the morning."

"Your platoon leader sees and understands the impact on you but withdrawing from your work and friends is not the way forward. Don't feel alienated from our cause and your involvement. Life will look better with time, and some change might help. I'm here to ask you to come with me and join a small group working for the PLA Intelligence Bureau. It's based in a quiet village in the eastern foothills."

"How can the PLA even exist now, Aduan? Look at the conditions in this basement. These men couldn't fight anyone. We don't see much effort being made to put things back together."

"No, Ali. The Israeli attacks were very violent and damaging to us, but every effort is being made to regroup. I've spent the past months with the Intelligence Bureau. You will understand that few people must know where I am assigned, so I haven't told you before. I need help and would be glad to take you as my assistant."

"I'd be pleased to work closely with you, Aduan. I'm willing to try." Ali bowed his neck and rubbed his forehead. "I will do what I can."

"Good, Ali. That will give you other things to think about, and you'll rarely be in active operations against the Israelis or Lebanese. There are valuable roles to play, and you'll be able to make a contribution to the cause. I've already spoken to the commander of the Intelligence Bureau and your platoon leader here. They agree. Gather your things."

CHAPTER THIRTY-SIX

CAIRO, AUGUST 1978

"Salim, I am glad to reach you. I've been here in Cairo for a couple of days but have been too busy to be in touch. How are you? How do you feel now that you've finished your law classes? It must be a relief to complete your courses. I remember the feeling well."

Salim grinned into the phone. "Grandfather, I am delighted to hear from you, and of course, I want to get together, if you have the time. Now that I've finished my degree, I have more time and am starting to think about a job. The past few months have been so busy, and I've been so focussed on my final exams, that I haven't looked ahead as I should have."

The old man chuckled softly. "Well, that may be resolved sooner than you think. I have been here for consultations with our colleagues on the outcome of the Egyptian Israeli Peace Treaty. Once more, we were left out of the discussions, and the interests of the Palestinian people were disregarded. Our colleagues, notably Farouk Abu Abbas, our Director of Political Affairs, whom you met in Cairo, were impressed with your participation in the discussions we had in Tunis a short while ago to prepare the PLO position when the Egyptian-Israeli Treaty was under discussion."

"That was extremely interesting, Grandfather. You probably know that I've done some speech writing for the Palestinian National Committee in the meantime."

"Yes, I do, Salim. Your help in drafting various speaking notes for our leaders has been much appreciated. The years you spent at school in the United States have given you a fluency in English that we can benefit from."

There was a quiet satisfaction in his grandfather's voice, and Salim felt a surge of pride in himself.

"Grandfather, you brought me up to respect our cause and to do my best to contribute to it, as has been our family custom. I am honoured."

"Yes," Yazid said. "We need your help once more, and this looks as if it could lead to a more permanent position. Farouk has asked me to see if you'd be prepared to go back to New York to assist our delegation, during the coming session of the General Assembly, to rally the support against the capitulation by Egypt and the effect it has had on us."

"This sounds like a great opportunity, Grandfather. I am more than pleased to accept." Salim could hardly believe his luck. This had been his dream since he'd had those few opportunities to go to the delegation in the summers while he was at school.

"It means leaving in the next two weeks, **Insh'allah,** Salim, so you need to get organized. Go with my fondest wishes, my son."

"**Shoukran**, Grandfather."

Salim thought immediately of the attractions of New York. He had seen little of them during his school days and summer breaks but would now be in a position to enjoy them.

CHAPTER THIRTY-SEVEN

NEW YORK

"Alex, I've just had a call to say that we can expect a meeting at the Office of Military Affairs this afternoon. We'll get confirmation within the hour," said Colonel Geoff Walker, military adviser on the Permanent Delegation. He stood at the door of Alex's office in a grey suit, tall and slim, as always looking as if he had left his uniform at home only by mistake, as his posture betrayed his long service in the military.

"All right, Colonel. I just had a call as well and am ready anytime. We can let each other know when we hear the details."

Walker looked as if he was about to salute but caught himself and disappeared with a nod of his head.

In March 1978, in response to the Israeli invasion of South Lebanon, the UN Security Council had adopted Resolution 425. The resolution calls for respect for the sovereignty, territorial integrity, and political independence of Lebanon; for Israel to withdraw from the area; and the establishment of the United Nations Interim Force in Lebanon (UNIFIL) to supervise the Israeli withdrawal. The purpose was to assist the government of Lebanon in reasserting their control over the area.

The Israelis did withdraw, turning over the areas they had occupied to Haddad's Army of Free Lebanon, leaving behind some two thousand dead Lebanese and Palestinians. Haddad was very pleased to have his own strip of country after the Israeli withdrawal, a narrow band across southern Lebanon that he intended to rule personally. In mid-April,

Haddad's forces had asserted their intentions by shelling a UN observer post, killing eight blue-helmeted UN soldiers.

Later that day, on the higher floors of the iconic UN headquarters building in New York, people filed into a conference room for the meeting to be chaired by the UN Under-Secretary- General for Military Affairs, Edward Fuller. A distinguished former British army major in intelligence services during WWII, Fuller had worked closely with the UN for many years. He was involved with the first major UN peacekeeping force deployment in the Suez in 1956 and had worked with the Office of Military Affairs ever since.

Wearing a Christ Church College, Oxford, navy-blue silk tie with the red crest and his usual dark-blue, chalk-striped suit, Fuller languidly leaned forward from his position at the head of the gleaming wooden table. Political and military liaison officers, from the delegations of the dozen countries that had provided the first forces for the UNIFIL operation in Southern Lebanon, jostled for seats around the table.

Fuller brushed his thick, grey hair to the right side with his hand. He cleared his throat to attract the attention of the chatting people in the room. "Ladies and gentlemen, as you are aware, Israel started to withdraw after UN Security Council Resolution 425 was passed, once they were sure of their control of various areas in Southern Lebanon. Major Haddad's forces, however, have been harassing our operation in Southern Lebanon since we first borrowed officers and troops from other regional UN operations and established our headquarters in Naqoura. There have also been attacks from random groups that remain to be identified. As you are aware, Haddad's forces attacked our HQ yesterday. This tragic incident will be discussed in detail later in a meeting between your ambassadors and the Secretary General.

The assembled diplomats shuffled in their seats and some murmuring broke out.

Fuller raised his hand in a calming gesture, and the room settled again. "The Secretary-General has made the usual protests publicly, and he's on the line to the Israelis privately. The press in all our countries has undoubtedly featured the incident. It has been proposed that a small group of us should go to Naqoura to highlight the incident and underline the role of UNIFIL. I intend to lead the group myself to emphasize our concern over recent events." There were nods of approval around the table, and Fuller looked pleased at this show of support.

Alex raised his hand and asked a question. "Under-Secretary-General, Canada will fully support such a mission and considers it imperative that the UN and members be seen to be taking this matter very seriously. Could you tell us what timing you have in mind?"

"Thank you for your delegation's support, Alex," said Fuller. "The final decision to proceed with a mission to the area will be taken later today. As for timing, I suggest we move as quickly as possible. I should add that I propose we meet with Haddad. We will undoubtedly have to include the Lebanese government and the Palestinians during our calls. Since Arafat met with our UNIFIL commander the other day in Beirut, we want to encourage whatever cooperation we can from them. After all, that meeting was, in effect, the first substantive recognition by the PLO of a ceasefire that involved Israel."

Fuller rose from his chair. "You are in a position to include all this information in the briefings for your capitals and ambassadors, and whoever attends the meeting this afternoon. Thank you, ladies and gentlemen. I expect you all have places to be."

Colonel Walker and Alex walked back along First Avenue toward the delegation offices, chatting through the prospect or likelihood of a successful operation in the area. Back at the delegation offices, they went into the ambassador's outer office.

"Is the ambassador in, Celine?" Alex said to her assistant. "We've just come back from the UNIFIL briefing and want to bring her up to date."

Celine buzzed the interphone, spoke briefly, and turned back to Alex and the colonel. "She'll see you right away."

The ambassador opened her door and invited them in. "Celine, please ask Rob to join us," she said, leaning out of the office.

Once the deputy, Rob Davis, had arrived, Alex ran through the discussion at the meeting in Fuller's office, reporting comments from the Under-Secretary on the Haddad raid and the proposal that a delegation from New York should visit the area.

"I've just received a call about the meeting this afternoon with the Secretary-General and was very positive about the idea," said Mme. Tremblay. "Colonel, do we have any more information about the attack on UNIFIL?"

Colonel Walker went through military reports he had received from Naqoura and agreed that they needed to draw wider attention to the situation. "There is no doubt, Ambassador, that UNIFIL will need to be enlarged and re-supplied in the coming weeks. I'll get on to National Defence in Ottawa to discuss their ability to take on an enhanced role for Canada."

"And, of course, I will report to Foreign Affairs as well and raise the possible expansion of our role," said Alex.

"I agree in principle that a group from New York should visit the area and that it should be done quickly," said Mme. Tremblay. "We need to be part of it. Alex, as it's your area of prime concern, you would be the logical representative for us. In the meeting this afternoon, I will suggest that. In the meantime, be sure that Foreign Affairs is onside."

Alex was pleased at this show of confidence in him. "Thank you, Ambassador. I would be glad to go. It's almost five years since I left my posting in Beirut. Since then, the civil war has officially broken out, and the security situation has badly deteriorated. While, in official terms, I am said to have been posted there before the civil war began, I don't expect that the people in our building who were killed in the fighting while we were there would agree. I would very much like to go and see what has happened since."

Ambassador Tremblay smiled at Alex's comment and added, "I expect you're glad that you weren't killed either." They all chuckled at the black humour.

About six-thirty that evening, the ambassador walked into Alex's office having just returned from the meeting with the Secretary-General. "Well, Alex, as we would expect, the Russians and the Chinese don't want anything to do with this mission, but they won't stand in the way either. Otherwise, there was strong support from all the troop contributors. I was the first to speak up about being a part of the mission and suggested you would be our representative."

"Thank you, Ambassador," said Alex. "I believe it's important that we take part."

Mme. Tremblay continued, "Some delegations still need word from their capitals, but it sounds as if it will be Fuller, one person from the Sec-Gen's office, and four or five delegations. They hope to get it organized to leave within a week. It was agreed that, from the political perspective, the only way to go is to fly through Beirut, then go to Naqoura by UN helicopters."

"Sounds like a good plan," replied Alex. "It will be an extremely interesting trip, and I strongly agree that the UN has to stand up for itself."

CHAPTER THIRTY-EIGHT

LEBANON

The Middle East Airlines plane slowed and shuddered as the rudders lowered and the aircraft began its approach to the Beirut airport. Alex heard the whine of the wheels going down and looked out the window as they banked to the right and started to flatten out toward the airport. Flying just off the coast, Alex was astounded to see the devastation in the city from years of civil war. It was barely recognizable in some areas. Hundreds of buildings had been destroyed and many streets were full of rubble.

Alex was sitting beside his Norwegian colleague, Martin Fredriksen who had come to New York from a posting in Tehran several months earlier and had become a valued colleague on Middle Eastern issues. Alex found Martin to be knowledgeable on the area, and they exchanged views frequently.

"Martin," Alex said, peering out the scratched window and gesturing at the carnage below, "the city looks as if it's been bombed, not just shelled with artillery. My God, look at the St. Georges Hotel out on the point! It was once the best-known landmark in the city. It looks totally burned out. We used to walk along the corniche nearby with the children and buy *kaak*, a street delicacy that foreigners called 'hepatitis rings.'"

Martin looked bemused at the description.

Alex laughed. "It's really a large, crispy-baked hollow ring, covered with sesame seeds and shaped vaguely like a purse. When you buy one, the vendor breaks a hole in it and pours in a thyme-based ground spice called za'atar. Then they shake it, so the spice goes around the circle. Delicious, but not always handled with the greatest concern for hygiene!"

"The Iranians serve something like that at their New Year celebrations, Alex, but it's a sweeter pastry," said Martin. "I won't comment on the hygiene." They both laughed this time.

Moments later, the plane settled onto the runway and reversed engines. Alex saw two large, white helicopters with UN letters painted on the side. The aircraft slowed and turned, taxiing back toward the side of the terminal. Stairs were wheeled out and a cordon of soldiers lined up on both sides, forming an aisle between the plane and the terminal. As the door to the plane opened and the warm spring air flowed in, a smart and well-decorated Lebanese officer came in and asked for the UN delegation to identify themselves. He asked that other passengers stand aside while the group left the aircraft. Descending the stairs into the brilliant sunlight, Alex and the others could see four light-armoured vehicles at the base of the plane with soldiers manning machine guns on top.

A civilian wearing a slim-cut, dark, well-tailored suit stepped forward. He identified himself as Salim Said, Director General of the Foreign Ministry. He shook hands and then swiftly guided the delegation into the terminal. More soldiers were stationed inside and stayed on their guard as the group was escorted to a VIP lounge with heavy, upholstered furnishings set around the sides of the room. The Ghanaian commander of UNIFIL, Brigadier General Kuweku, and two aides were there. They welcomed Under-Secretary-General Fuller and introduced themselves to the others on the delegation, including Anil Sharma from the Office of the Secretary-General and officers from the delegations of Ireland, Bangladesh, Norway, Finland and Canada that had contributed troops to UNIFIL.

Tired from the stuffy, five-hour flight from London, where they had spent a night enroute, the New York-based delegates settled into the huge, soft armchairs upholstered with garish, sateen damask and gold fringes. Waiters appeared with massive trays of mint, sweet ginger, and other teas. These were followed by large glasses of cooled fruit juice and plates of sweet pastries, nuts, and dates, and then more rounds of tea.

As the delegation enjoyed their refreshments, Brigadier Kuweku stood and addressed them. "I am pleased to welcome you to Lebanon. After a short period here to relax, you will be flown on UN helicopters to Naqoura, where you will stay in very comfortable accommodations in a private house. We will have a further briefing on the program once we arrive at the residence. However, to start it off, our understanding of the incident that led to the deaths of our troops last week is that a new, local commander in Haddad's forces let things get out of hand, and they now regret the incident. That is their claim, in any event."

Eyes were raised in disbelief among the delegates. Alex blew out a puff of air.

Fuller returned the thanks for the welcome. "Brigadier, we so appreciate you making the arrangements for us on short notice. The attack on your troops was deplorable. We're here to ensure that the Palestinians, Haddad, and the Israelis take UNIFIL seriously. Our message is that such an attack will not happen again without serious consequences."

After an hour of pleasantries and discussion, they boarded the helicopters and flew south, seeing below a low surf washing up on beautiful beaches, and brilliantly clear views of the pine-covered hills. This gave the impression of peace and security, contrasting with the chaos and conflict they knew was on the ground. Forty kilometres south of the airport, the beautiful city of Sidon unfolded before them. One of the major ports in the era of the Phoenicians and a centre of their vast trading empire, over the millennia, Sidon had seen a host of invaders. Jutting out from the stone front corniche, they saw a magnificent limestone castle built by Crusaders in the thirteenth century, seemingly floating on the water. Some further fifty kilometres along, the Litani River spilled into the sea; then the city of Tyre appeared, a major Phoenician port, later important to the Romans. It was a magnificent sightseeing tour. Alex's mind conjured up memories of visits there in more peaceful times, sitting with his family at wonderful seafood restaurants on the boardwalk, eating fresh grilled fish and huge prawns, and drinking cool, light Lebanese wines.

The pilot interrupted Alex's reverie by announcing their imminent arrival in Naqoura. Moments later, the helicopter swept inland and descended noisily onto a large parking area behind a tall house, looking out toward the Mediterranean.

"What an introduction to Lebanon," said Martin to Alex as he moved toward the door with him and their other colleagues. "In all the times I've been in and out of Tehran, I've never had the opportunity to fly via Beirut and see anything of Lebanon. I'm sure the city looked better in the past, but this countryside and the coast are beautiful."

Alex agreed, still basking in his glorious reminiscences.

As they descended from the helicopter, a young soldier wearing a blue UN beret anxiously said in a Scandinavian accent, "Please leave quickly, as the second helicopter must land here. Please walk across the grass and straight into the house."

Alex left the helicopter feeling the sudden strength of the sun. Ahead of him, a three-storey, yellow stone house sat half-covered with the stunning scarlet and purple flowers of the bougainvillea vines climbing to the red-tiled roof. He entered a large entrance hall, was struck by the cool breeze coming at him across a dark tiled floor, gleaming with polish, and sensed the smell of beeswax. The arrivals were drawn through a large reception room by the magnificent view through wide-open, floor-to-ceiling windows. Beyond was a huge, covered porch set with chairs and tables laden with bowls of fruit, sweet pastries, and a variety of soft drinks. As others did, captivated by the astounding view, Alex walked straight to the front. He looked over a lovely grassy garden shaded by pine and palm trees, cascading down the steep with the Mediterranean beyond.

A UNIFIL officer appeared. "Dinner will be at 8:00 p.m. on the terrace. You will be joined by several UNIFIL members. Tomorrow morning, you will have the opportunity to visit the headquarters and two outposts."

Dinner with the delegation and members of the UN force was a relaxed affair. Alex enjoyed the spirited discussion of the challenges of the local situation and personalities as well as the politics in the UN building in New York. It was past eleven o'clock when everyone retired to their comfortable accommodation. It had been a long day.

***

The next morning, Alex awoke to birdsong in the garden. The air held the scent of the many flowers around the house and the tang of the sea. *Quite different from the smoke and exhaust in the air in New York and the clamour of sirens that never stops*, he thought.

After breakfast, two armoured cars and a pair of white fourteen-passenger vans, with UN on the side in large letters, arrived at the house. The diplomats, wearing the casual pants and shirts that had been suggested, assembled on the front porch for a photo and then climbed into two vans and were taken to the nearby UNIFIL headquarters.

They entered the bland, three-storey concrete building, which must have been a school, and were escorted into a room that lacked only the small desks they imagined would be there.

Brigadier Kuweku made a ritual speech about the role of UNIFIL and how pleased they were to receive their visitors. "We're a long way away, and I particularly must note my appreciation that UN headquarters in New York is aware of the difficulties we're facing with this deployment. I am pleased to introduce Lieutenant Colonel Byrne, who is my number two on the ground. He is very experienced in the region, having joined us on a transfer from the UN Disengagement Observer Force on the Golan Heights." The brigadier took a seat to one side.

A smiling, burly and fit ginger-haired Irish officer stood and took over the podium. He crisply acknowledged the visitors and went straight into his presentation. Byrne went over the maps, providing a view of UN emplacements. He took the group through recent activities of UN and SLA forces in the area as well as of Israeli forces with their overwhelming strength mere kilometres away. He finished with a detailed account of the attack by Haddad's forces on the UN offices and brought up prospects for the coming weeks.

The group then spent an hour discussing the needs of the UN force, expected deployments by the Israelis, Haddad, and the Palestinians, and the upcoming program. The New York delegates now had a better idea of the demands on the UN force and prospects for the effectiveness of the operation.

Taking a break and a cup of coffee at the back of the room after the briefing, Alex said to Martin, "I thought the Under-Secretary was clear and offered the leadership I expect of him as he led each intervention. The UNIFIL members were impressed and seem grateful for the visit. This will be a stimulating trip."

"I can only agree, Alex," said Martin. "With leadership like that, this operation will be very effective, whatever the challenges and resources available."

Piling back into the two vans, they were escorted by the two light-armoured vehicles and drove off to see UN outposts in the West Sector. After twenty minutes of driving through dusty back roads and pine-treed slopes, the vehicles mounted a promontory, looking over farms below, and pulled to a stop. A white-painted cement block building, and walls with huge UN markings, was built around a good-sized square. This was surrounded by a white cement, brick, and sand bagged wall, over which flew a huge UN flag. Barbed wire was rigged around the main opening to the wall, and the entrance road was set at an angle so that no vehicle could be driven straight in.

The New York group was readily received by officers and men of the different countries having contributed forces. A Peruvian major, Alois Fernandez, gave the group a tour of the outpost. They squeezed into small concrete rooms, below ground, containing communications equipment and the command centre with a viewing platform above. The diplomats took turns on top of the outpost, looking through the telescopes as the major urged them to look at

Haddad's and Palestinian emplacements across the valley and into the hills.

Down the hill, a few small, dusty villages dotted the farming area. Many of the buildings had collapsed roofs and evidence of walls crumbling from earlier attacks by Israeli and then Haddad forces. Alex spotted people working in the fields, and donkeys pulling ploughs, and commented on them.

"These farmers only come into the valley during the day," said Major Fernandez. "As the day ends, they go back north, maybe fifty to sixty kilometres, across the Litani to where they and their families have been living ever since they were driven out. Not an easy life."

The group digested this thought in silence.

The troops later laid out a table of sandwiches and drinks for lunch in the square. The UN soldiers on duty at the outpost and the delegates from New York exchanged views, the former responding to many questions about life on the line.

The delegation's final stop of the day was a second outpost farther east. This one was on a clifftop overlooking a main road coming from the border with Israel. In the distance, they could see Israel itself with a high, electrified fence on the border and a wide strip of vacant land before heavy Israeli military equipment parked at military installations. That discussion with UN force members centred on Israeli movements and exposure and the relative strength of Palestinian forces. Returning to Naqoura late in the day, they drove along mostly dusty roads strewn with burned-out military vehicles as well as cars and trucks damaged during various attacks. Alex flinched involuntarily as they passed one horrifying group of ten badly damaged and burned personal vehicles, apparently pushed aside off the road by bulldozers to clear an intersection.

Under-Secretary Fuller spoke up as they finally returned to their residence around dusk, saying, "Time for a drink!" Everyone agreed. *After seeing the disruption and devastation that this conflict causes, I could really use that drink,* thought Alex. *Fuller knows what he's talking about.* They later ate whole, grilled fish with a garlic sauce and lightly grilled vegetables on the terrace. The evening was spent talking through the day while they enjoyed the magnificent sight of the sun setting over the Mediterranean.

CHAPTER THIRTY-NINE

UNIFIL HQ

Alex woke up before dawn the next day when the birds were still quiet. He dressed and wandered into the main reception rooms, where a man in a white jacket with gleaming brass buttons was setting places at the tables and had just brewed the coffee. Alex took a mugful out onto the terrace, where he found two of his companions already there, watching the rising light play on the sea in the distance.

The group had been advised to dress well, as they would meet government officials during the course of the day. Alex was wearing a light, tan-coloured summer suit and anticipated being warm but hoped for fresh air, as he heard they would have a longer drive into the more mountainous East Sector. First, they would visit a third UNIFIL outpost. From there, they would carry on to Marjayoun, where a meeting with some Lebanese government officials and religious figures was scheduled.

After breakfast, as the convoy prepared to move out, USG Fuller announced that there would be a stop of perhaps an hour at a farmhouse outside the village of Kfar Kila, a small agricultural community virtually on the border with Israel and within a stone's throw of the Israeli town of Metulla. He confirmed that there would be a meeting with Saad Haddad, the SLA leader.

Alex was excited to hear this news. They hadn't been sure that there would actually be an opportunity to meet Haddad, and everyone in the van from New York bubbled with enthusiasm and not a little nervousness at the prospect.

THE STRUGGLE CONTINUES

As they approached the area, after an hour's drive from the outpost, the vans and accompanying vehicles turned into a small road through an olive grove and bumped along a dirt track toward a cluster of buildings. There were half a dozen well-armed UN blue berets at the front of the house, and they could see UN vehicles parked there. Several armed soldiers in Lebanese army fatigues were at the other end of the house, standing around a couple of four-wheel-drive trucks and a pickup. The vans stopped, and Fuller got out, shaking hands with one soldier who then walked briskly into the house, guiding the Under-Secretary. Alex and the others followed. The warm air was heavy with the scent of vegetation and animals. It was a plain farmhouse, built from local stone, and had a tiled floor cracked with age and well worn from generations of boots. A short, fortyish, lean man with a heavy, dark moustache, who was wearing Lebanese army fatigues, rose from an overstuffed chair in the corner and held out his hand to Fuller.

"Excellency, welcome to my land. I am Major Saad Haddad. I am pleased that the United Nations recognizes my position in this region that I control for the security and territorial integrity of Lebanon." Haddad's English was accented but perfect. His vowels were more British than American.

Fuller resisted rising to the bait and shook his hand firmly.

"I would like to offer some refreshments to you and your colleagues. I have only limited time. Did you have a good trip from New York? Do you find the weather agreeable?" asked Haddad.

There were ritual exchanges of niceties. Haddad seemed to want to talk about everything but the issues at hand. Fuller finally interrupted to say, "Major, I appreciate that convivial exchanges such as this are important so that parties get to understand each other, but we too are pressed for time. We must deal with the matters at hand. May I first say that the attack by your forces on UNHQ in Naqoura recently, which resulted in deaths of eight of our troops, was deplorable and will not be tolerated in the future."

"You recognize, Excellency, that that was only a minor difficulty that will not happen again," said Haddad, somewhat more stiffly.

That hardly deals appropriately with the issue of eight UN troops you have just killed, thought Alex.

Fuller bristled at Haddad's tone. "I want you to understand, Major, that we take the incident much more seriously than that. I can assure you that it will not happen another time without serious consequences. Our troops are well trained and experienced and have the appropriate military equipment to respond. They have been issued orders to defend our operations. That could mean pursuing attackers as far as necessary."

Haddad appeared about to speak but held his silence.

Fuller continued. "The United Nations and the international community recognize that the political and military situation in Lebanon is extremely difficult. You take positions on those disputes upon which I will not comment, but along with your allies in Israel, you have imposed an enormous burden on at least 100,000 Palestinians by pushing them off the land where they had taken refuge. I cannot imagine that those same allies of yours want to see further destabilization of the area. I assure you that there are member countries of the UN that take this seriously. If you want to avoid greater outside intervention, you will ensure that such an attack never happens again." Fuller's face was reddening as he laid out his points, but the diplomat in him maintained his composure, and his features rearranged themselves into a controlled veneer.

Haddad's features had remained impassive throughout Fuller's remarks.

I wonder if Haddad really understands the seriousness of what the Under-Secretary is saying, thought Alex. *He needs to make a better effort at indicating penitence rather than just staring blankly at him.*

"Excellency, I can tell you that we are pleased to have the UN in situ in Southern Lebanon," Haddad replied. "We too value the stability of the region. Let me say that we will support the efforts of the United Nations to maintain peace and security in the area. We are pleased to work closely with you." He shrugged his shoulders and leaned forward with a smile. "I appreciate this opportunity for us to deal directly with each other. I have had a long army career and have had the pleasure of visiting Britain and dealing with your military. I acknowledge their centuries of loyal service to the Crown and can only view them with the greatest respect. You can depend on the full cooperation of my forces."

Fuller rose from his seat, and after reiterating the assurances of cooperation that Haddad had offered and bidding him goodbye, he walked out and got into a UN vehicle. "Bloody hell!" he said as the vans started up. "Haddad reached an entirely new level of obsequiousness in that exchange. We shall see what it means in the coming months."

In Marjayoun, they met and had lunch with district Lebanese military commanders and various religious leaders. The delegation's reception was extremely cordial, even with the information that Fuller and his delegation had met with Saad Haddad. They drove back to Naqoura late in the day, had a final debrief with the UN contingent, and settled in for a quiet evening, rehashing the meetings of the day over drinks and dinner.

The next morning, the helicopters returned to take the group back to Beirut. They flew along the coast and landed within a secure perimeter, where they were met as usual by UN force representatives and Lebanese protocol, then walked into the VIP lounge to await their return flight to London. Bags were off-loaded and placed under the care of some UN troops while the group settled in, waiting for their flight with the standard juices, teas, and pastries.

Martin Fredriksen asked that his bag be brought to him, explaining that he was planning a day or two in Beirut to see colleagues before returning to New York. "A driver from my embassy is to pick me up at the main arrival area. Many thanks to you, Under-Secretary, for an extremely interesting visit to Naqoura. I thank you for this opportunity to appreciate first-hand the challenges that the UNIFIL mission is facing and look forward to seeing you all back in New York."

The others bade Fredriksen farewell as an officer from the Lebanese Office of Protocol guided him toward the arrivals area.

CHAPTER FORTY

As Fredriksen approached the exit doors at the arrivals area, he said, "Oh yes, there's a van with a Norwegian flag on the windshield." He thanked the protocol officer, who gave him a half salute and went back into the terminal. On the curb beside a grey van waited a lightly bearded man of middle age, wearing a somewhat crumpled and worn brown suit and unpolished shoes. He was carrying a neatly lettered sign with Fredriksen's name on it. A brief exchange took place as the man took Fredriksen's bag.

A second man, heavy and moustachioed and wearing a loose canvas jacket, was sitting in the passenger seat. As the sliding door was opened, sitting on the other side of the back seat Fredriksen saw an impressively large, fit, third man with a heavy black beard wearing combat style pants and a t-shirt.

"You are Fredriksen. I have your photograph," he said. "Call me Farhad. The others you do not need to know. We are here to take you to your destination. We have a drive of some hours and have brought food and water."

Fredriksen noted that there was an automatic rifle leaning against the door on the far side. Farhad was holding a heavy pistol in his lap. A brown canvas bag that undoubtedly held further weapons was beside him. The van pulled away from the entrance and drove into the city in the direction of Bourj al Burajni. Fredriksen shrugged off his suit jacket to be more comfortable.

From his side view, the looks on the faces of the others in the van were cold and distant. Fredriksen got the message and stayed quiet.

No one spoke except the red-faced driver, who became flushed and sweaty as he yelled and gesticulated non-stop at other vehicles. He dodged from one side of the road to another, roaring into the tiniest of possible openings and braking suddenly, then lurching ahead as he manoeuvred through the intense traffic. All this was with his left arm out the window waving madly and making impolite hand gestures, as many other drivers did. Taxis spewed exhaust and endlessly honked their horns, either in anger at other cars or to attract riders for their shared routes. Small trucks and vans clogged the route. The streets were full of men wearing military fatigues. Many intersections had corners where sandbags and coils of barbed wire surrounded a protected area, and there were often wooden viewing platforms above. The identifying marks on these posts were flags and banners representing various factions, but all the men in them looked alike. It had proven better during the civil conflict not to identify yourself with any permanence as the militias fought back and forth across the city. What was your land one day was someone else's the next. Huge numbers of buildings on the narrow streets showed signs of fire and destruction. Fredriksen coughed frequently as the three others in the vehicle smoked incessantly.

The driver turned on to a more major road at Hazmieh and sped up intermittently on the road east. Fredriksen saw periodic signs to the town of Aley, which proved to be fifteen kilometres away, most of it up the sharply rising Mount Lebanon. Cars and trucks raced up the two-lane, winding road, paying little attention to the sharp bends and turns hanging over the coastal plain below. At the top, the air was markedly fresher and cooler. Beautiful stone villas dotted the hillsides with magnificent views down across the city to the water. Long a retreat from the stultifying humidity and heat of Beirut in the summer months, Aley was a prosperous city that had avoided much of the conflict and bombardments in the ongoing civil war. People crowded the streets and shops, looking relaxed, stopping in coffee shops, and lingering to talk with friends.

Fredriksen's driver continued through the rising hills, along with the other drivers doing their best to honour the Lebanese belief that driving with speed and aggression are essential to maintaining their manhood and not wanting to take any chances.

Over the coastal mountains and dropping down the curving road into Chtoura, they entered the beautiful farmlands of the Bekaa Valley. Passing signs for a winery on his left, Frederiksen thought he would appreciate a good, cool bottle of wine at the moment. He assumed that such a suggestion might not be appreciated by his escorts. They drove through rich farmland for another half hour and then pulled off onto a small farm road in the foothills of the **Anti-Lebanon**[12] mountains pushing up against the Syrian border. The vehicle bumped and lurched down the track for a few minutes and then pulled into a dry, grassy area under some trees.

"We will stop here and eat," said Farhad.

The front passenger, who had not said a single word, brought a carton from the back and set it down. All four sat on the ground as he opened the box. He unfolded a cloth containing several kinds of vegetables cut in large pieces. There were containers of baba ghanoush, a blend of roasted eggplant and tahini, olive oil and lemon juice, along with hummus and some cold falafel. The driver leaned over and took a package of soft, flat pita bread out of the box and tossed it into the middle. All took some and tore off small pieces to use to dip into the spreads and pick up vegetables.

After they had eaten, Farhad spoke for the first time since they'd stopped, saying they would now sleep and then continue later. The driver first got out a few tools and changed the licence plates from Lebanese to Syrian, throwing the tools and plates in the back of the van. The others lay down on the ground. Soon the sounds indicated that the other men were fast asleep. Fredriksen stretched out and leaned on one raised arm, wondering what was ahead of him. Later, not even realizing he'd been asleep, he felt a boot touch him in the side, and the silent passenger motioned with a wave of the hand for him to get in the van.

---

12 Mountain range in Eastern Lebanon.

They crawled back to the main road, the sky still brilliantly blue in the late afternoon, and turned right in the direction of the looming Syrian mountains, still sunlit on top. Before long, they were climbing quickly and saw the border post ahead.

"When we get to the border, say nothing," said Farhad. They approached the barrier slowly, and two Lebanese soldiers came out to look in the car. A quick exchange of words with the driver, some friendly chatter, an envelope passed out the door, and they were through.

One hundred metres ahead, they went through largely the same ritual at the Syrian entry post.

Several kilometres down the hill past the border post, the van turned off the highway to the south and went through a small, primitive village. At the far end was an old, small, stone house built partly into the hillside. They stopped just short of the building, and the passenger got out and walked ahead to the dark house. He looked in the window and rapped on the glass. A face appeared at the window and looked out. Whoever it was then moved over and opened the door. The passenger waved at the driver to come forward, and he turned into the yard, leaving the van hidden under a sloping wooden roof.

"Out," said Farhad.

Fredriksen joined the three of them and approached the door of the house.

In the entranceway appeared a tall man of about thirty-five years, dressed in a pair of wide woolen pants, a loose rust-coloured shirt, and a sleeveless jacket. Around his waist was tied a black cotton *kamarband,* a garment that Martin knew had long ago been anglicized and adopted as a "cummerbund."

"My friend Martin, please come in. Take some tea," the man said, raising his arms in greeting.

"Khawaja Davoud, I am pleased to see you," said Fredriksen, embracing the man.

Frederiksen had been told—through a message delivered to him via the Iranian Permanent Mission to the UN in New York—that his friend Davoud Shirazi would like to meet with him when he went on the UNIFIL mission. Fredriksen had developed an intellectual interest in Shirazi during his posting in Tehran after having met him at an Islamic study group. Over many coffees, they had come to realize they both agreed that the Shah was a dictator and had no interest in Islam. Shirazi had studied religious history and faith in depth for years and taught the principles of Islam, hence his honorific, Khawaja, and Fredriksen knew he was politically involved.

The men entered the gloomy house, little more than one room with a rough stone counter and sink on one side. There was a blackened fireplace on the back wall and some mats for sitting and sleeping on the stone floor. The low fire produced some light and heat. Half a dozen rough-looking men stood in the shadows.

"Let me introduce you to some colleagues," Shirazi said, motioning for Fredriksen to come further into the room. "These two are with the Intelligence Bureau of the PLA. You know their people are suffering badly from the Israelis and their lapdog, Haddad. I understand that you met him during your mission to Southern Lebanon."

Fredriksen looked up in surprise, shocked that only hours later this information would be known.

A heavy set, fiftyish man of medium height with the traditional six- or seven-day beard stepped forward. He had a white and black kaffiyeh around his head and put out his hand to shake. "Abu Fadl," he said, with no expression on his face whatsoever.

"His colleague is Aduan, and that young fellow is his assistant," added Shirazi.

They sat on the mats, and Shirazi spoke quietly but insistently. "We have little time, as we must move from here, but I wish to bring you up to date on some matters. Martin, you will recall that I have long been a follower of Imam Khomeini. He lived, wrote, and studied for many years in Najaf, in Iraq, after he was exiled from the city of Qum by the Shah. In the last year, he was expelled from there by Saddam Hussain and is now in France. This will not be for long."

"Davoud, you know that I would like to see the Imam return to Iran to lead his people," said Fredriksen. "Although I am from a privileged family and a wealthy country, I was brought up to believe in the value of the poor, who are the real citizens of a nation. I was sickened during my time in Iran at how the people suffered under the Shah. Governments should ensure they work strongly in the interests of the workers. In the case of Iran, I appreciate that means within an Islamic framework."

"Yes, Martin. Loyal followers support the Imam's views that Islamic rule is necessary if the people of Iran are to see justice. Corruption must be wiped out and a framework of clerical rule installed. As you realize, the Imam sees it as his duty to support the poor and the oppressed and encourage them to live their lives within a framework of Islamic beliefs. The people must be governed by Islamic law, and foreign powers must not be allowed to interfere. While the Imam's first interest is the people of Iran, he also sees the Palestinians as being in much the same position. People have been forcibly removed from their land by the Jews and left to find refuge elsewhere."

He paused, took a sip of his tea, and continued. "The Imam has supporters in Syria and contacts with certain religious figures in southern Lebanon. He has undertaken to work with them to better the lot of the poor there. He also wants to ensure that his fellow Shias among the Palestinians are able to maintain their interests. The Imam wishes to work with the clerics in South Lebanon to develop a movement that will play a greater role in the complicated conflict. Arms and money can be provided. The Intelligence Bureau of the PLA has been designated to work with us. Our friends here have come to discuss these matters with me and to meet you. You will appreciate that there are many interests at play, and we must be careful to know who our friends are." He paused again and looked expectantly at Martin.

"Davoud, you know that I am a supporter of the principles that the Imam espouses and that I deeply share your desire for real change in Iran. The time of the Shah is long past, and the interests of the poor he has so oppressed must be put in the forefront. I understand the parallels with the Palestinian cause and appreciate why the Imam would like to reach out and provide assistance," said Fredriksen.

"Then you can help these people and the movement," said Shirazi. "You are able to go beyond sharing the cause of the oppressed. Your position in New York allows you to acquire information that is of interest and assistance to our friends in the Intelligence Bureau. The United Nations has contacts with all of the players, as your recent meeting with Haddad shows. We would like you to maintain contact with us and provide information on political and military issues that can assist the Palestinians in their efforts to help their people."

Martin was puzzled. "How could I do that?"

"A contact point in New York will be identified for you, whom you can periodically meet with to provide information. You can be sure that your position will be protected, and your help will be greatly appreciated. We only need to keep abreast of military developments on the ground."

"Yes, Davoud. I would be pleased to offer what little assistance I can. I respect the desire of the Imam to aid the oppressed in this region." Martin's eyes shone in the gloom.

"Excellent, my friend. The Imam and others will be very pleased to know of your cooperation. You will be contacted in New York sometime after your return. I regret that I am not in a position to offer you food and a bed here, but I too must leave quickly, as must our Palestinian friends. Farhad and his men will drive you back to Chtoura tonight, where a hotel has been booked for you. They will leave you there, and you can easily take a taxi to Beirut in the morning and continue your travels."

Shirazi stood up a little stiffly after the long discussion. Martin did also, and the two men hugged briefly but warmly.

The Palestinians, who had not said a word during the meeting, aside from the leader saying his name, mumbled only their *ma'a salama* salutations. Fredriksen walked out and got into the van with Farhad and his two companions.

"That seems to be promising," Davoud said to the Palestinians. "*Insh'allah* we will all benefit from his connections and his faith in the Imam."

CHAPTER FORTY-ONE

NEW YORK

Fredriksen walked up Second Avenue to the address, just off 46th street, that he'd been given in the phone call that morning. Coming in out of the windy, overcast day and the noise of late afternoon traffic, he entered a small convenience store in a dilapidated old building in need of paint. The store was cluttered and dirty. A vaguely rancid smell lurked in the atmosphere. A small, bearded man stood alone behind the counter. He didn't greet or acknowledge Fredriksen. The Norwegian looked around for the rotary stand of pocketbooks, where he had been told his contact would meet him. He looked at the books, mainly well-thumbed cheap novels with covers promising sex and violence.

After several minutes of embarrassment at being in such a place, Fredriksen felt someone approach. He looked around to see that a man in a long-sleeved brown shirt, buttoned to the neck, and wearing cheap denim pants, and incongruously, a pair of yellow, high-top sports shoes, had appeared beside him soundlessly.

"You are the friend of Davoud?" the man murmured.

"Yes."

"Go through that door," the man said, gesturing to the back of the store with his right hand.

Fredriksen walked through an opening covered by strings of coloured beads to keep the flies out. The room appeared to be an ill-lit storeroom, oddly better organized than the front of the shop.

"Sit," said a man, who was sitting in a chair in a gloomy corner. He motioned the Norwegian toward a faded, red-plastic lawn chair.

Fredriksen sat inelegantly, the chair balancing on uneven legs. The sloth-like man in the corner was wearing a pair of well-worn tan pants and an unpressed grey suit jacket. Fredriksen saw that he had a full beard and disheveled white hair that looked dirty and itchy. He spoke up. "You will call me Barzin. Your assistance in furthering the aims of the Imam will be appreciated. The oppressed people of Palestine will benefit."

"I am willing to offer some assistance, as I appreciate from my time in Tehran that the people of Iran seek ways to better their lives, and that there are parallels with the Palestinians," said Fredriksen, feeling ill at ease and over-dressed in his business suit in front of this man.

Barzin leaned forward in his own plastic chair. It creaked ominously under his bulk.

"We need information on the movements of forces controlled by Haddad and plans of the UN forces as well. This will identify opportunities to assist the Palestinians in protecting their people and advancing their cause." Fredriksen sensed rather than smelled cigarette smoke and sweat in the fetid atmosphere.

"Yes, Barzin, there is a summary of military movements in the region prepared periodically in the Office of Military Affairs. There will be information in those reports of interest to you, which we could discuss." Fredriksen felt his upper lip prickle with sweat. He began to feel claustrophobic in the small room.

"We will not discuss them. I want the reports. We have a place where documents can be delivered. When we call you, go across from the UN building beside the restaurant called La Bibliotheque. There is a stairway going up to Tudor City apartment complex. Go up." Barzin looked at Fredriksen searchingly, seeking confirmation that he understood.

"Yes, I know where that is," Fredriksen replied.

"Good. Continue straight to building number five, backing onto a small park on Second Avenue. You will be met. I do not expect we will meet further. We can contact you by telephone when you are needed." Barzin stood up with a sigh and stretched his back, with a grimace on his face. The audience was over.

Fredriksen walked out of the shop, thankfully into the daylight. His shoulders were taut with the tension of the encounter. Outside the cool, windy air hit him with a blast. The traffic was heavier and the sidewalk busier than he remembered. While he felt everyone passing seemed to be looking at him, he forced himself to walk confidently. He walked for a half hour through heavy pedestrian traffic, randomly crossing streets and keeping an eye out for anyone he saw more than once. Twice, he felt light raindrops, but it didn't turn into anything beyond threatening. Finally, he found himself back on First Avenue at 49th, where he entered John's, a trendy restaurant where he was a regular and often went for a lunch of an onion and cheese omelette with crisp, fried potatoes, and occasionally, a drink after work.

"Hi, Martin, what can I get you?" said Anne from behind the bar.

"I've had a long day, and it isn't over yet. Give me a double vodka on the rocks, please."

She reached into the freezing unit under the counter, brought out a bottle of Smirnoff, heavily coated in frost, and poured it liberally over four ice cubes.

The glass was cold and the liquor colder, Fredriksen was pleased to find. The vodka slipped down his throat with the potency it should have, and he straightened on the stool, taking a deep breath. With his finger, he traced the wet mark the glass had made on the wooden bar and thought through his day. He mentally raised his glass to himself, silently toasting: *Quite a day and the beginning of a new phase.*

"I'll have another," he said.

CHAPTER FORTY-TWO

SOUTH LEBANON

As the sun began to rise, an exhausted Ali dismounted from his sweating horse and unsteadily walked down the three concrete stairs and into the basement room of a large, run-down house. The plastered cement walls were pockmarked with bullet holes around the windows and doors, and an old wooden terrace from the main floor was twisted and half collapsed into the untended garden.

"Aduan, I'm back," he said to his friend, who was sitting at the table. Ali sat heavily in a chair, wiped the sweat from his forehead with the back of his sleeve, and grabbed a bottle of water. He handed an envelope to Aduan. "It took me two hours to get to the rendezvous spot on the Syrian border and three to get back, thanks to patrols of Haddad's men. One time, I had to take the horse into a wooded valley and try to keep it quiet while I could hear them above. These mountains are difficult once you get off the trails." Ali took a long swallow from the bottle and then rested it against his forehead and closed his eyes, enjoying the coolness.

"Fine. Let's see what they have for us." Aduan opened the bulky envelope, which was heavily creased from being in Ali's pack. Spreading the papers out and reading by the faint light in the room, his face broke into a smile. "This looks very good, Ali. It should be useful. Stay here and have something to eat and then get some rest. I'll take this to Colonel Abu Khalid, or should I say, Abu Fadl, as he introduced himself that night a few months ago? He will be pleased to see some return on the meeting we had with Davoud and that fellow from New York."

Aduan climbed the concrete stairs and walked into a small room on the main floor above. "Sir, Ali has returned from making his contact with the Iranians," he said. He handed over the envelope to the colonel, who was sitting in fatigues behind an old, crudely painted table, drinking coffee from a pot on the table.

"Watch out for my coffee, Aduan. It is early in the morning, and I have to make a start. Have one yourself." He indicated where to find another cup.

"Yes, Colonel, thank you," said Aduan, pouring his own and adding a generous portion of sugar. "This document sets out a pattern of movements of Haddad forces. Most interestingly, it indicates places where they meet with Israeli forces to secure supplies and when they do so."

The men studied the document on the table with concentrated interest and pleasure, clinking their coffee cups.

"Aduan, this material will be useful in our effort to disrupt Haddad and the Israelis. It seems to cover most of a month's activities, and we ought to be able to act on the pattern. Let's pay a visit to Operations and see what they say."

CHAPTER FORTY-THREE

NEW YORK, 1980

On his way to the weekly Western Group meeting, Martin Fredriksen walked through the Indonesian Lounge in the UN building. The Counsellor on the Iranian delegation, Parviz Esphahani, a well-dressed, tall man with a thick, black moustache, fell into step.

"Parviz," Martin said, "I haven't seen you for weeks—months, actually. How are things at the delegation with all the changes in Iran?"

"Hello, Martin." The Iranian's English had a hint of a British accent. "Not surprisingly, most of us have been recalled to Tehran for 'consultations.' What the clerics really have in mind is a litmus test to see if we support them and the new regime or are supporters of the Shah. I had the dubious pleasure of being asked to make the trip home."

"What is the mood in Tehran these days?" said Fredriksen.

"The people have spoken. Since the referendum in March, in which the people overwhelmingly, about 98 percent, supported the Ayatollah Khomeini and his proposal to make Iran an Islamic Republic, things have ground to a halt. People likely felt they had to support the Ayatollah or would be found out."

"What does that mean for diplomats who served under the Shah?" asked the Norwegian.

"The ambassador here was discharged almost immediately, as you will have heard, and frankly, we hardly know what the policy is from day to day. And as for policy, as long as it sounds anti-American, we are all right for the moment," the Iranian diplomat said in a matter-of-fact manner.

If Martin was surprised at the Iranian's open and frank tone, he didn't betray it. "Do you have any plans?"

"I know where I stand. I have been in France, arranging a teaching position in the international relations faculty at the University of Grenoble. I went straight there on my way back from Tehran. The Foreign Ministry, it seems, thinks I may not be sufficiently supportive of the religious establishment to be trusted as a representative abroad, so they told me my assignment here was at an end. I can only agree with that, or perhaps it is my taste in fine British tailoring, now so out of fashion in Iran, but I am officially unemployed as of next week. I am just awaiting a confirmation from Grenoble."

Esphahani held the door for Martin as they left the lounge area and continued down the hallway. "There have been a lot of changes since my time in Tehran, Parvez," said the Norwegian. "It's difficult to imagine how much change there has been, but your countrymen must be pleased to have someone like the Ayatollah so committed to a better life for the people after the Shah."

"That remains to be seen, Martin," said Parvez. "We have been a united and cosmopolitan society for centuries, and we have always played a major role in the region. Iranians have never had religion at the centre of our society before. We will see how it affects society with time. It is always good to talk to you, Martin, as someone who knows our country."

"And I always enjoy our discussions about Iran, Parvez."

"If I don't see you again before I leave, keep an eye out for our interests. All the best for the rest of your assignment at the UN. It is such a great place to meet interesting people, exchange views, and learn about the interests and values of other members."

"And my best wishes to you."

They shook hands and Fredriksen continued on his way. As he walked, he mused to himself, *Yes, an intelligent, polished man with a fine European education. His family must have been strong supporters of the dictatorship and shared in the looting of the economy along with the Shah. It's a wonder they let him out of the country. He should have been incarcerated. Perhaps incinerated. I am doing the right thing, helping the cause of the Ayatollah Khomeini. The people of Iran and the Palestinians will benefit.*

CHAPTER FORTY-FOUR

SOUTH LEBANON

Shortly after Colonel Abu Khalid and Aduan had discussed the intelligence with the Operations Group, a tall, well-built man of about thirty years was called into the office of Colonel Abdel Nour, Director of Operations.

"Sir," the man said, saluting. "You wanted to see me?"

"Yes, Bashar," said Colonel Abu Khalid. "We have received important information about the supplies that the Israelis are sending to Haddad. It would seem that every other Wednesday night, the Israelis cross just over the border into Lebanon at Metulla to bring arms, food, and other supplies to Haddad. This map shows where one of the routes is. I want you to take fighters to be ready to intercept the shipment next week before Haddad's men can distribute the supplies. The shipments are small, and they take back roads to avoid being noticed."

"Yes, sir. It would be my pleasure."

Five nights later, Bashar and ten fedayeen left their camp for a ride in the back of a large truck. Ali joined them to provide a report to the Intelligence Bureau. He was to stay with the vehicle on the orders of Colonel Abdel Nour, who wanted only Operations personnel involved.

They drove for close to an hour, south and east into the farms and hills near the border with Israel. They carried backpacks loaded with munitions and automatic rifles, making their burden heavy but manageable. The packs included shovels and unarmed anti-tank mines. When the group got out of the truck, they walked through the darkening, dry hills for twenty minutes. They avoided people or farms where they could, as there was no way to know who supported, worked for, or reported to which party in the conflict.

On Bashar's orders, the men dropped to the ground in a grove of trees and drank from their canteens. They sighed with relief at the break, pulling bread and dates from their packs.

"Hami, Nasir, come with me," Bashar said after several long pulls of water and eating a piece of pita bread that he had in his pack. He had been consulting his map. "We are going to scout the road at this point to see where it is best for our attack."

The three men climbed a small, treed hill and looked over toward the Israeli border point some six or seven kilometres away. Its lights were still just visible in the distance. There was no traffic on the dusty side road, nor people or animals in sight. The local farmers were settled in their houses at the end of their long day of work. Bashar looked up and down the road and surveyed the hills on each side through his binoculars. Some one hundred metres farther on, he saw that the road took a sharp, more than ninety-degree turn where the road became a narrow cut between two large hillocks, covered with thick trees and bushes coming right to the sides of the road. Behind the knolls on one side was a large grove of olive trees and a small waterway lined with banana plants.

A place to escape through, Bashar thought, *leading to our pickup point.* "Hani, bring the men. We will set up just over the hills up there," he said, pointing to the narrow cut in the hills. "Nasir, stay here as our lookout; in fact, go there, on the next hill toward the border, and call me on the radio if you see anything on the road."

Sensing the fight that was to come, the men rose eagerly from their rest and grabbed their equipment. Bashar took four men with him and walked down the side of the hill and along the road to his selected position. "I want six devices planted in the road on this side of the turn and another six on the other side around the corner twenty metres ahead," he said. "Stagger them so they'll be under the wheels of their vehicles no matter where they are at this turn. The mines can be set off by radio. I will hope to do so to separate the convoy as it rounds that turn. This could cause confusion, as the ones at the front and back won't be able to see easily what is happening to the others."

The other men took up guard positions on the two hills as the sound of picks and shovels bounced up from the road. Bashar looked up frequently to see if there was any sign of life on the road or a signal from Nasir. Shortly, the first grouping of mines had been laid and triggers set. One of the men took branches and swept the spots where they had dug, scattering sandy soil and dust from the edge of the road to mask the new, darker soil they had taken out. Others laid the second set around the corner. When the last mine was laid, the men stepped off the road into the foliage after giving it one last sweep to obliterate footprints.

"Good work, men. Hani, Nasir, and I will stay here on this hilltop, which gives us a clear view of the road," said Bashar. "The rest of you, take the gear and cross the olive groves. Continue around that hillside for about half a kilometre. There's another road where the truck is to meet us. That's where the small stream cuts across that road. With only three of us here, we'll be able to activate the mines and follow you quickly before the Israelis can get helicopters in the air searching."

The fighters trudged off down the hill and into the grove and were soon out of sight. Bashar radioed his unit and confirmed that the truck would meet them. Hani and Nasir settled themselves with him into the grasses and watched the road. The mild evening was comfortable, and no sound was heard except the chirp of cicadas, and occasionally, the rustling of a small rodent in the dry grass. They ate a little more and drank some now-warm water, watching each way on the road but seeing nothing moving.

About 2:00 a.m., Hani sat up. "Did you hear an engine?" he said to his comrades. The three of them listened carefully.

"Yes, yes," Bashar said. "That is definitely an engine—a light, armoured personnel carrier, I would think."

A brief flicker of headlights was seen in the distance toward the border. The sound of engines became louder. From the lights, there appeared to be at least six vehicles. They came closer along the farm road at a moderate speed. Soon the Palestinians could make out the outlines of two APCs, one each at the front and back of four light trucks.

"Get ready," said Bashar. "I hope the front APC and two trucks will slow at the sharp bend in the road. We will blow the mines first at the front. A second later, we will do so at the back. *Insh'allah*, they will disappear in front of our eyes!"

"*Insh'allah*," both of his fighters replied.

"We will then immediately go into the grove and run to meet our comrades."

The vehicles approached. Half a dozen men could be seen in the APC in front. The four trucks looked laden with goods. The APC at the rear also had armed men on top. The vehicles slowed as they reached the turn in the road, as Bashar had hoped. The rear lights of the second truck went around the corner, and the others geared down. Bashar pushed the activators. First one, then another. The sky turned into a huge flash of light, and instantaneously, their ears pounded with the concussion of the explosions. Fire leapt high in the air, highlighting the trucks pushed off or collapsed into the roadbed and burning brightly. They saw two men in Lebanese fatigues slide down beside the trucks on the far side, lying amongst the bodies of others.

"*Yellah*, my friends!" shouted Bashar. The three of them scrambled down the hill and were in the grove before they heard any arms fire. They ran through the cover and soon reached the partially hidden truck, with their fellow fighters sitting anxiously in the back, awaiting their arrival and eagerly wanting to know all about the explosions. Bashar, Hani, and Nasir laughed as their friends pulled them into the back of the truck and under the canvas cover that had huge white letters printed on top: UN.

"We have five kilometres to drive," said Ali delightedly, leaning back from the passenger seat. "We can then pull under an animal shelter next to an unmanned UNIFIL base under construction. If any helicopters see us, they will think we are just going back to our base." He laughed. "I'm glad I could come on this operation, Bashar. I can see that this intelligence has value."

Indeed, the first sound of a helicopter was heard only as they turned off the engine, fewer than ten minutes after the operation.

The next morning, Bashar's platoon and Ali returned to their base and reported on the success of the mission to the Operations and the Intelligence Bureau. "Congratulations," said Colonel Abdel Nour. "The guidance of Allah was with you." Then with a grin and a nod toward Colonel Abu Khalid, he added, "And a little good intelligence information didn't hurt."

"Yes, Colonel," said Abu Khalid. "May the flow of information continue."

CHAPTER FORTY-FIVE

NEW YORK

"At five o'clock this afternoon, you will be met. Walk north on Second Avenue from 56th street on the west side. You know what to bring with you. Carry the envelope in your left hand."

"But what about my earlier instructions? Why do they change every time?"

"Listen to me. Do not ask questions."

Fredriksen started to perspire and felt the knot in his stomach tighten as he hung up the phone. This had happened every time there was a contact over the months. The meetings were different every time. The rest of the afternoon, his mind couldn't focus on anything but the call. As he left the office about 4:40 p.m., he almost stumbled on the curb at the first intersection but caught himself. *I must pull myself together*, he thought. *I'm early, and I have time for a drink.*

He turned into a tavern advertising happy hour drinks and appetizers. It was quite dark inside and few were in the establishment except a group of five office workers, joking and laughing at one end of the bar. A morose, middle-aged man in a creased brown suit, tie loosened and hair tousled, sat alone at the far end. *How appropriate*, Fredriksen thought. *I don't know which group I belong to. I'll sit between them.* He ordered his usual large Smirnoff with lots of ice and downed it quickly. "Again, please," he said to the bartender, who—perhaps seeing the strain in his customer's face—had hovered nearby with the bottle.

THE STRUGGLE CONTINUES

Forcing himself to drink more slowly, he tried to convince himself that he was about to do something positive and should not be nervous. In a few minutes, he stood up, left the tavern, and walked up First Avenue, crossing at 56th, and then along the block to Second Avenue.

Fredriksen stopped at the corner and looked to the far side and up the block. Everything looked normal: office workers on their way home, others ducking into small shops in search of something to warm up for dinner. Nothing unusual. Nothing threatening. He reached into an inside pocket of his suit jacket and took an envelope in his left hand.

The light changed, and he crossed the street, turning north on Second Avenue. He walked smartly, falling into step with the human wave moving along. In moments, he crossed the next street and continued up Second Avenue to 56th, the wide intersection at 57th, and 58th. The pedestrian traffic was busy. He was momentarily distracted by an attractive, well-dressed young woman walking his way and carrying several packages. As they passed, she brushed his arm and dropped one bag. Reflexively, he stopped and leaned over to pick it up, as did she. He heard a soft voice say, "You have been helpful," as she took his envelope when they both reached for the fallen bag. He instantaneously realized that this was the contact and that the exchange had taken place. She disappeared into the crowd.

He was astonished, having thought he was only being polite to a woman in distress. Taking a deep breath, he walked on another two blocks before he had processed what had taken place. He hadn't seen the man on the far corner of 58th taking a photograph.

Fredriksen walked home more slowly, conflicted and tense. At home, he realized that his heart was still beating rapidly. He sank into a chair with yet another vodka, leaving the bottle at his elbow.

How long can I do this? he asked himself.

CHAPTER FORTY-SIX

AL BASSAH, ISRAEL

Southern Lebanon settled into a long pattern of attacks and reprisals. Haddad's forces took up more positions along the Israeli border and further east, in the hills up to Marjayoun where, in the comfort of the lovely hill town, they made their headquarters. They built themselves up with arms, ordinance, and supplies that continued coming from Israel. Many officers and men in Haddad's military went to Israel for training. Haddad was perhaps more interested in Lebanese politics during their civil war than in the Palestinian-Israeli conflict, although his forces harassed the Palestinians regularly. The Palestinians were poorly organized and lacked supplies. Their most aggressive military action was to fire rockets at Israeli settlements close to the border. The Israelis would reply with strikes from the air on Palestinian positions and Lebanese villages—a disproportionate response and devastating.

The Palestinians were continually urged to do more by the small detachment of Khomeini's Revolutionary Guards, who had been sent to the area to run training programs. They upped the ante, urging more frequent, violent raids into Israeli-controlled territory in attempts to kidnap Israeli soldiers or civilians. Little changed on the ground, and it was the civilians who suffered from the disruption on both sides of the border.

Davoud came to the area to see how the Iranian troops were doing. He met with Aduan and Colonel Abu Khalid. "Colonel, I know my men have been active in training and providing equipment to your forces. What operations have you planned with the information we have provided? Does it continue to be useful?"

The colonel was very direct. "The material you have provided has allowed us to undertake some operations that have been more targeted than before. Our enemies are powerful, however. Whatever success we have is met with such massive military responses that we are no further ahead. Few operations can be duplicated. We are about to launch an operation into Israel tonight that is based largely on our own intelligence. I will show you later what we have planned."

***

Toward the end of the day, Colonel Abu Khalid returned to the headquarters with Davoud and went into the Operations rooms, where he introduced him to Colonel Abdel Nour. "It's a pleasure to meet you, Davoud," said the head of operations. "I can confirm that the intelligence that comes through you, as well as from our own sources, has been of value to us.

"I will demonstrate this to you. We have a plan arranged for the next mission, and I have asked the platoon leader to come to the office. He is waiting in the back. Come this way." The sergeant stood to attention and saluted smartly as the three of them walked into the room. "Sergeant Khoury, we have a mission for you."

"Sir," replied the short, youthful man in fatigues.

"I am told that your family was originally from the village of Al Bassah."

"Yes, sir."

"I am about to give you the opportunity to visit your village and avenge the tragedy of the actions of the terrorist Haganah when they drove your family from the village in 1948. The Haganah was supposedly being converted into the Israeli army at about that time, but their commandos, the Palmach, terrorized and looted many Arab areas for their own profit, yours among them."

"Yes, sir. In the name of my grandfather and namesake, Elias Khoury, who with his family was driven out and sought refuge in Lebanon, I would be very pleased to take on the responsibility." The sergeant's eyes never moved as he spoke. His face was a mask. His voice was devoid of the emotion he felt inside.

"You will take your platoon tomorrow and cross the border to deliver a message that Palestinian territory is Palestinian territory, and the expansion of their kibbutz must end. The Jews destroyed the entire ancient village in 1948 and ensured that none of the local population remained. As your family would know, the fields had always been lush and fruitful with wheat and other grains, cotton, and citrus trees. The ugly new buildings and the Jews in the field now are an affront, as they claim the area was abandoned desert. We will send them that message. Prepare your men."

Khoury snapped out another salute and stepped back into line with another, "Yes, sir."

Soon after, with great enthusiasm, Khoury brought his men together and went over the details of the plan for the operation.

In the Intelligence Bureau down the hall, Colonel Abu Khalid later brought Aduan into his office. "Operations is preparing a raid on the kibbutz of Al Bassah, Aduan. We have information from a worker in the area, who says that the Israelis are planning to convert an old school building into a laboratory to store and distribute chemical weapons. I want Ali to join Khoury's group to go there and speak to our contact. He might even have an opportunity to see the building."

"Yes, sir," said Aduan. "Ali will be pleased to go on an operation like that. He is always eager to prove that the intelligence we receive is valuable."

Late in the afternoon, Sergeant Khoury ordered seven men from his platoon into the back of an old open farm truck. They were dressed in well-worn and dirty civilian pants and shirts that made them look like farm workers. Ali joined them.

The evening light was fading as they set out for the border area. They passed through Aalma el Chaab, and coming down off the ridge, turned south and drove by thick groves of pomegranate, olive, and fig trees, and then small fields of grain. In a few minutes, they turned into a farm road and stopped before a complex of old stone buildings, animal and equipment shelters, storage sheds, and a small house. The yard was littered with rusty equipment, and they heard the low murmur of clucking as the chickens scratched for insects.

The driver and Khoury got down from the truck and approached a man who had emerged from the house. Likely in his seventies, he was tanned and lined from the sun and dressed as they were. He raised a hand, fingers stained yellow with years of nicotine, and saluted them with a cigarette. "I am Ahmed. Welcome to the border, my friends," he said, gesturing toward a high wire fence not much more than a hundred metres through the olive trees behind the storage sheds.

"And I am Sergeant Elias Khoury, from the village of Al Bassah."

"Bring your men inside, and we will talk." The old man turned and walked back into the house.

The group followed. Inside, after their eyes adjusted to the gloom, they could see a table that had bread and some small plates of food on it. A wood-burning stove crackled under the coffee pot.

"This is my son, Bassam," said Ahmed, warmly taking the arm of a smiling, darkly tanned, broad-shouldered man in his mid forties. "We have time to take coffee and eat a little. We will discuss your mission before you go."

Sergeant Khoury sat in a soft, leather chair and told the story of his grandparents and their expulsion from the area of Al Bassah. Ahmed and Bassam listened intently, as did Ali and the fighters from Khoury's platoon. It was a classic story that many families could feel a part of.

Ahmed told them his recollections of the time. "I know of your family, Elias, and well recall when the Israeli criminal gangs forced everyone out and torched the village. Several families came here through the fields, and we gave them shelter for a few days. Those who later were sent to work that land knew nothing of local conditions. They had no idea of the force of the sun or the methods to preserve water that we have learned over centuries. It seems that farming in Russia or Poland does not have the same challenges. In those days, we could easily cross the border and see what the Jews were doing, and we would watch. It took many years for them to regain the level of harvests that we always remembered."

"Ahmed, tonight we will cross the border and deliver a message to them that they will remember for some time," said Sergeant Khoury. His eyes hardened and a look of determination set his face.

"Even the fences the Jews have put up across our land are not enough to prevent our passage," said Ahmed. "In fact, at the end of my land is a waterway we have used forever for the farm. It was cut off when they erected the border fence. But we have a way to cross it. The farmers on the other side know of this, but in this sense, appreciate that we who deal with the land must have access to water. When we go there to tend to the water lines that become clogged or broken, no one ever sees us or says anything about it." The old man grinned with satisfaction.

"Your crossing point must be quite close to Al Bassah," Khoury probed.

"Yes," said Bassam. "The walk through the fields will not take more than a few minutes. There is good cover of bushes and fruit trees along the watercourse that they have dug from our stream, so you should be able to approach quietly. We will show you the way after dark."

The Palestinians went into a nearby shed and checked their weapons. Most carried rifles and two had machine pistols. Some carried rocket-propelled grenades, and one a small flame thrower that the Iranians wanted them to try out.

Bassam came into the shed and said it was time to go. The group assembled, left the farmyard, and walked behind the buildings into the grove of olive trees. Bassam spoke softly to Khoury as they approached the fence and walked along a path protected by bushes and tall marsh grasses, just a few metres out from the barrier. He halted and raised an arm to the side to quiet the group. They stopped and listened to the night. Far in the distance, they heard a vehicle start up and move away. A dog barked on a distant hill. No other sounds were heard. After a long two minutes, Bassam suddenly turned into the brush and was immediately beside the fence.

"Look at this. My father did this after the fence was built," Bassam said. "He first connected the lower three wires, about two metres to the left, to a higher one so that the electrical circuit would not be cut. They are attached the same way just to your right."

"And that keeps the electrical circuit in contact?" said Khoury.

"Yes," replied Bassam. "Even more clever is that he then removed the lower wires here at the post and put a small extension on each. The wires fasten behind the post and are simply hooked onto it where they cannot be seen. From the other side, it gives the impression that the wiring is continuous. All we have to do is release a few, and we will be through. We have crossed here many times."

Bassam leaned forward and unhooked the wires. Khoury crouched beside the crossing point, offering a word of encouragement to each of his men as they slipped through the opening in the wire. He felt the heat increase markedly with the tension as the men crossed into Israeli-occupied territory. Bassam led them off to the right a hundred metres, joining the bank of a small waterway. "You can now see the lights of the settlement, only a ten-minute walk ahead. Keep to the path and close to the reeds and bushes as much as possible. The first building you will come to used to be a school. I will return now. May Allah be at your side and your mission be successful."

The group of fighters spread out and walked slowly into the night, following the water line.

"Ali," said Khoury softly, "you know where you're supposed to meet your contact?"

"Yes. I was told he would make himself known to us about half a kilometre from the kibbutz, at a point when we have to cross a small bridge."

The men walked on cautiously, seeing no sign of movement and not hearing anything but the soft pad of their boots on the path. After a few minutes, Sergeant Khoury motioned for them to stop and waved at Ali to look ahead. "Ali," he whispered, "there is a small bridge ahead just before the path turns."

"Yes. Oh look! I saw a tiny flash of red light over there," Ali whispered, pointing.

As they looked for it again, the figure of an old man emerged silently from the reeds. *"A salaam a leikum,"* he said softly.

"Wa aleikum asaalam," replied Ali.

In an instant, a bright red hole appeared in the man's throat, and his body was thrown backwards. Automatic-weapons fire opened up on them from behind the bushes only metres away. The Palestinian fighters fell to the ground, crawling down the short bank to the water and returning fire with their weapons. Ali spread himself out on the ground, clawing for his weapon. He had just grabbed it when the convulsing body of Khoury fell over him, the back of his head blown open. Ali rolled for cover and to get away from the horror of Khoury's body. He felt a massive sting on his cheek as a bullet grazed him. The fighter with the flame thrower released a hideous blast of burning chemical at the bushes across the path. Two men rose out of their hide, weapons in hand. Their clothes flared in full flame as they fell and tried to roll, screaming piteously.

The Palestinians scrambled to stand and run back along the pathway. Four, including Ali, were able to run. They ran wildly, leaving their fallen colleagues behind, but there was no more firing at them or by them. Soon they saw the fence and rushed toward it, some shoving to get ahead of others and stumbling on the rough path. When they reached the point where they joined the path on the way in, they crashed through the side bushes and ran at full tilt toward the break in the fence.

Ali slid feet first into the opening and then got up and dove into the bushes on the Lebanese side. The others joined him, and they lay on the ground under cover, panting with fear and desperately short of breath. They could hear the rumble of approaching vehicles. Ali crawled back on his stomach and re-hooked the wiring on the fence to cover their exit point. After a minute to catch their breath, they returned to the farmhouse, by then totally in the dark.

Ahmed came out of the house and saw how few men had returned. "I heard the gunfire and am surprised any of you made it back," he said. "Bassam, you drive their truck; we must all leave immediately."

Bassam and Ahmed quickly got into the front seat, and the Palestinian fighters climbed in the back. The truck left the farmyard in a swirl of dust, went back along the farm road, and turned left toward the town. Ahmed knew where they could find friendly faces and hide themselves. He guided Bassam into a back street, where his son pulled the truck to a halt under the cover of trees. Ahmed jumped out and pounded on the door of a large, wooden animal shed.

"Arif! Arif!" he called out, trying to wake his contact.

A hulking, sleepy man opened the door. After exchanging words with Ahmed, he motioned for them all to enter. Only then did Ali notice that his shoulder was soaked in blood from a wound in his cheek where the bullet had grazed him and opened up the side of his face.

As they settled themselves onto straw on the floor of the shed, Ali slumped over, holding a dirty rag to his throbbing, bloody cheek. His head was pounding. His clothes clung to him with sweat and were caked with dirt. He was devastated by the loss of so many of their fighters and the futility of the operation.

Ali spoke to what he hoped was the spirit of Khoury in paradise. *Elias, my friend, not every operation can be successful. You can, however, feel that your ancestral family must now know that you have tried to take the terrorist attacks of the past to the enemy. The Khoury family will not be forgotten in Al Bassah.*

CHAPTER FORTY-SEVEN

ZAHLE

"Ali, my love, it is so long since I have seen you. How are you? Have you been involved in the fighting? Where are you?"

Hearing Fatima's voice down the telephone line made Ali's heart soar. "Fatima, I can't stay on the telephone more than a minute or two. I long to see you. I've had some difficult times, but I'm safe. I can't give you details of where I'm stationed or what I've been doing." He rubbed his injured cheek where his wound was slowly healing after a period of infection. "I must go to Zahle, in the Bekaa, next Friday to meet with someone, and I wonder if we could get together there for the day."

"Oh yes. I so want to see you. I could go that day. It's been months!"

"I will meet you at Saydet Zahle at 10:00 a.m.," Ali promised.

"A Christian shrine? You make me laugh, Ali." Fatima's genuine laugh was music to Ali's ear.

"We can walk and talk together."

"Yes, until then. Goodbye, my Ali." Fatima hung up and turned away from the phone, tears of joy welling up in her eyes. She thanked Said, the owner of the restaurant who had brought her to the phone from her home when Ali called, and then hurried back home.

"Mother! Mother! Ali just called me. He wants to meet in Zahle. I can take the bus and go there," Fatima said, doing a pirouette in joy.

"Oh Fatima! All these months of wondering if he is well!" Dalia clasped her hands to her ample bosom with delight. "What an opportunity! You two should be together."

"We will just have the day together, but I need to see him, Mother."

***

On the Friday, Ali anxiously paced back and forth around the monument with Our Lady of Zahle looking down on him and the beneficent smile of the Christ Child in her arms beaming at him. His face was throbbing, but today, for the first time, he had been able to remove the bandages, seeing that the wound had left a raw, four-centimetre blotch of scar tissue on his cheek.

Having arrived in Zahle in the pre-dawn hours for his rendezvous to pick up papers from an Iranian contact, Ali had sat drinking coffee, at a chipped and rickety table in a smoky café full of truck drivers and warehouse workers, until he felt his presence might be noticed. He had then walked through a local park in the morning light until he became anxious that Fatima would arrive early. He went to the monument and sat on a nearby bench in nervous anticipation. Shortly before 10:00 a.m., he saw her crossing a busy main road, dodging honking taxis and trucks belching smoke, and moving his way. He felt he had never seen such a lovely vision and realized he had missed her even more than he thought.

"Ali! Ali!" called Fatima when she spotted him rising from the bench. She started running in his direction and threw herself into his arms.

"Fatima! My Fatima," he said. Though it was against their social customs, he didn't hold back from hugging her. He looked into her face with joy and saw the look warmly returned. She suddenly reacted with shock at his disfigured face. "Oh, what has happened to you? This injury must have been quite terrible!"

Ali told her without details that he had been in an operation and suffered a bullet wound. "Don't worry, Fatima; all is well now," he said, rubbing his cheek gingerly. "The abrasions and scarring will reduce with time."

They stood, their faces close, absorbing the pleasure of the moment and trembling with joy. "Ali, I have missed you terribly," Fatima said softly.

Ali looked back, deep into her eyes, unblinking, until he forced himself to tear his gaze away. "Come, let's walk in the park. Bring me up to date with your news."

"Life has been quite good, Ali. Mother sends her best wishes to you and anxiously awaits my report on your health and activities. My injuries from Tel al Zaatar have healed, although my arm still doesn't have the range of motion that I had before. Nonetheless, I am again able to work at the health clinic in Damour."

"That's very good. You felt so useful when you worked at the clinic in Tel al Zaatar," said Ali.

"It's not the same, though. With all the foreign doctors and qualified nurses who have come to the town because of the new Palestinian military installations, I'm back at the beginning and do very little actual nursing work. I'm more of a comfort to injured and ill patients. I spend quite a bit of time talking to them and discussing how their illness or injuries will affect their lives. Many just seem to want to have someone to talk to. I've seen so much in the clinics and can empathize with them and offer encouragement."

"They would enjoy talking to such a pretty young woman with such a radiant smile."

"Oh, Ali," Fatima said. She broke into a broad but shy smile, and her cheeks reddened.

Ali thought she had never looked so lovely.

Holding hands self-consciously, they strolled slowly along the pathways to a pond and looked at the waterfowl. "Aside from work, life in Damour has been very quiet," said Fatima. "Few people I used to know are there anymore, so there is little to do in the village. It's so full of fighters, it's not comfortable to walk the streets by myself, so I stay close to home. Now that I'm working again, and Mother continues with her vegetable cart, we get along at home all right, but all we talk about is how the fighting is going in the south and what you might be doing." She stopped abruptly, as if realizing that she was doing all the talking. "Tell me, what are you doing every day?"

"I'm very busy with my work, notwithstanding this injury," he said, unconsciously rubbing his jaw. "It seldom involves actual fighting. All I can say is that my work helps organize military activities to counter Haddad and his army and to take the fighting to the Israelis. We have become more active and successful in recent months, but as always, we are quite overwhelmed by the power of the Israelis and all the weapons they give to Haddad."

"Is there ever going to be an end to this?" Fatima's frustration boiled over at the words. "Can we ever hope to return to Palestine and to peace? What does the future hold, Ali?"

"The future doesn't promise much change or a better life for us, Fatima. The only thing I want is to be with you. Since Marwan was killed, the only person I know from the past is his uncle, Aduan, who has been good to me, and I see him almost daily. He has kept me away from most of the active conflict."

Fatima's features clouded with sadness. "It is so tragic that Marwan was killed, Ali. You two had such a wonderful time together as boys. He was too young to die."

"Yes, very sad, but as I say, Aduan has been good to me. We work together, and I hope this will continue. So many people have been displaced and killed that I don't want to try to make friends for fear that I'll soon lose them. Enough despair, Fatima. Let's find some lunch and enjoy our time together."

Fatima broke into a run across the grass, laughing as they made their way out of the park. They found a bright but shaded patio and enjoyed a mezze of fried cauliflower; pickled onions and vegetables; crisp radishes and peppers, with olive oil and sage sprinkled over them; some tabbouleh made from bulgur wheat, parsley, mint, tomatoes with olive oil and lemon juice; nutty arugula; and some dense, dark, lamb sausages and kibbeh.

As the afternoon wore on, they slowly walked back into the centre of Zahle, looking for a bus or taxi that Fatima could take back to the coast and on to Damour.

Fatima turned her face up to Ali, and her fingers gripped his forearms tightly. "I have not had such a wonderful day in a very long time. We must try to meet more often."

Ali didn't want Fatima to hold out any false hope. "I would love that, but it's easier said than done. I can't tell from one day to the next what I'll be doing or where I'll be, but we'll try." As a shared taxi drew to a halt in front of them, he quickly determined that the driver and three other passengers were bound for south Beirut, where it would be easy for Fatima to find transport to Damour.

"Yellah! Yellah!" shouted the driver as Ali and Fatima hugged quickly, and she slid into the back seat.

"Thank you, my dear Ali. See you soon," Ali heard as the taxi screamed off into the swirl of honking traffic in a cloud of blue exhaust. He watched as Fatima's hand briefly came up to the back window, and then he turned away, feeling the emotion of their separation. He took a deep breath and crossed the street to find his own transport.

CHAPTER FORTY-EIGHT

SOUTH LEBANON, NOVEMBER 1980

"Ali, the contacts with our friends from over the mountains are more and more useful. Tomorrow, we leave very early and will meet them in the hills. This time, there are more than documents to be delivered to us," said Aduan.

At 4:00 a.m., Aduan came into the small room at the back of the schoolhouse where Ali slept with two others from the intelligence unit. "All right, all of you, we're off for a drive."

The men stretched and got up, rubbing the cobwebs of sleep from their eyes. After a quick stop in the food tent, where the old women were just arriving to start preparations for the day, the men collected water bottles, bread, baba ghanoush, and fruit, and then grabbed their rifles and went outside. A battered, grey Land Cruiser was waiting. They hauled themselves up and inside with the old and cracked brown leather seats protesting the cold and early morning disturbance.

The engine gave a deep-throated growl as they turned into the gravel road behind the building and started up the steep incline. A little less than an hour later, Aduan, sitting in the passenger seat in front, told the driver to slow and turn off the road onto a desolate track. They went several hundred metres and then turned sharply into a grove of trees.

Aduan jumped down from the Land Cruiser onto the dry pine needles. "Davoud, I am so pleased to see you again," he said as the tall, well-built man, dressed like a farmer, came forward out of the trees and embraced the Palestinian.

"It's my pleasure. And good to see you too, Ali. I bring the good wishes and blessings of Ayatollah Khomeini. These trucks behind me have arms, medical supplies, and some new communication equipment that he offers to the fighters for the people of Palestine. You must know that the people of Iran look with warmth to their fellow fighters and to the dispossessed and poor who wish to return to their own villages and property in Palestine. Our drivers will deliver the supplies to the camp for you if the route is secure."

"That's not a problem, Davoud," Aduan replied. "My people can only offer their gratitude for the blessings of the Imam and support of the people of Iran. These supplies will indeed be valuable in furthering our cause and bringing justice to the region."

"My brother, there is much to be done, but we can hope that the near future will bring us ever closer to our goals." Davoud grasped Aduan by the shoulder and pulled him closer, the gesture sealing their pact.

Aduan returned the embrace with warmth and strength. "I also offer my admiration for the struggle of your fighters and believers, which has led to the return of the Ayatollah to Iran. We recognize the changes that he has brought over the months since his return. Indeed, the future looks very bright for you and your people. With your cooperation, we hope to see the same for Palestine." Aduan's eyes were bright with fervour.

"Yes, the people of Iran bring the spirit of their revolution to you with this modest assistance today. With this first shipment of many, we will help strengthen the fighters of the people of Palestine." Davoud lowered his voice, and his tone became more serious. "The most important aspect is that the Ayatollah has agreed to send a contingent of trainers from the Revolutionary Guard to help you with training and strategy. This will happen in the coming weeks. In the meantime, I know that the information from New York has been useful, and *insh'allah*, long may it continue."

CHAPTER FORTY-NINE

NEW YORK, AUGUST 1981

Fredriksen's phone shrilled harshly at four o'clock in the morning, shattering the silence in his Upper East Side apartment. He picked up quickly, his head foggy, his voice raspy. "Who is this?" he said, looking down at the telephone.

"You will meet me at eight o'clock this morning at a park bench behind the Metropolitan Museum." The phone went dead.

Fredriksen hung up and sagged back onto his bed. It was Barzin, his Iranian contact. The voice and accent were unmistakeable. This request to meet was unusual. Fredriksen ordinarily called a number himself and left a message when he had papers to pass on. He would then get instructions on where to leave it. He had only met Barzin once and had been told that would be the only time.

He recalled with a shiver the first time he had actually met a contact on the street, never imagining it would be an attractive Western woman. Exchanges in person must be the most dangerous kind and made him the most nervous. Since then, he had most often been instructed to leave an envelope in a specified place.

Sleep was now impossible as anxiety crashed in waves over him. By all reports, things were going well in Iran, and the Ayatollah had firm control. Fredriksen could see that the conversion to an Islamic state was proceeding apace. He had done his part to help the Ayatollah spread his word and influence amongst the Palestinians by providing periodic reports on military movements. Maybe he'd done enough. He couldn't deal with the stress. Maybe he would tell them he would no longer do so. *I will tell Barzin today,* he thought.

Well before seven o'clock, unable to sleep or sit and read, Fredriksen decided he would leave his Upper East Side apartment and walk to Central Park for his meeting. He could grab a bite to eat along the way if he thought he could keep it down. He wore a tan Burberry raincoat over his grey slacks and navy jacket. A pair of highly polished, rich brown Church's shoes completed the outfit. The streets were quiet, with few people around except those walking their dogs or making deliveries to commercial establishments. The vehicular traffic looked so much more orderly than usual.

Crossing Lexington Avenue, he entered a deli where steam coated the windows. Inside, the New York hustle was already in full flight. Several people were standing at the counter, calling out what they wanted, and the two men behind it rushed back and forth, preparing orders, shouting loudly to each other, and intimidating the customers.

Walking back into the crisp morning with his cup of coffee and a hot, iced cinnamon bun, Fredriksen made his way uptown to 82nd Street, where he turned west to see the beautiful stairs and pillars of the Met, several long blocks away. He looked at his watch for what must have been the twentieth time: 07:45. He decided to go to the meeting place. *I'm early*, he thought, *but perhaps Barzin will be also, and we can get this over with.*

Following the path around to the left and behind the Met, Fredriksen passed several benches, seeing no one except a homeless, older man sorting out his belongings and rolling up a sleeping bag. He walked the full way around the path to the north side and turned to look around. A few people walked by, but no one who looked like Barzin.

Fredriksen returned to the mid point of the half-moon path and sat on a bench that would give him a view of anyone approaching from either side. His back was to the bushes, and the building was in front. Eight o'clock passed: 8:15. No sign. He felt the morning cold and had the urge to move around to keep warm. He squirmed a little on the bench and then walked away fifty yards and came back and sat down. By 8:30, he had convinced himself he should leave, but he didn't. Ten minutes later, a heavy man dressed in a shabby dark coat, and wearing a black scarf around his head that obscured his face, appeared unsteadily out of a small trail in the bushes and stopped in front of him. No one else was nearby.

"We have work for you," Barzin said abruptly. "Tell me what you know about Egypt and President Sadat," he said, sitting heavily on the bench and taking a deep breath.

"What do you mean? I'm not a specialist in Egyptian affairs." Fredriksen's face went pale.

"If you're not, you need to educate yourself quickly," barked Barzin, and then he coughed. "We need information on the security establishment and what they know of the Islamic movement. We're aware of many things but want a view from the outside. Speak to your American counterpart and inform yourself. They have the agencies that can read messages and hear phones and radios. They'll know what we want to know."

"I can't do that. My involvement is because my heart lies with the people of Iran and the rise of Ayatollah Khomeini. You said that I could help the Ayatollah's cause by providing information that would help the Palestinian people. I've done that, but now I must stop," said Fredriksen nervously. His voice cracked a little as he faltered through the short speech he had rehearsed since 4:00 a.m. "I cannot take the stress of this anymore."

"No," said Barzin, his tone brooking no argument. "You will continue because you work with us. You are not in a position to say no. We have photographs of you. Others could find out what you've done. You will report in five days. Not one extra day. Leave the park by that way," he gestured. "I will expect your reply quickly." Barzin heaved himself up and waddled back into the bushes, not looking back.

Fredriksen sat on the bench for a full twenty minutes until his heart stopped hammering in his chest. He got up unsteadily to his feet, wiping his brow with a handkerchief. Despite the early morning chill, he was drenched in sweat.

CHAPTER FIFTY

NEW YORK, SEPTEMBER 1981

"Salim, it is so good to see you again," Ambassador Obeidi said as Salim came into his office at the Palestine Observer Mission to the UN. "I know that you've been helpful to the National Council during your time at university in Cairo, but I'm pleased to see you return to New York. There is no end of work to be done here, as you know. We need your writing skills and your insight from your time with our leadership in the Middle East."

Salim shook the older man's hand warmly, placing his left hand on top of the other one. "Ambassador Obeidi, it is exciting for me to return to New York. Working with the delegation is something I only dreamed might be possible someday."

After inviting Salim to sit down in one of the comfortable, dark leather chairs in his well-appointed office, the ambassador got straight to the point. "The annual session of the General Assembly requires a good deal of work, and your help will be important. You will work directly for my deputy, Ghassan al Hamoud, whom you already know. He is an excellent colleague and knows everyone in the United Nations system who has anything to do with our issues."

"Yes, Ambassador. It will be a pleasure to work with Ghassan."

"He's at the UN building right now, but later, he'll be back and will tell you where we want you to start. First, my new assistant, Mariam, who I must say manages things very efficiently, will set you up with an office and everything you need. She will also give you the keys to an apartment. It's one where we have a long-term lease, so everything is ready to go. Welcome, Salim."

With that introduction, the ambassador pressed the intercom. The efficient Mariam appeared and swept Salim away. Salim spent the rest of the morning under her tutelage, and she indeed seemed to have the operation of the mission under firm control.

Just after 1:00 p.m., Ghassan returned to the mission, sought out Salim, and embraced him warmly. "My friend, welcome back to the delegation. I hear that you have more than proven in Cairo that you have a good deal to offer to us."

Salim smiled and was about to reply but Ghassan hurriedly carried on. "From my point of view, the usual ten or so hours a day that I spend in meetings or the halls of the UN during the GA, plus the social engagements afterwards, are more than enough. That time will not be reduced with your arrival, as there is always a great deal more to do, so we will keep you busy. Now, come with me, and we'll get a quick bite to eat on the street. Then we have people to see back at the UN building."

"I look forward to it," replied Salim with enthusiasm.

Ghassan, who seemed to move only in high gear, was already going out the door.

They ate huge egg-salad sandwiches, heavy with mayonnaise on dark bread, while sitting on a bench in the square under the plane trees at First Avenue and 48th street. Ghassan explained that the coming days would be spent preparing for the influx of heads of state and heads of government, as well as many foreign ministers, for the annual opening of debate. He emphasized the need to establish contacts in national delegations to ensure that bilateral meetings were arranged, and Palestinian positions were well understood.

Salim was fascinated to have this insight into the mechanics of diplomacy at the UN, which to that point had been something of a mystery to him, even though he'd had some exposure during the summers when things were quite quiet.

"This year, Salim," Ghassan continued, "our focus will again be a response to the Camp David Accords. While much of the world and the amazingly naive President Carter welcome Camp David as a step toward peace in the region, we know that Palestinian interests have been put aside. That is how the parties reached agreement."

"Yes, Ghassan. I have been involved in some discussions in Cairo that dealt with these issues. I understand that our interests have been largely ignored."

Ghassan raised a hand and regained control of the conversation. "Sadat hopes to gain politically from a normalization of relations with Israel that would reduce the pressure on his regime. I concede that he needs to pay more attention to domestic social issues and economic development. His slogan 'Fewer weapons and more food for the people' has a ring to it. Additionally, the return of the Sinai and passage of Israeli ships through the Suez could help Egypt, but for us, nothing."

Salim was familiar with many of these points and looked for an opportunity to get a word in to ask the main question on his mind. "Ghassan, the international community seems to have bought the view that the Camp David Accords are a step toward peace. I know the media in the US has given Carter a great many unquestioning kudos for brokering the agreement. But how many delegations here are prepared to look beyond the headlines?"

Ghassan looked pleased at Salim's question, but the response was grim. "This is not easy for us in New York. Few delegations understand our position or speak critically of the accord. So many countries would like to see a settlement that they are unwilling to question the headlines. That's why we need to speak to as many delegations as possible."

Salim nodded, and Ghassan continued. "As for Camp David, you know the agreement calls for an autonomous self-governing authority on the West Bank and Gaza. Can you imagine proposing that without including the people of Palestine in the discussion? That is both insulting and unrealistic. Egypt, Israel, and Jordan are to agree on the modalities for the authority, although they generously agree that Palestinians can be included on their delegations. Probably to make the coffee." Ghassan's contempt for this generosity was palpable.

"Finally, you know that Camp David ignores the issue of Old Jerusalem, destined to be our capital. We must keep reminding delegations that it was captured in 1967 and is illegally controlled by the Israeli government under the clenched fist of the military. Very few countries recognize this seizure by the Israelis as legitimate, but we have much to do to advance our interests."

Salim finished his sandwich, feeling that he needed to polish his own presentation if he wanted to keep up with Ghassan. The two of them walked quickly back to the office and prepared for the afternoon round of appointments to which Ghassan wanted Salim to accompany him.

CHAPTER FIFTY-ONE

SOUTH LEBANON

"Davoud, welcome. Please sit there. I thank Iran, your leadership, and the assistance you have provided to our people and to my Intelligence Bureau in particular." Colonel Abu Khalid snapped his fingers, and a boy came forward carrying a brass tray of glasses of tea and small pastries. Aduan sat at the end of the table, eager to hear the exchange. Ali sat in the back of the room with a pair of aides to the Iranian intelligence officer.

"Colonel Abu Khalid," Davoud said, raising his hand and taking a glass of mint tea from the tray. "It is my pleasure to be at your headquarters again and to have the time to enjoy your hospitality. The pressure of our work and causes does not always allow time with our friends. Many thanks to you for this." He took a sip of the hot, sweet tea appreciatively.

"My friend," said Abu Khalid, raising his glass of tea in a gesture of respect, "we have worked well together, and the information you have periodically provided, as well as the supplies and trainers you have sent, have made a difference to my forces on the ground. I thank your great leader and you for your support."

"Colonel, you are aware, I realize, that clerics in South Lebanon are creating a growing demand for a group of believers who can further the principles of Islam. The clerics support the Ayatollah and want our help to act even more directly against your Israeli oppressors and their dogsbodies of Haddad's forces. I am here to speak to the clerics and determine if we are able to assist them in reaching their goal. We shall see how the talks unfold."

THE STRUGGLE CONTINUES

Davoud set down his now empty glass before continuing. "You will also recall, Colonel, that the Ayatollah has been a strong supporter of the people of Palestine from before he was brought back to Iran by his acolytes, who asked him to lead them to a better life. Much progress is being made to bring about reforms. Our leader remains devoted to spreading his message throughout the Muslim world. While we will continue to support your cause, there are opportunities and rising desires amongst other populations for change and support for the Islamic state. Egypt is a prime candidate for that change. Disturbances and demonstrations have unnerved Cairo for months. I should add that there is support in the Egyptian military for change. Islamic forces have encouraged dissent amongst left wing and religious followers opposed to the treaty that Sadat signed with Israel in 1979. We want to offer our assistance to them." Davoud looked up to see how the colonel was reacting to his comments.

"I realize that, Davoud," said Abu Khalid. "I know that the treaty has been rejected by the Muslim Brotherhood. My own colleagues in Cairo tell me that their activity and level of support for the Brotherhood is increasing daily."

"And we in Iran want to encourage them," said Davoud. "You realize that the Egyptian President Sadat was a close friend of the Shah. He increased his support for Sadat following the 1973 war with Israel. Iran even helped clean up the damage to the Suez Canal and sent oil to Egypt to help in the rebuilding."

Ali's eyes widened as he heard this exchange. He had no idea that Iran and Egypt were such close friends.

His eyes glittering with hatred, Davoud continued. "In later years, Colonel, you will know that Sadat even allowed the Shah to live in Egypt after he was deposed. That is where he died and was given a state funeral. This was an insult to Islam. Anyone who is such a supporter of the man who enslaved and impoverished the people of Iran, economically and spiritually, does not deserve to be in power. The Ayatollah wants to see Sadat removed from office."

The colonel's tone was sympathetic. "The Palestinian people have had great difficulty with Sadat since he visited Jerusalem and then signed the American treaty with Israel. I can understand that the people of Iran hold him in contempt."

Davoud looked pleased. "Yes. We in Iranian intelligence have sought information about the level of dissent within the Egyptian armed forces. There is a group in the army calling itself El Jihad that is said to be preparing the elements of a coup. Our colleagues in the Muslim Brotherhood, now recasting itself as Islamic Jihad, have been preparing their own plans and are close to taking action. If there is any information that comes your way that would be helpful, we would appreciate learning about it. We are asking others as well."

Colonel Abu Khalid rose, saying, "I have found our discussion of great interest, but now I must attend to other issues. If information comes to the bureau regarding Egypt that would be of value to you, I will ensure that it is passed on."

Ali stood up and shook hands with the Iranian aides and Davoud. They all left the room, and Aduan fell into step with Ali. "Quite an important discussion, Ali. The assistance from Iran comes with a price, it seems. They will be asking for our help further."

CHAPTER FIFTY-TWO

NEW YORK

Alex put down his coffee cup and answered the telephone. "Hello. Matheson here."

"Hello, this is Salim al Omeri from the Palestinian Observer Delegation. I am following up at the request of Ambassador Obeidi to introduce myself, as I have only recently arrived to join the delegation. I believe the ambassador spoke to you earlier to say that I would be in touch."

"Yes, he mentioned that a short while ago. Welcome to New York. With my responsibilities for political affairs in the Middle East, amongst other regions, we clearly have mutual interests," said Alex.

"Mr. Matheson—"

"Please call me Alex."

"And me Salim. Would you be available for a coffee tomorrow morning? I'd like to explain my mission." Salim hesitated, wondering if the Canadian diplomat would be prepared to meet with him.

"Yes, that's a good time for me. I'll look forward to it," Alex replied.

Salim was relieved and continued. "I propose nine-thirty at the Wayfarer's coffee shop at 51st and First Avenue. Would that work for you?"

"Yes. How will I know you, Salim?"

"My ambassador pointed you out to me yesterday as we passed on the long escalator at the main entrance to the UN building, so I will recognize you."

"All right. See you tomorrow."

The next morning, Alex donned a raincoat against the early autumn wind and walked to the coffee shop for his meeting. He opened one side of the large double doors and stepped into a replica of a turn-of-the-century country coach stop. There were panelled walls, dark, upholstered furniture, and wooden posts covered in bright brasses. He paused, looking around, his eyes adjusting to the dark interior. A young man of medium height, likely in his mid-twenties, wearing a well-cut, navy blue suit, came into focus and approached him.

"Alex, I am Salim al Omeri," he said, exchanging a firm handshake. "It's nice to meet you. I have a table just over here." He motioned to a corner table overlooking the busy street.

A waiter in a sparkling white shirt, black vest, and a long, white apron, tied around his waist, came over and took their order. "I will have a cappuccino," said Salim. "And you, Alex?"

"The same, please," Alex said to the waiter.

"So, Salim, where were you before coming to New York?"

"I was in Cairo, where I earned my law degree. I've been based there since that time, doing work for the Palestinian National Council. The work provided me with opportunities to travel and meet many people who are involved in Middle East issues. I've been attached to the delegation here before, on a summer co-op project, so I have some idea of how things are done at the UN."

Salim's flawless and American accented English surprised Alex. "That's an interesting background. I'm sure you'll enjoy working on these issues at the UN. I must say, unfortunately, that it doesn't look as if you'll be out of work for some time."

"Regretfully, I must agree with that, Alex, but living in New York has many advantages. I went to a boarding school in Connecticut and later NYU, so I know the region quite well, although I was then too young to enjoy all that New York has to offer."

Ah, that explains it, thought Alex.

"So, tell me, Alex, how long have you been in New York yourself? What do you think of the work here?"

"I arrived two years ago and enjoy it immensely. There are so many thoughtful and experienced people here on the delegations.

It's really the one place where everyone can come together and discuss the issues very directly. The atmosphere allows all perspectives and views to be aired and exchanged. So many people without knowledge of what goes on here are ready to say the UN is a failed organization—I'm not one of those."

"I have to say that I've heard that label put on the UN before," said Salim.

"Yes, 'the UN,'" Alex said, gesturing with his hands to put in quotation marks, "is often blamed for not dealing with so many dreadful things that happen in the world. But the UN is really just a forum and framework for discussion, a place where people like us can exchange views and seek solutions to the most intractable problems."

"I agree with that. The UN really does play an invaluable role in the international community. You will appreciate that the Palestinian position is that not all the decisions of the UN, particularly those of the Security Council, are good ones, but many are."

"You know, when critics say the UN has failed to stop this or that conflict, what they should really say is that the *members* of the UN—*the international community*—have failed. Not the UN, per se. I do feel that the organization is an overwhelming success in protecting human rights, in refugee care, providing health care, food, housing, water, and endless practical things to serve millions of people on a daily basis. Where the UN really fails, in the view of many, notably in the United States, is in meeting the expectations of the public, politicians, and the media on matters of international peace and security." Alex paused and took a sip of his coffee. "The problem is that the international community doesn't always agree with the US policy or approach."

Salim was quick to concur. "I can see how true that is. So much of what is said at the UN is only a reflection of domestic politics in member countries. I am sure you would agree."

"Exactly, Salim. A classic case was the political and media uproar that occurred last year when the American ambassador was seen meeting with your Ambassador Obeidi. There was such an outcry from the pro-Israel lobby that the American ambassador lost his job! Yet he is a man with an outstanding reputation. Just because of a meeting! The ambassador had a deep appreciation of why the United States is a member of this organization and what can be done here to further domestic as well as international interests and objectives. Most of the objections from US politicians and the media are because they don't always get their way." As seasoned a diplomat as he was, Alex didn't want to show his frustration over this point, examples of which were all too frequent.

"You will realize that the affair with the US ambassador, and the uproar it caused, was greeted by the Palestinians with a certain pleasure, as it should have embarrassed both the Americans and the Israelis," said Salim. "That is even though we too had a great deal of respect for him as an individual. The issue was that he and Obeidi were seen in public, not really just that they were talking because, of course, that happens."

Salim's nuanced understanding of this delicate political situation surprised Alex. He was impressed by the young Palestinian diplomat and answered, "Notwithstanding the frustrations we encounter here, talking about these issues and attempting to understand the range of factors and interests behind them is a much better way to proceed than the alternative of fighting it out."

"I agree, Alex. We have much to discuss. As a troop contributor to UNIFIL, you are aware of the pressure my people are under in Lebanon with the civil war going on endlessly. The activities of Major Haddad and the South Lebanon Army, not to mention incursions by the Israelis, are causing enormous anguish and economic and social difficulties for large numbers of our refugee population. This will be a central focus for me in the coming months. I hope we can meet to exchange views on that from time to time, and I want you to be completely open with your views and comments."

"I will be, and I would urge you to do the same. Please feel free to call anytime if you have any questions. This has been enjoyable, and I hope we'll soon meet again. I must get back to the UN building. Are you going that way?" Alex stood up and indicated that Salim should lead the way.

They put on their coats and walked out of the coffee shop into the busy traffic on the sidewalk toward the UN building. "I understand that you were once posted in Beirut, Alex," Salim said conversationally as they strolled down First Avenue.

"Yes, it's coming up to ten years ago since we went there. That was a fascinating assignment, although at that time, there was a good deal of Lebanese-Palestinian conflict, and the civil war was just ramping up. The Christian forces were reacting to what they saw as the huge Palestinian refugee population creating a state within a state, and that was becoming a code phrase for removing the Palestinians. You know all that. Interesting times, as they say."

"I grew up in Beirut myself. Where did you live?" Salim asked.

"In Raouché, near the Shell Building. I'm sure the area has changed since the civil war has devastated so much of the city."

"Really? I lived in that area until my mid-teens."

Alex stopped and stood back, looking with amazement at Salim. "Al Omeri." He paused, "Was your mother Amina al Omeri?"

Salim's voice softened as he spoke. "Yes, God bless her soul. She was murdered in a targeted attack when she was trying to secure peace with the Lebanese, and we never learned who was responsible."

"Salim, my deepest condolences. If that is the case, we lived in the same building! I remember well the horrific attack on your mother. My family and I were in the apartment the night that happened."

"That is an incredible coincidence, Alex," Salim said, his heart beating faster. He was stunned by the memory and the realization of this connection with Alex. "We must discuss this further when we have the opportunity," said Salim shakily. They walked into the courtyard in front of the iconic UN building and parted, warmly shaking hands and pledging to meet soon. Salim felt unbalanced as he walked away, thoughts of the horror of the night his mother was murdered swirling through his mind.

CHAPTER FIFTY-THREE

NEW YORK, NOVEMBER 1981

The deep voice and distinctive accent on the telephone got straight to the point. "You did not provide us with the intelligence I asked for weeks ago."

"I told you that I didn't have any information on the subject you asked about," said Fredriksen.

"I told you to ask others who would know," Barzin persisted.

"I said I wouldn't do that." Fredriksen felt braver over the phone than in person. He trembled and perspired heavily. He could feel the drops on his neck. He forced his voice to remain calm.

"But I said you would. Time has gone on. You will have heard the news from two days ago. In the future, you will provide information as I request. You would not want your capital or colleagues here to learn what your role has been." The threat was clear.

Fredriksen felt a stabbing pain in his forehead and bile rise in his throat. Since Egyptian President Anwar Sadat had been assassinated days earlier, Fredriksen was fearful that his contacts had something to do with it. If he was being honest with himself, he knew they did. The press speculated that it was a combination of some officers in the military and the Islamic Jihad who had worked together. *It must have been*, he thought, *and the Iranians must have played a role.*

Shakily, Fredriksen plowed on, determined to say his piece before he lost his courage. "I will no longer deal with you. The situation in Southern Lebanon has become more and more chaotic. Your goals and those of your supposedly glorious leader have been perverted.

You are doing nothing for the welfare of the Palestinian people. I didn't agree to help you to see my own countrymen killed. I am finished."

"You are not. I want—"

Fredriksen slammed down the phone, clasping his aching head. He slumped in a soft chair and sobbed, hands over his face. He staggered to his feet and went to the kitchen, where he filled a glass with ice and added a liberal quantity of Smirnoff's from a bottle in the freezer. He gulped it down quickly and poured a second one. He returned to the living room and sank weakly into his chair. He awoke with a jolt, seeing it was already dark and two hours had passed. He was lost in despair and felt a deep sense of loneliness.

CHAPTER FIFTY-FOUR

EIN EL HILWEH

An increasing number of raids from Lebanon by Palestinian fighters on Israeli settlements in the late seventies and early eighties brought strong retaliation from the Israelis. These incursions and harassment from Haddad forces put heavy pressure on the Palestinians. Many of their forces moved farther north, including to an ever-expanding camp at Ein el Hilweh, near Sidon. Originally established in 1948 with the first influx of Palestinians, the camp had become a city of some 75,000. With a regular influx of Palestinians seeking living space, much of the town looked like a hastily erected Lebanese town with concrete and stone buildings. At the edges, however, it had become a shanty town. Thousands lived in corrugated iron shacks or huts built from random lumber and plastic sheeting. There were few amenities or services.

PLO fighters moving to the area built well-fortified bunkers and outposts and gradually developed a Palestinian controlled area where no Lebanese authorities dared enter.

On the border, retaliatory attacks plagued the area. Israeli Force commanders in the Northern District became increasingly hostile to the harassment of Israeli settlements and started arguing for more punishing operations directed at Palestinian military installations.

The commander of Israeli Forces in the northern district, emboldened by the election of General Ariel Sharon to the Knesset, and his appointment as Minister of Defence, intensified the pressure to push back even more strongly against artillery and other attacks by the Palestinians on Israeli settlements.

THE STRUGGLE CONTINUES

***

"Ali," said Aduan, briefing him on the plans to relocate the Intelligence Bureau to Ein el Hilweh, "it will take some time for us to settle in and organize all our documentation and offices. I want you to go there today and see what space we are being offered. If we aren't actually on the site, we are likely to get nothing. Take two of the men and have them stay there to guard it for us, but come straight back to organize the move."

"Yes, Aduan, you are right. I understand the need to be there to claim our space. We know our fellow fighters all too well!" Ali said with a shake of the head and a broad smile.

"All right, Hafiz, find Maalouf," Ali said to one of the drivers for the unit as he walked out of the cement-block building where the Intelligence Bureau was based. "Get some gear and food for you two, enough to last a few days, and the pickup. We're going to Ein el Hilweh."

Hafiz scurried off in search of his colleague and the provisions.

Half an hour later, their faded, red Toyota pickup swept along the dirt back roads with Hafiz driving and Ali in the front seat. Maalouf sat in the back, holding tightly to the bags of stores as the vehicle careened through the hills. Ali explained their mission to Hafiz, who was pleased that the unit would be moving, as he had some family in the camp already. Hafiz hoped that this would mean some good food once in a while, prepared by someone who had some idea of how to cook rather than one of his fellow fighters, who had been told to do it but knew not how.

As they approached the lowland camp, they enjoyed the green and deep, rich smell of foliage and animals in the peaceful farm area. They passed easily through random Palestinian manned checkpoints and stopped as they drew up to the well-defended gate in the fence on the outskirts of the camp. Four heavily armed men walked out to the pickup and surrounded it. The guards rummaged through the bags that Maalouf was holding in the back and ran a long-handled mirror underneath the vehicle. A more senior officer examined their documents and asked Ali to explain why they were there. The officer seemed satisfied and directed them to follow another soldier, who mounted a motorbike and set off through the narrow, crowded, and noisy streets.

The fetid air from crowded conditions, uncollected garbage, and lack of a proper sewage system contrasted sharply with the freshness of the country they had enjoyed passing through only a few kilometres away. Turning suddenly into a small square, they stopped and climbed out of the pickup. The soldier pointed to a long, stone building that might one time have been stables, with a second storey of storage. Hafiz and Maalouf stayed with the truck.

Ali was escorted down a long hallway with small offices where the administrative units apparently worked. Halfway down the hall, he was told to stop beside a pile of boxes, behind which were two men and a woman in what was the accommodations section.

Having identified himself, the plain woman at the desk replied to Ali, barely looking up. "Your unit has been designated some rooms across the street at the side of this building. Down the hall and turn right. Go out the door at the end. Cross the alley and enter the door on the left. Sign this," she said, pushing a paper toward Ali, who did so. "Oh yes, take this," she said, tossing a huge, old fashioned, rusty key at him.

With that welcoming reception, Ali went back to the square to find Hafiz and Maalouf leaning against the pickup, smoking. "I have a key to our space. Bring the pickup down the alley on that side of the building," he said, gesturing to the right side. "I'll go through the main building to make sure I get to the right place. I'll show you where to go."

Ali re-entered HQ and followed the directions he had been given. Opening the final door, he walked out into the blinding light and crossed the alley to a stone building with a peeling, grey, heavy wooden door. Hafiz had started down the alley. He brought the Toyota forward slowly and stopped a few feet away, the truck leaving not much more than room for a person to squeeze by.

Ali stuck the weighty old key in the rusty lock and heaved against the door to open it. He walked into a large, stone-tiled room, perhaps fifteen metres square. He felt the mustiness and lack of oxygen of a long closed and sealed room. A dozen bare lights suspended from wires in the ceiling made little difference when they were turned on. A feeble, brown-tinged light tried, largely unsuccessfully, to make its way through the filthy windows. Thick dust motes moved in the air, admitted through the open door. The walls were a smoky green, peeling and bubbled in many places like festering sores. The floors were littered with paper, old clothing, hundreds of cigarette butts, food wrappers, and bottles. There were several nests of rugs and blankets where men had slept, seemingly long ago. Since then, rats had clearly moved into the luxuries left by the previous occupants.

Maalouf almost gagged as he came in from the outside. "What have we done to earn this?" he said, coughing.

"Welcome to the fighting forces," added Hafiz.

Ali laughed and crossed the room, where he opened four additional doors that led into small but no cleaner, airless rooms. "Not bad," he said. "You two will have some time to clean all this up."

A fifth door revealed two heavily stained toilets and a yellowish-brown, crusted urinal. There was even a seemingly broken and rusted shower hanging in the corner. Ali turned on a faucet and heard a sharp burst of air, followed by a trickle of thick, brown water. The last door, with two heavy bars crossing it, led to a back area off the next street, where there was room for perhaps three vehicles if they cleared out the shacks that had been built there.

"This has real potential, my friends, but it needs some work, which you are volunteering to do. I must go back to HQ and talk to them about other administrative matters. You can bring in the cleaning tools and supplies from the pickup and get to work. This is home until we make the move."

Ali crossed the alley again, relishing the fresh air outside. He found that the door he had exited in HQ would not open from the outside, so he had to walk the length of the alley and enter the main door.

As he re-entered the lobby, he felt the compression and then heard the *whump whump* sound of helicopter rotors overhead. He sensed, more than saw, the bustle of activity as people noisily dove under their desks. Others ran toward him, trying to leave the building. In a second, he heard the hiss of rocket fire, followed by a huge flash of light that burst from the ceiling as a missile hit a top corner of the building. Concrete, tiles, and beams thundered to the ground, unleashing a thick cloud of dust. Ali dove for protection under a heavy wooden staircase going up to the mezzanine. His senses were assailed by the shouting, screaming, and automatic-weapons fire, uselessly blasting into the air from the street outside. As he crouched, the large windows above the staircase shattered and rained shards of glass on the stairs. With a brief pause, he saw his opportunity and rushed back to the main door and into the square, crossing it with dozens of others seeking safety.

Five helicopters with Israeli Defence Forces markings on them were circling above, directing rocket fire into HQ. Flames were roaring from several hits on the main structure. More explosions appeared through the red-tile roofs of adjoining buildings, two of which collapsed in a frightening slide to the street. In moments the helicopters ceased firing, seamlessly formed a diamond formation, and swept out toward the sea. By now, the flames had engulfed the headquarters building. Although emergency services attempted to contain the flames, the effort was clearly futile. People on the streets stood in helpless horror.

Ali ran to his right to the alley alongside the remains of HQ. Stepping over rocks and debris from the attack, he looked ahead to see the rooms where he had left Hafiz and Maalouf minutes earlier. The side of their building had collapsed, leaving the door and its heavy frame standing forlornly. Ali jumped over the fallen rocks at the entrance. There was little of the main room left. The roofing had almost entirely collapsed, and beams were burning; under it was a body, not moving, the upper part covered in fallen stones. Ali tossed stones and roof tiles to the side, revealing a bloody torso and Maalouf's smashed head.

Ali vomited into the rubble. Shaking with fear, he looked around, hoping that Hafiz was alive. He stumbled over the smoking debris, shouting Hafiz's name. Finally, he saw a shirt all but buried in the stones and dirt. He scraped away the rubble and uncovered what proved to be Hafiz's lifeless body, lying on its back with wide eyes and a look of horror on his face. Ali fell sobbing to the ground.

CHAPTER FIFTY-FIVE

SOUTH LEBANON

"Fatima, I returned from Ein al Hilweh yesterday. I so need to talk to you. I have to tell you that I was there when the Israelis attacked the PLA headquarters. Two men with me were killed. I am very shaken because I found their bodies."

"Oh no, that must have been so terrible. Are you alright?" asked Fatima.

"Yes, it was horrible, but I'm not injured myself. The entire headquarters building was destroyed. Thanks again to your friend in the restaurant that I can reach you on the telephone. How are you?"

"Oh, I'm fine. This all sounds terrible. Will it never end?"

"There has been a huge build-up of Israeli forces in the north of Israel, and we are concerned that they're planning a major move. We also hear that there has been an increasing amount of rocket fire from Israeli naval vessels off the coast. The Israelis are also said to have struck farther north last night, and that even Damour was a target. Is everything all right there?"

"As I said, Mother and I are fine. There was an attack on the PLA training base at the other end of town, but nothing near us. This morning, the word was going around that civilians should seek safety in the camps near Beirut, where there are already thousands of people. Many are packing to move. My mother and I think we could go to the Shatila camp, where she has a cousin who will take us in. At the clinic, they tell me that they need workers there even more than here. The Gaza Hospital in Shatila is desperate for help, they say."

"I am very concerned about the coming weeks, Fatima. The Israeli build-up is enormous. They have the best equipment and a huge number of soldiers. There have been hundreds of Israeli air attacks across southern Lebanon in the past few months and so many interventions by their troops into the south. They could overwhelm us in hours."

"That is very scary, Ali. What about the Palestinian forces? Can they do nothing?"

"I have never been so conscious of our military weakness, regardless of the bravery of our soldiers. The Israelis now have so many of those naval vessels in the sea between Tyre and Sidon and are firing rockets day and night. The events at Ein el Hilweh were only a practice for their attack helicopters. There is great concern that they will move farther north along the coast. I'm worried that they might go all the way to Beirut. The Israelis are also supplying more and more artillery pieces and vehicles to that crazy man, Haddad. There are independent militias popping up everywhere here, and few know whose side they are supporting."

"Haddad is terrible. The Lebanese hate him too." Fatima's voice sounded vehement.

"A few days ago, an Israeli artillery unit shelled a UNIFIL outpost near us, killing several Norwegian soldiers. That's outrageous. The Israelis were actually firing from within a Haddad compound! Our contacts from across the border tell us that, since Ariel Sharon was appointed Minister of Defence, he is the reason behind the growing Israeli troop strength in the northern district. He claims to be acting as God's protector of illegal settlements. He has made many assurances that the settlers on our land near the border of Lebanon will soon be free of attacks."

"This all sounds very dangerous. I don't know if we should stay here or not."

"If you go to Beirut, how can we maintain contact, Fatima? Do you know how we can do that?" Ali was desperate to avoid losing contact with Fatima, the only person he really cared about.

"We must decide to go or not quickly, Ali. If we do move, I will contact you as soon as we reach Beirut. I can always try to write to your unit as we have done, wherever you may be."

"That will find me. Go with my love, Fatima. Take care." Ali hung up. His shoulders dropped, and he stared at the ground.

At the other end of the line, Fatima did much the same. He didn't hear her say softly that she sent him her love as well.

CHAPTER FIFTY-SIX

NEW YORK

Under-Secretary Fuller walked into the room briskly and brought the meeting of UNIFIL contributing countries and permanent members of the Security Council to order. "I'm afraid I have more bad news from UNIFIL this morning. My most sincere condolences go to you, Ambassador O'Regan, for the deaths last night of two of your soldiers who were serving with UNIFIL. This is a tragic follow-up to the recent killings of the Norwegian troops. A third Irish soldier was also kidnapped during this event at their base in Tibnin. Our first reading is that this seems to have been carried out by a Palestinian group, but we don't know who is actually responsible. Our contacts overnight with PLA headquarters provided no further information. They claim not to be aware of the incident at all but are looking into it, as are we, of course." Fuller's distinguished face was clearly troubled.

The Irish ambassador nodded as he followed Fuller's comments, and then he responded. "Under-Secretary, Irish troops are proud to serve with UNIFIL, and we are all aware that this comes with risks. You will understand that there will be questions in the Dail Eireann, our Lower House of Parliament, today. However, I have instructions from Dublin to assure you and our fellow troop contributors that my government fully supports a continued role for Ireland as a contributor of troops for UNIFIL."

"That is much appreciated, Ambassador," Fuller responded. "We are all aware that our entire UNIFIL contingent has had a difficult time in the past few months. The involvement of Iranian forces and their aggressive new methods of attack include a great deal less respect for UN troops. In addition, kidnappings and some suicide bombings have upped the ante. The Iranians, including men from the Quds Force of the Revolutionary Guards are, amongst other things, apparently training Palestinian militias and urging them to be more aggressive themselves."

"The growing Iranian involvement in South Lebanon is a matter of great concern in Washington, as you might imagine," interjected the American Deputy Permanent Representative.

"Yes, I understand," said Fuller. "Their involvement has led to increased activity by both the South Lebanon Army and the Israelis themselves, some against our troops as well. The shelling of a UNIFIL position recently from within an SLA camp was excused by them as being the responsibility of a new officer who didn't know the area. That is preposterous. As I have mentioned, there also seem to be more independent groups forming, giving themselves grand names, and trying to prove themselves with random attacks."

"If I might ask, Under-Secretary," said Fredriksen, "is there any further news about our two soldiers who were kidnapped just last week?" He looked tired, flushed, and stressed.

"I was just going to get to that," said Fuller. "We have heard just this morning, Martin, that the person behind the kidnapping may have been a Lebanese working for an Islamic splinter group. The players on the pitch are increasingly difficult to identify. You will know that we are doing everything possible to find your soldiers and will continue to pursue this. I appreciate your cooperation and understanding. We will ensure that you are informed immediately when we have further information.

"I think that is all, unless there are further questions," said Fuller, looking around the room. "Thank you. We will undoubtedly meet again soon." He rose from his seat.

On the way out, Fredriksen walked beside Alex Matheson. "There is no doubt that capitals will be concerned about the latest incident, Alex. I'm under a lot of pressure from Oslo to provide details on the kidnapping, but we really have no idea who is actually responsible.

It's hard to imagine that we will find anything except two bodies." Fredriksen looked very depressed.

"I must say, you do look under pressure these days," Alex said. "Are you feeling all right?

"I'm okay, Alex, but there is no doubt the squeeze is on from Oslo. We've been troop contributors across the world for many years, but the loss of our troops is always punishing. The idea of a kidnapping is particularly difficult to deal with."

"Martin, the incidents in the past few weeks have indeed been onerous. With the Iranian involvement and random militias, it's so chaotic in southern Lebanon. As if trying to keep the Palestinians and the Israelis apart isn't bad enough!" said Alex.

CHAPTER FIFTY-SEVEN

NEW YORK, DECEMBER 1981

Alex and Salim shared a window table in La Biblioteque restaurant, perched above First Avenue and overlooking the UN building. The restaurant was a popular spot for diplomats to have lunch after one o'clock, when committees took their lunch breaks. Even on a day of broken cloud, light streamed through the many windows, and waiters scurried from table to table through the noisy crowd.

"Thanks for the invitation to lunch today," said Alex. The waiter arrived with a tall glass of sparkling water with lime, clinking with ice cubes, for Salim, and a generous glass of Saint Nicolas de Bourgueil red wine from the lower Loire, for Alex. "We've had some good conversations about the Middle East over the past months. I appreciate your openness and willingness to hear different points of view. The situation of the Palestinian people is indeed dire. Better minds than mine have spent years trying to reconcile divergent positions."

"Alex, we have developed a real understanding of the positions that each of our delegations takes on resolutions in the GA and discussions in committees. The fact that you served in Beirut and saw the Palestinian-Lebanese conflict of the time, first-hand, has given you a feeling for our situation. Of course, having lived in the same building gives us a special relationship." Salim and Alex both smiled, raised their glasses, and touched them.

"Yes," Alex said with a laugh. "As I've said before, as we passed in the foyer of the building from time to time, your mother was friendly, but I didn't realize who she was or her position with the PLO. I wasn't aware that she had a young son and couldn't have imagined we would be sitting across the table from each other years later!"

"Well, now you know," Salim said with a smile. "We are very concerned about the increase in Israeli forces in Lebanon itself. They are conducting operations farther and farther north. We're concerned that they might invade Lebanon as Sharon incites."

"That would set off a very violent conflict, Salim."

"Sharon claims that an operation like that would be in self-defence," continued Salim. "We wonder what would become of our population if that happened. The personnel of the PLA and other armed militias is one thing, but the hundreds of thousands of civilian Palestinians have nowhere else to go. Alex, think of the children living in terrible conditions. Food, clothing, housing—in some areas, it's almost medieval. They are rarely able to get proper schooling. What kind of citizenry does the international community think we can develop without education? Our people in Lebanon are under immense pressure from the Lebanese as well as the Israelis, but what can we do?"

"I fully realize how difficult the situation is, but what we can or should do about it is not at all clear."

"The social fabric of Palestinian society has been badly torn, Alex, almost destroyed. There is virtually no opportunity for employment. As I said, access to education is extremely hard to find, and really, there is none in the context of Palestinian culture. Think how important that is to society," Salim said, leaning forward over the table to emphasize his point.

Alex could sense the weight of hopelessness in Salim's words. "I appreciate that is very difficult."

"Since our people were driven from their land in the 1940s, we've been able to focus on little more than basic existence. Most of our population has grown up in refugee camps. How can we create a society that looks at anything but its daily bread? We don't want all our young men to grow up into lives of violence and conflict, but there seems to be nothing else open to them."

"Salim, it does seem as if the level of military conflict is bound to increase in the region. From their perspective, the increase in attacks from Lebanese territory in recent months gives the Israelis an excuse to be more bellicose. The kidnapping of Israeli soldiers that we have seen lately is a particularly intense flashpoint in Israel. From the New York point of view, kidnapping of UNIFIL troops is a huge issue. Under-Secretary Fuller is thinking of another trip to UNIFIL to ensure that we in New York are knowledgeable and demonstrate our concern over the situation. At the same time, we see that the pressure on the Israeli government is strong. This isn't just a military issue for them either. They see that their settlers need security to develop their communities and become a part of the society of Israel."

"Yes, I know. Fuller has been in touch with Ambassador Obeidi. If there is another group going out there, he wants our delegation to join it. If that happens, I will be the one to travel."

"Good. My capital would expect me to go as well. This is very political at home, and we have to be seen to be closely involved. We'll see how the major countries and the UN plan to react in the next few days."

CHAPTER FIFTY-EIGHT

SOUTH LEBANON, APRIL 1982

As Israeli forces greatly increased their troop strength, and armoured vehicles were massed near the Lebanese border, the exchange of rockets from Palestinian forces and replies by the Israelis became more frequent. The rising tempo of the exchanges was reaching a crescendo.

Heavy and deadly attacks on PLO-held buildings in Beirut became frequent. Shells fired from naval vessels offshore found hidden arms depots. Air attacks throughout South Lebanon targeted Palestinian military infrastructure. The attacks on Beirut were clearly aimed at the Palestinian leadership and support from their community.

"Ali, hurry and pack these files! We have orders to leave as soon as possible," said Aduan, running into the room.

Ein el Hilweh had come under periodic artillery and rocket fire in recent weeks, but today the word was going around that a huge force of Israeli armed units had crossed the border and was moving north towards Tyre.

"Oh no. Another move," said Ali to three colleagues in the Intelligence Bureau offices. "Where do we go now?"

The Intelligence Bureau, established in Ein el Hilweh for only a matter of months, was again on the move. The men threw boxes of files into a truck, and with accompanying armoured personnel carriers, tore off into the mountains, where they sought refuge for their men. After a tense drive, tearing toward the mountains along the rough roads, all the while keeping a lookout for Israeli aircraft, they pulled into a narrow valley.

Aduan and Ali piled out of the truck into the shelter of an overhang where a natural cave had been hollowed out and extended, providing protection from the air. Men started pulling the boxes off the truck and taking them deeper into the cave. The two of them carried on a whispered conversation while they supervised the unloading.

"We Palestinians are in the most exposed position our people have been in for many years," said Aduan. "I don't know where we go from here, but we're not going to get much help from our leadership in Beirut. From the radio contacts we have had, they will be fortunate to escape the rain of shells and bombs at their headquarters. I think we're on the verge of a major change in our situation."

"I agree this is desperate," replied Ali. "How can we possibly stand up against the massive military machine of the Israelis? We know that Sharon is determined to eliminate us if he can. What will happen to our people? Most are not involved in the conflict and don't want to be but have such a hard time living from day to day. This will only get worse. I can see no hope ahead."

***

The Israelis moved on, soon surrounding Ein el Hilweh and pounding it from the air and sea. Bringing in more armour, including hundreds of their new Merkava tanks, they shelled the camp relentlessly. Tanks and armoured vehicles choked the coastal road. The radio reported devastating air battles between the Syrians and the Israelis further north. Scores of Syrian MIGs and surface-to-air missile sites were destroyed at virtually no cost to the Israelis. Radio communications from PLA forces, occupying the heights of Beaufort Castle, talked of heavy battles, hundreds of Israeli tanks, artillery barrages and airstrikes, little ammunition, and dwindling food and water supplies.

Using a radio connection, Ali tried several times without success to call Said, owner of the restaurant in Damour near Fatima's house. He was unable to get any answer. Ali trembled at the thought that Fatima and Dalia might have gone to Beirut after all, as the days went on and Israelis kept up the bombardment of the Palestinian controlled parts of the city. He needed to know that she was safe.

The Intelligence Bureau personnel were cut off completely from the advancement of Israeli military power to the east and west of them. They spent days in the cave with other PLA fighters, going out only to find food and other supplies but unable to do anything to help their cause. In the meantime, Israeli forces swept by them, ignoring the small Palestinian emplacements that were poorly armed.

"Aduan, I can't stay here and not know where Fatima is or how to contact her. She is all I have in the world. The Israelis are pushing farther north. Those messages the other day that the Gaza Hospital in Shatila has been all but destroyed by bombing and long-range artillery terrify me. That's where Fatima hoped to be able to work if they went there."

"We all heard that an American negotiator has been trying to arrange a ceasefire," said Aduan. "The Israelis are so dependent on American military and economic aid that they have to listen. If there is a ceasefire, we may be able to leave, and you can find out what has happened to Fatima."

"But I must go to her, Aduan. I'm desperate."

"I understand, but I can't have you go try to find her. The reports are that the Israelis are focussing so much on shelling Beirut that fewer of their forces are occupying the south. Colonel Abu Khalid had a message yesterday to say that we might soon be able to return to Ein el Hilweh or a place farther south. We have to wait to see if there is a ceasefire."

CHAPTER FIFTY-NINE

BEIRUT, JUNE 1982

The Israelis briefly halted near Ein el Hilweh and then again around Sidon. Both were short delays. After a barrage of artillery from ships, they made a major landing north of Sidon and pushed north to Damour, only a few kilometres from the Beirut airport. Their heavy equipment rumbled through farm areas and villages. Some 1,500 armoured personnel carriers were engaged. Children came out from houses and shacks to see the immense military power on the move, waving at them and begging for candy, a few waving Israeli flags. The entire area was enshrouded with fine dust kicked up by the vehicles. The grinding noise was unending, and the earth trembled. The Israelis installed huge artillery guns south of the city. Only a short period after invading Lebanon, the Israelis had all but encircled Beirut and appeared ready to destroy the city.

The guns opened up. Day and night, the bombardment of Palestinian controlled areas of Beirut continued. The Palestinians were entrenched in the midst of the local population and had built extensive networks of tunnels connecting areas and buildings. Huge explosions would periodically erupt, killing fighters and civilians alike in neighbouring buildings. Many of these collapsed from the relentless barrages, but thousands of fighters fought on with their rifles and RPGs against the might of the Israeli forces with their own and American weapons.

An American envoy, emphasizing the damage that the Israelis were doing to their own reputation as well as to the huge numbers of civilians in peril in the city, rushed from player to player, seeking a ceasefire. The Palestinians were being wiped out. The city was on the verge of complete infrastructural collapse. Hundreds of thousands of Lebanese and other civilians were in mortal danger. The Israelis were seen to have conducted a massive offensive campaign against small, ill-equipped Palestinian forces. Much of the world only saw the destruction and the deaths of tens of thousands of innocent civilians.

A ceasefire was brought about with the media attention and the collapse of the Palestinian resistance to the Israelis. Included in the terms was agreement on a multinational force to supervise the departure from Lebanon of the majority of the Palestinian fighters. Ships were sent to load the Palestinian leadership and take them, via Cyprus, to Tunis, where they would establish a new headquarters, and some would go on to other Arab countries. Thousands of fighters went along the Damascus Road in trucks and buses to camps in Syria or Jordan. The Israelis tightened the noose and moved closer to the Palestinian camps as the fighters left.

CHAPTER SIXTY

DAMOUR, AUGUST 1982

"Aduan, with a ceasefire supposedly in effect and things looking quieter here, I want to go to Damour now to see if I can find out what has happened to Fatima. We have nothing to do here but stay in place. I want to take a motorcycle and go there. I can be back in a few hours."

Aduan looked at Ali, seeing he was anxious and about to leave even without permission. "All right, Ali. This time I will say yes. There is indeed little we can do here. Take the back roads, and keep out of the sight of any Israeli or Lebanese forces. God go with you."

Having filled the gas and oil tanks, Ali, dressed in an old pair of black pants and a checked flannel shirt, mounted the battered, green Yamaha DS7 two-stroke motorcycle. He stomped on the starter, and the motor came to life with a choking burst of exhaust. "I'll be back early evening, Aduan. *Insh'allah,* I will have news."

He took off on the dirt trail, heading north through the countryside toward the Sidon to Jezzine road. Ali passed through a couple of small hamlets, looking as they had for hundreds of years. People sat on their door stoops, and children bounced balls along the rough road, which was nothing much more than a path. Old men sat hunched over small tables, playing tric trac, the clatter of the pieces breaking the stillness of the hot afternoon. Virtually no one looked up. *What do these people even know of the war?* Ali thought.

A matter of minutes later, he reached the main road, stopped, listened, and looked carefully, seeing nothing but one wandering donkey. He booted his motorcycle across the highway and followed a small trail through the pine trees that, by his reckoning, would lead to the Awali River. There he stopped briefly to drink and duck his head into a small, cool pool in the otherwise low water level of the river. He remounted, following the path north and east along the hillside above the river. All was quiet in the countryside. The town of Beiteddine was his next goal.

As Ali approached it, he moved cautiously. Down the hill, he could see the sultan's palace. Originally built at the site of Druze historic grounds in the seventeenth century, the palace had been used as an administrative centre by the Ottoman Empire in the nineteenth century, and later by the French after WWI. It had been all but destroyed in conflict between various Lebanese factions in recent years. Ali went slowly around it so as not to attract attention, even though he saw only one Lebanese-marked military vehicle and four armed soldiers in the palace square. He circumvented the town on back lanes and farm roads and then crossed the valley, heading west over the next range of hills.

As he crested the last rise, which brought him to the top of the hills along the coast, Ali thought back to the days when he and Marwan had wandered these hills as boys, never venturing quite far enough to see the training area where there was said to be a private militia base. Now he could see the actual installation farther north and turned away from it without being seen. Down the trail, he passed the golf club where he and Marwan had scavenged for balls. He entered the lowlands covered with banana plants and citrus trees.

Ali stopped his motorcycle on the edge of an abandoned farmyard beside the main coastal highway on the outskirts of Damour. He hid his bike in a pile of drying canes and stepped cautiously across a narrow field to the highway. A pair of Lebanese armoured cars sped past him from the north, and he ducked into the bushes. An Israeli truck with a canvas top, loaded with wooden boxes, came from the other direction. Seeing a break, Ali ran across the road and ducked into a lane between small buildings.

Apprehensive about the presence of the military, whether Israeli or Lebanese, Ali moved cautiously. Many of the buildings were burned or had walls and roofs caved in. The lanes were covered in rubble, the evidence of a battle or shelling. As he approached a more central road, he saw locals going about their days in a normal fashion, but the road was quiet. He took a deep breath and walked into the street and down a small hill, as if he belonged, trying to look as if he had something to do there.

Farther along, there was more damage to buildings and even fewer people. The stench of burned wood and materials filled the air, clearly a long time after the fire itself. He stopped and looked ahead to see a small, completely collapsed and burned building where Said's restaurant used to be. There was no sign of Said or other people. His heart in his throat, Ali turned quickly into the small lane on the right where Fatima lived. He broke into a run and then saw that the end of the lane was blocked by debris. He scrambled over the top of blocks from a fallen wall and into the small square where Dalia and Fatima had their shack. The place where it had been was now a pile of burned debris and twisted pieces of corrugated iron, which had been on the roof. He walked closer, tears welling in his eyes. Kicking aside some rubble, he picked up a faded yellow shawl that he knew had belonged to Fatima. There was no other sign of life or death.

Suddenly, he heard a cough and what sounded like a sob. He looked around to see a very old woman heavily wrapped in a blanket, even in the heat of the day, sitting against a broken wall.

Ali walked to her, bent over, and asked if she knew what had happened to Fatima and Dalia. "Where are they?" he said. "What happened?"

"Gone."

"Where? When?"

"Gone."

The frustrating pattern continued through several questions, the old woman's only answer being, "Gone."

Ali felt frantic. He finally decided that she must be talking about her own family who had left her to die. She was very faint. Her eyes were milky from glaucoma, and he realized she may not have seen or known anything about Fatima at all. Ali gave the old woman a drink from his water bottle. She grabbed at it, her dried, claw-like hands shaking, so desperate was she for the liquid. Her head then dropped on her chest with a great sigh. Ali realized that she would not be able to give him any information.

He walked away slowly, his head pounding and thoughts swirling, overcome with the fear that Fatima had been killed in the attacks, not knowing yet fearing the worst. As light fell, he retraced his ride to the camp, barely aware of where he was going.

CHAPTER SIXTY-ONE

BEIRUT, SEPTEMBER 1982

In Beirut, senior Israeli military men met on the top floor of a building overlooking the Shatila camp. Defence Minister Sharon and his chief of staff gathered their senior officers.

"In light of the targeted explosion that killed President Bashir Gemayel last night, our friends in his Phalange militia are more than outraged with the Palestinians. We've been talking to their leaders this morning. Bearing in mind that this conflict is about their country, not ours, I am prepared to accede to the Phalange request that their forces be allowed to enter the Shatila camp. They want to rid it of the terrorists that they say the camp is training and harbouring," said Sharon.

"Should we then draw back our forces from the district, Minister?" asked a colonel who was there commanding a contingent of paratroopers.

"No, Colonel. We have agreed that our forces will surround the camp to ensure that no terrorists are allowed to escape. We will control access as well while the Phalange forces enter. We can expect that they will be prepared to launch their operation in the next forty-eight hours. We will watch from our command centre here, overlooking the camp."

"No further questions?" said the chief of staff, looking around. "Dismissed."

CHAPTER SIXTY-TWO

SOUTH LEBANON

A few days later, a messenger delivered some documents and mail to the Intelligence Bureau, which had returned to their quarters in the southeast.

"Ali, there is a message here for you!" said Aduan, who had received the mail. "Fatima's mother left a note with one of our men still at Ein el Hilweh, hoping it might reach you. This was received only two days ago, so she might still be there!"

"Oh Aduan, *alhamdulillah*! Give it to me!" Ali's hands trembled as he unfolded the note, written in pencil on piece of grey, crumpled paper.

"I need to see you," Dalia had written. "I will be at Ein el Hilweh for some days. Come now."

"Look, Aduan," said Ali, holding out the paper. "She will still be there. I must take the motorcycle again and go to the camp to look for her!"

"Well, the Israeli agreement to evacuate Beirut and Lebanon is proceeding quickly, so they are thinking only of going home. We have nothing to do until we get orders to move, which will likely mean we leave Lebanon completely. The coastal road must be plugged with military vehicles, so if you stay away from that, you should be quite safe. Go ahead."

Ali rushed out and started up the old Yamaha. He sped along gravel roads and farm paths to Ein el Hilweh, urging the most speed out of his 250cc engine and ignoring the dangers of possible military activity or patrols. Finally, he made it through the unattended and badly damaged gate and into the main square. The extent of destruction was devastating. Buildings that had housed thousands were now burned piles of stone and timbers. On a side street, he saw a line of people waiting for food handouts at a Red Cross stand under a green umbrella. Desperate, totally ravaged, and stressed civilians, and others with tattered, partial uniforms, stood numbly in line. Ali left the motorcycle leaning against a pile of stones and walked the line, asking everyone if they knew Dalia. No one did.

He walked to the nearby square, where at one corner, there was a fountain. Surprisingly, it was working, so he had a long drink of water and washed his face. He sat on the edge, wondering how he could find Fatima's mother. Some minutes later, he looked up and noticed a seemingly elderly woman hobbling across the square, headed for the food line. She was dressed in rags and looked as pitiful as the old woman approaching her death whom he had seen in Damour days earlier. The woman looked up as she came closer, and he heard a wild cry of "Ali!"

Ali slipped from the fountain's edge in surprise and looked up, realizing that this old woman was Dalia, who would only be some fifty years old!

He rushed to her, taking her in his arms. "Dalia, Dalia. Yes, it's me! Where is Fatima?"

She sagged against him, letting out a deep sob. "Ali, our beloved Fatima is dead. She was murdered by the Phalangists in Shatila."

Ali howled in pain like a wounded animal. He cried to the heavens, shouting out his anger. Gasping for breath, he grabbed and shook Dalia, crying out, "You must tell me what happened. Speak!"

She slumped to the cobblestones. Ali picked her up and helped her to the fountain, where she sat on the ledge, her head sagging. He got her a drink of water and splashed cool water on her face while she rubbed her eyes and gradually brought herself together. He then did it again to himself.

"Tell me. Tell me." Ali couldn't stand it. He trembled with anticipation.

THE STRUGGLE CONTINUES

"We left Damour when the Israelis were increasing their attacks on coastal towns. Fatima had called you days earlier. We walked to Shatila to stay with my cousin. We'd been there only a few days when Fatima went to Gaza Hospital to look for a job. She was taken in immediately. The hospital was overrun with wounded, both military and civilian. It was horrible. Everything in the camp was extraordinarily crowded. The streets were jammed with refugees. Food and water were scarce. Fatima worked fourteen to eighteen hours a day and often collapsed in the hospital to sleep. She only returned to my cousin's house every two or three days.

"One day I went into Beirut city to search for food. The ceasefire was in place. Thousands of Palestinian fighters had been expelled. I saw a huge and wild demonstration in Martyrs' Square. The new president of Lebanon had been assassinated the previous night. Thousands were there, waving Lebanese flags and chanting support for the Christian Phalange. The emotion, noise, and energy of the crowd was incredible. I was very afraid. Speakers were blaming the Palestinians for his killing.

"I knew I had to get off the streets," she continued. "I hid until after dark in a partially destroyed building and then went back to Shatila. As I got close, I could see that Israeli soldiers were guarding the entrances. No one was allowed to pass in or out. I was so frightened that I couldn't even walk the streets to go to my cousin's. I found another place to hide and slept the night alone."

Ali was mute with shock.

"The next day, I saw hundreds of Phalangist fighters enter the camp. The Israelis then closed off the gates and allowed no one in or out. I stayed close by. I could hear a great deal of shooting, screaming, and cries. It went on through the afternoon. All that night, the Israelis shot flares into the sky. The area was as bright as day. The screaming and shooting carried on. Fires burned. The following day was much the same, and then suddenly, the Phalange formed up and left, as did the Israelis." Dalia paused to catch her breath and gather strength to carry on.

"Ali, I cannot tell you how horrible it was. For much of the day, no one moved. Some people straggling out of Shatila were so shocked that they couldn't speak. Many had bloody wounds, and their faces were filled with horror. The Phalangists had been on a rampage. Hundreds of young men had been tied up and shot. Many young women were raped, then massacred, one man said, because the Phalanges claimed they would only breed terrorists. Babies and children were bayoneted, and their bodies left on the streets."

"Oh Dalia, I cannot bear this. What about Fatima?"

"I hated to go into the camp, but I had to look for Fatima. There were bodies everywhere, mutilated and savaged. Hundreds, thousands were killed. I went straight to the Gaza hospital and saw that it was burning fiercely. A medical attendant came out, limping badly. He was crying openly. He said that the Phalangists had broken in, dragged people from their beds, and butchered them with savage cries of victory and joy. He said that they had attacked many of the nurses and violated them sexually before killing them. I had seen evidence of that in other places on the way to the hospital. He confirmed that Fatima is dead."

Ali threw himself on the ground and wailed.

"Ali, he said the Phalangists had laughed at him in the hospital and said they would let him live only because he could barely walk from his injuries and was no danger to them. They said someone had to tell the other Palestinians what would happen to them if they stayed in Beirut. This atrocity must be the greatest massacre anywhere in the region. The Israelis had control but let it happen."

Ali was numb. He groaned and writhed with the horror of it all, collapsing on the street and pulling Dalia down. They lay there, holding each other, images of the horror flashing through their minds. At last, as night was falling, they struggled to their feet. "I must return to my unit, Dalia, but my life is over."

"I have an old friend who lives close by, and I'm staying with her in the remains of her house, Ali. My life is also ending with this tragedy."

Crying, they hugged again. Ali mounted his motorbike, shaken with emotion, a savage hatred and anger engulfing him.

CHAPTER SIXTY-THREE

Ali rode back, his mind enveloped in a fog. Finally, back at the unit, he collapsed to the floor, sobbing uncontrollably. His head felt like it would explode. His heartbeat was rapid and irregular. He gasped, seeking air, but his lungs didn't feel as if they could take it in. Ali smashed his face into the floor, opening the gash on his cheek from where he'd taken a bullet at Al Bassah, an injury that had never fully healed. Blood spurted onto his clothes.

"Ali, Ali, what is it? What news?" called Aduan, coming into the room. He looked at Ali, startled. The wailing intensified as Ali wrenched from side to side, covering his face and kicking his legs. Hearing Aduan call to him, he rolled onto his stomach and folded his arms over his head, his shoulders shaking and heaving.

Aduan ran across the room and knelt beside Ali. "What has happened, Ali?"

Ali did not immediately reply. Finally, he gasped for air. "My Fatima is dead. I saw Dalia. The Israelis and the Phalangists have destroyed Shatila. Everyone I have loved is dead—my father, my mother, Marwan, and now Fatima. We only sought a time to be together in peace, and now she is dead. The evils brought by this conflict are never ending."

"Oh Ali, I can only imagine your pain. Come with me. Lie down in the back and rest," Aduan said, lifting Ali to his feet and hugging him. "The horror of this news is too much."

Others ran into the room, hearing the commotion. "Get out, get out," said Aduan waving them away. "Ali has had dreadful news, and he needs time and quiet."

Aduan settled Ali on a cot in the back room. He soaked a cloth in cold water and tried to wash the blood from Ali's face.

After a few minutes, Ali stopped sobbing and lay on his back, his body still heaving. "I cannot go on, Aduan. My father was killed at Karantina, my mother died in Tel al Zaatar, Marwan killed by the Israelis, and now Fatima. Go. Leave me."

CHAPTER SIXTY-FOUR

NEW YORK, SEPTEMBER 1982

"Colonel Walker," said Alex, leaning into the office of the Canadian Forces military attaché, "I just heard from Under-Secretary-General Fuller's office that he wants a meeting on UNIFIL today at 6:00 p.m."

"I'll go over there with you, Alex," Walker replied.

"Good, Colonel. Ambassador Tremblay is coming as well, and she wants both of us there, given the fluidity of the situation and threats to UNIFIL."

"Oh, good. Fuller must be ready to go to Lebanon again. National Defence has been very tense and wants to know what happens to UNIFIL with the Israeli invasion," Walker said.

"Foreign Affairs, of course, agrees completely," said Alex. "At least the Israelis have started withdrawing from Lebanon." Their faces were grim.

Just before the appointed time, Walker and Matheson left the Permanent Delegation offices and walked up the hill past the park to the UN building. Ambassador Tremblay would meet them there. They ran into the Norwegian ambassador, Anker Falk, and his deputy, Martin Fredriksen, as they entered the building at the main doors.

"Ambassador, good afternoon," said Matheson. "I'm sure that Oslo is anxious to see a delegation launched to visit UNIFIL."

"Indeed, they are," said Falk. "Developments on the ground have become so confused, and politicians don't like to have our soldiers in that kind of situation. The killings were bad enough, but the more recent kidnappings are also dreadful. Now there is complete chaos with the Israelis and the Phalange. We definitely need to show support for our contingents."

"You won't be surprised that Ottawa feels the same way, ambassador," added Walker.

"Martin, you look quite disturbed yourself," said Alex as a quiet aside to his colleague as they walked across the marble-floored lobby.

"I have to admit I am, but I hope that Fuller can provide some direction for us," Fredriksen said. "We have to do something more to protect our troops."

"You're right. The UN peacekeepers are so exposed to attacks from either side," said Alex. "With a mandate to stand between opposing sides that have allegedly agreed to a ceasefire or a limit on operations in certain areas, UNIFIL really has no authority to take the fight to them if attacked. The Israelis have clearly violated the understanding by invading Lebanon again."

They went to the thirty-sixth floor and settled into the SG's conference room. Ambassador Tremblay had arrived already. "My colleagues," began the Under-Secretary, "we are in a difficult position. The Secretary General has had many calls from your heads of government and foreign ministers in the past few days. He looks to me to review the role of UNIFIL and make some sense out of the confusion on the ground. By 'me' I mean 'us.'" He looked around the room. There were expressions and gestures of confirmation around the table from the assembled diplomats.

"Accordingly, we must organize an immediate trip to the region, and I hope that several of you will join me and my staff. I plan to leave in the next three days. That will give us one business day tomorrow to make practical arrangements and the weekend to contact interlocutors at the other end. Monday we will leave. Comments?"

"Thank you, Under-Secretary," said Falk. "This will be much appreciated in capitals, and your good offices are important to be making the right contacts."

The Irish ambassador added his agreement. "Whom would you suggest that we see?"

"I think we should first visit UNIFIL HQ, where we can meet some of the contingents and get a briefing on the ground from our military. Arafat is no longer available, as he is on his way to an unexpected holiday in Tunis with most of the PLO leadership." Several participants lightly snorted at the reference to the expulsion of the PLO leadership from Beirut. "Senior Palestinian military and intelligence officers are likely to be available in the south, however, as they're doing little more than keeping their heads down. We could meet with Major Haddad if he isn't in Beirut shaking hands with the Israelis and having photos taken. I have real reservations about him personally, but he will be looking for the press coverage of a meeting with us." Fuller was always shrewdly aware of the importance of the media to the Israelis and to Haddad.

Fuller continued. "We will have to see what the situation is in Beirut in the coming hours and whether a visit there is viable and useful. I really think it's unlikely that a visit there would be productive in any way. Goodness knows who is in charge." He looked down at his notes and then carried on. "Finally, we should think through whether at least some of us should go to Tel Aviv to meet the prime minister and Ariel Sharon, the Minister of Defence, if he has returned from Beirut and will deign to see us. We would, of course, not consent to meet in Jerusalem because of the capital issue, although the Israelis will propose it. Agreed?"

"Ambassador Tremblay?" Fuller acknowledged that she wanted to speak.

"Thank you, Edward," the Canadian ambassador said. "I just wanted to assure you that Canada fully supports the UN in this debacle. The invasion of Lebanon by the Israelis is a complete change in their professed strategy. They have gone much too far by invading and occupying Beirut. They are no longer operating as the 'Israeli *Defence* Forces,' as they like to be known."

A murmur of agreement passed through the room.

"All right," said Fuller. "I would appreciate being informed tomorrow by close of day who from your delegations will participate. I would note that Ambassador Obeidi from the Palestinian Observer Delegation has already asked if one of his officers could join us. I have agreed. I trust there is no objection. Good afternoon," he said, rising and gathering his papers.

CHAPTER SIXTY-FIVE

SOUTH LEBANON

"Davoud," said Aduan as they walked together toward the Intelligence Bureau's site, now back in the southeast foothills where they had worked for years. "Ali is a broken spirit. I can barely get him to eat or drink. He doesn't come to work. He doesn't want to talk. He doesn't wash or care for himself. He's in a profound depression. I don't know what can be done for him. He is convinced he has lost everything in his life, and he sees no future."

"Perhaps I can help, Aduan. We've had a good relationship over the months and have had some conversations about bringing him more actively to the faith. He has been receptive, and it could be some comfort to him. I will talk to him."

"That might be useful. He's in his quarters in a separate room where you can talk quietly."

Later that evening, Davoud softly knocked on the door of Ali's room. Hearing no answer, then waiting, he opened the door. The lights were off, but in the moonlight coming through the window, he could see that Ali was lying on his bed with his eyes open but unfocussed. He looked grey and drawn from lack of food and sleep.

"Ali. It is Davoud. I want to talk to you. I understand why you are in this mood. Tell me how you are feeling. What the story is."

Ali didn't say anything.

"Ali, everyone is concerned about you. It's time to take hold of yourself. I lost many close family members and friends in the struggle to liberate Iran from the Shah. I know how you are feeling. My sister was an activist. I was very close to her. At a demonstration one day, she was arrested. I wasn't there, but I tried to find out where she was and what had happened. I never saw her again. I think of her every day and pray that her soul is at peace."

With effort, Ali tried to roll on his side but failed to boost himself up on one arm. He looked up. His eyes were sunken into deep, dark circles, and his face was gaunt. "Then you will understand, Davoud. My life is finished."

"No, Ali, there is much more to be done. You live for a reason. Eat some food. Take this water. I will make tea. You need to strengthen yourself to face life. Eat. Drink. We will walk in the hills together."

"No," Ali grunted, turning away and closing his eyes.

Davoud visited Ali again the following morning with oranges, bread, hummus, and tea. Ali grudgingly slurped the tea and ate. He rallied somewhat when Davoud, who would not take no for an answer, helped him rise and go out for a short walk in the fresh air. As his visits to Ali continued, Ali's strength began to return, but he said little and talked to few, except Davoud.

Several days later, Aduan again ran into Davoud in the parade square. "Davoud, I see that you are really helping Ali. He has agreed to come back to work. Although he is very quiet and withdrawn, at least he comes. He also sounds as if he's more aware of Islam and what faith can do for all of us. You are indeed bringing him along and giving him a reason to resurrect the Ali we have known."

"Thank you, Aduan. I will continue to do what I can to encourage him."

CHAPTER SIXTY-SIX

"Davoud," Aduan said as they crossed paths the following day. "Thinking about our discussion yesterday on how Ali is coming along, I am organizing the meeting with the UN delegation coming at the end of the week, and I think I will include him. I hope it will help bring him out of his shell."

The next day, Davoud led Ali into the hills for their daily walk as the sun was setting and the air cooled. "Ali, I feel we have developed an understanding that transcends your deep concern over the difficulties that life has brought you, and your fears of the future. The people of Palestine have suffered immensely. Neither the Lebanese nor the Westerners seem prepared to do anything to help. The Israelis are in control. Your appreciation of the importance of the faith of Islam has matured, and I think you're ready to look ahead."

"The Islamic beliefs we have talked through have given me a new perspective on life and on the enlightenment of the prophet Mohammed, peace be upon him. Indeed, I am developing an appreciation of the guidance he provides and the framework for our lives.

"The coming days will provide you with an opportunity to prove that faith, and to demonstrate the strength it provides to you," said Davoud with a tone of gratification.

"Yes. Thank you. Aduan has suggested to me that I should help to organize and participate in the meeting with the United Nations in the next few days at our headquarters. It is time that I resume my work."

"Excellent, Ali," said Davoud, his arm around Ali's shoulder. "We will talk again before that time."

CHAPTER SIXTY-SEVEN

NAQOURA

The heavy, white UN helicopters flew in over the coast and settled into the landing area at the UNIFIL headquarters in Naqoura. A choking dust swirled about as the rotors slowed. The delegation had transited through Cyprus instead of going to Beirut due to the intensity of the conflict there.

"Well, finally, we're here," said Alex to his Norwegian colleague, sitting beside him. "It was alarming to see the number of Israeli naval vessels along the Lebanese coast. We didn't see that the last time we visited UNIFIL."

"It is good that we didn't try to go through Beirut this time. Lots of things will have changed there with such intense fighting," Fredriksen said.

The delegates walked stiffly down from the helicopter, stretching, feeling the warmth of the air, and noting the smell of the grasses and rosemary bushes. "All right, everyone," said the administrative officer from UNIFIL. "Please move away from the landing area quickly so that our other helicopter can land. Please go to the main desk, where you will be assigned quarters. You are all to meet in an hour in the central reception room. Drinks and appetizers will be served."

"Salim, are you staying at HQ with us?" Alex said as they jostled each other in picking up their bags.

"Yes, I am. I'll see you at the reception. I must say, Alex, I can hardly believe that I'm here and will be meeting frontline Palestinian forces. After years of involvement in policy issues, this is really my first opportunity to see what they mean to those in the field."

"Good. I'm looking forward to your views and observations during this trip. We've had some good conversations in New York, but it'll be different now that we're in your neighbourhood."

After time for a shower and a change of clothes, and re-energized with cups of tea or coffee, thankfully provided in their quarters, the delegation collected in the reception area, where drinks were served and trays of appetizers beckoned.

Under-Secretary General Fuller raised his glass of whisky and tapped it firmly with a teaspoon from a nearby table, drawing the attention of the room. "Ladies and gentlemen, I have had an opportunity to speak to CO Colonel Kuweku, to confirm the program for tomorrow. We will leave here at 09:00 and drive about twenty-five kilometres to a Palestinian base, where we will be hosted by Colonel Abu Khalid, head of the PLO Intelligence Bureau. We should expect to be there a good two hours. I would hope less than half that time will be just drinking tea and exchanging pleasantries." The delegates laughed at Fuller's comment, knowing how culturally appropriate it was.

"The situation on the ground has changed dramatically in the past ten days," Fuller continued. "The assassination of the Lebanese president just before we left New York has had a profound impact on the situation. The subsequent horrific massacre at the Shatila camp in Beirut rules out meetings with the Phalangists in government. The Israeli forces have now almost completely left Beirut, and the Palestinians are keeping their heads down. Our focus will be to support the UNIFIL contingents."

"Hear, hear," with accompanying sounds of support, was heard throughout the room.

Fuller took a long drink and held out his glass for a refill. "As for the Palestinians, Colonel Abu Khalid, whom we will be meeting, is waiting for orders to leave the area. Where they are to go is not clear, but it will likely be Syria. This may have been overtaken by events, notably the massacre at Shatila, but the colonel had been asked by my office to start his remarks with his perspective on the Israeli occupation of Beirut and the evacuation of the Palestinian leadership, and their armed forces, from Lebanon.

"I should add that I don't know how much of this is now relevant, but we do want to question him about recent Palestinian operations against the villages in northern Israel, now on hold, and the rise of independent Islamic militias, such as where they come from and who supports them. That will lead us into questions about the attacks on UNIFIL and the kidnappings."

"Under-Secretary," said Alex, "we all share a deep concern for the safety of the UNIFIL contingent and the viability of their mandate, so what do you think they will do from here on?

"Very importantly on this trip," Fuller replied, "we need to re-evaluate the status and future role of UNIFIL. Even if most of the Palestinians leave South Lebanon, we expect that UNIFIL will stay. There will be much to discuss after these meetings with UNIFIL command, as well as the growing number of players in the region."

The Norwegian ambassador, Anker Falk, interjected, "Edward, there is no doubt that the local situation is very chaotic. Security issues for our people in the region are extremely important to address. Even with the invasion of Beirut and recent attacks on UNIFIL, and the kidnappings, Oslo is fully supportive. From the perspective of my government, we agree that we are here to stay. I hope that is the message we will deliver here."

"Thank you so much, Anker. That indeed is the message. I've had contacts from other contributors that would endorse your position. I am fully aware of the domestic interests in capitals that come into play when the politicians get into these matters, but so far, everyone seems ready to stand firm.

"Finally," Fuller said, looking at his notes, "while many of the Palestinian forces have already moved to Tunis, Syria, and elsewhere, there are still many here, and they see strong challenges from the forces of Haddad, who now feels he has a great opening. Our CO says that the Palestinian colonel is a no-nonsense individual, reasonably articulate, and that we can expect him to be quite open. We will start with that meeting, which is about an hour's drive away. On the way back, we will visit a UNIFIL outpost where we can talk with the soldiers on the frontline as we did before. We will then return here for a late lunch to assess what we have heard. We are scheduled to meet with Major Haddad in the late afternoon. For the moment, have a relaxing evening and a good sleep. Breakfast is at 07:30. We reassemble at 08:45. Cheers!" Fuller raised his refilled glass, and the others followed suit.

Salim, Martin, and Alex left the reception together. "I have never met Colonel Abu Khalid, but the USG's description of him was positive," said Salim. "I must say I am quite excited. The situation has become so complex, it's difficult to see how it will evolve in the coming days."

"I can agree with that," said Alex. "We have clearly landed in the middle of it. UNIFIL is in a very difficult situation, and the reputation of the UN goes with it. What did you think of that briefing, Martin?"

"I really don't know what to think. There are so many players in the game that it's really difficult to see who might do what next," replied the Norwegian. "Indeed, you are from an interesting region, Salim!"

***

The dining room was bustling with activity by 07:30 as the delegation started the following day. Several officers from UNIFIL had joined them for breakfast. Discussions covered the issues expected to be on the agenda with the Palestinians later in the morning. The dozen delegates and some UNIFIL representatives boarded a line of white UN vehicles and set out across the dusty hills to the east, bound for the PLA Intelligence Bureau.

CHAPTER SIXTY-EIGHT

SOUTH LEBANON

A line of four senior Palestinian officers stood at attention in the main hall of a small, wooden community building where they were to meet the UN delegation. Aduan brought them to attention. "Colonel Abu Khalid, you wanted to address the group."

"At ease, gentlemen. The military situation has become very difficult. The Israeli invasion has made a huge change in Lebanon. Our leaders have been sent to Tunis. Our fighters are being sent away. Some have already been taken on the ships. Thousands of others are being evacuated to Damascus by truck and bus. We can expect that we will be moved before long, but we have no idea where to at present. The focus is on Beirut itself. The assassination of the president has led to an enormous outcry from the public." Colonel Abu Khalid held out his hands, palms up, and shrugged his shoulders in a gesture of uncertainty. "I hear we were not responsible." The officers shifted uncomfortably but said nothing.

"The Israelis organized the massacre by the Phalangist forces at the Shatila camp, and thousands of our family members and fighters have been killed. The Israelis are withdrawing their forces quickly, as they are rightfully being blamed in large part for the massacre, led by Ariel Sharon."

Aduan and the other officers murmured to each other under their breath, pleased that the Israelis were on the hook for the massacre.

"Quiet!" barked the colonel. "For the moment we must stay quiet while the follow-up to the siege of Beirut calms. We will not be planning any operations. However, we must guard against the

South Lebanon Army attacking us, and the activities of the random militias that are forming."

The colonel took a deep breath and carried on, looking very tired. "This meeting provides an opportunity for us to ensure that the UN knows what pressure we are under and that it is our troops and people who are under threat. You will be the face of the PLA. Ensure that you are professional and friendly. These people will report to New York, and we have many supporters there. We will receive a five-minute advance notice of the arrival of the delegation. You may be at ease until then. Dismissed." Abu Khalid turned smartly and left the hall.

***

"Ali, you are feeling well today?" said Aduan as he walked to the back of the hall to speak to him. "Your primary role is to stay close to the colonel as his assistant. He may need papers or want to pass messages during the discussions."

"Yes, Aduan. I'm feeling better and ready to fulfill my responsibilities. Excuse me, I have some things to do. I'll be back in a few minutes."

Ali walked out a door at the back, crossing to a nearby building.

"Ali, I am here," said Davoud, coming out of a small room, the first on the left. "Are you ready?" Ali slipped off his combat jacket, and Davoud embraced him. Then he helped Ali into a bulky vest.

"Yes, Davoud," said Ali. "I see this as my opportunity to uphold the tenets of Islam and pay my respects to Allah and the teachings of the Prophet, peace be upon him."

"You will indeed receive the blessings of Allah," said Davoud as he adjusted the vest and helped fit and rebutton Ali's loose combat jacket. "You are to be just behind Colonel Abu Khalid when the delegates are introduced to him. The best opportunity is when the ambassador of Norway is introduced. I expect that he will be among the first few people, given his seniority. The fallout of this action will focus the world on the plight of the Palestinian people and the loss of Fatima, whom you will join today in *Jannah,*[13] *alhamdulillah.*"

"And may God go with you and the faithful, Davoud."

"You also go with the Party of God, Ali. We are at the beginning of a new chapter that will bring justice to this region under the banner of our party, to be known as Hezbollah. The faithful will move forward and prosper. Our enemies will cower before the force of Islam. The Western powers at the UN have done nothing to help the people of Palestine. May Allah go with you, my son," Davoud said, carefully hugging Ali once more.

"And with you, Davoud. I am ready," Ali said, standing tall.

Insh'allah, thought Davoud.

Ali returned to the main building, walking purposefully along the back corridor. A grouping of a dozen heavy armchairs upholstered in bright, striped silks with gilt fringes had been placed at one end on beautiful, elegantly colourful Persian carpets. Smaller chairs were placed close by for note-takers and aides. Round wooden tables with drinks, fruit, and pastries were placed among them. A large table laden with carafes of tea and other food was on one side. The traditional photo of PLO Chairman Yasser Arafat was on the wall behind the chairs.

As he entered the hall, Ali heard an officer call out that the delegation would arrive momentarily.

The colonel moved to the middle of the room to receive his guests. Ali took his place close behind him. Abu Khalid smoothed his luxurious moustache, tugged at his sleeves, and adjusted the bottom of his jacket. On his right, two steps away, were two members of the Operations Group. Their colonel had already left the region. Two other soldiers manned the door, one standing on each side at full attention. Aduan walked to the entrance to receive the guests.

---

13 Paradise.

Minutes ticked by. Ali felt moisture on his upper lip. He blinked but was too nervous to wipe away the bead of sweat that ran down his forehead and then beside his right ear. The UN vehicles entered the courtyard, where PLA soldiers stood at attention. The UN security detail got out of the vans first and joined them at attention beside the vehicles and then opened and held the doors. The members of the delegation got out and stood, looking ahead at the building and sorting themselves out in order of precedence, as had been discussed. They chatted amongst themselves, commenting on the beautiful weather and expectations for the meeting.

Under-Secretary General Fuller walked forward and shook hands with Aduan, who had come down the three stairs from the entrance to welcome him. Fuller put out his hand and gave Aduan a firm handshake. "Welcome, Your Excellency. Please come this way," said Aduan, extending his left arm toward the entrance.

"Thank you. We are pleased to be here in these trying times." Fuller shrugged his shoulders to straighten the fall of his light grey suit and followed Aduan. They mounted the stairs and walked about ten paces into the hall. The rest of the delegation from New York followed a few steps behind.

Aduan stepped to the side and moved around to stand beside Ali as they approached Colonel Abu Khalid. "Excellency," the colonel said with a broad smile at the Under-Secretary General. "We are honoured to receive such a distinguished delegation." He raised his hand to shake, as did Fuller, and then, with a huge grin, Abu Khalid enveloped him in a hug, kissing him on both cheeks.

Fuller, his British diplomatic antennae quivering, stiffened a little but did not back away. "I appreciate your welcome and thank you for receiving the delegation, Colonel. We look forward to a useful exchange of views."

Fuller began introducing his delegation to the colonel as the others entered. "Colonel, you have already met Brigadier Kuweku, the CO of UNIFIL."

Ali felt his body stiffen in nervous tension as the introductions began. He blinked and held back the rise of tears.

THE STRUGGLE CONTINUES

The colonel snapped a smart salute for the superior officer and shook his hand with enthusiasm. The brigadier returned the salute and the handshake with a professional smile.

Aduan stood shoulder to shoulder with Ali behind the colonel, watching as the delegates came into the hall. He looked at his men at the entrance door. He was pleased, as he had never seen them so straight or their salutes so sharp. Out of the corner of his eye, he glanced at Ali and thought, *It is good that he has pulled himself together and come back to work to keep busy. It will be better for him to focus on moving ahead rather than dwelling on Fatima's death.*

Other delegates filed into the room behind the UNIFIL commanding officer. Salim was in his place at the back of the line, about to mount the second stair, quivering with anticipation at the prospect of the meeting and his eventual report to his ambassador, which would find its way back to the Palestinian National Committee. He saw Alex in a smart, light-weight suit, several places ahead, just waiting to go through the doorway.

Alex turned slightly and caught Salim's eye, an excited smile on his face. *Salim seems very pleased to be here*, thought Alex. *So are we all. Lebanon is such a mess. I am fascinated to see how we are received and what we determine will be UNIFIL's future.*

The Norwegian ambassador and his aide, Martin, stepped closer as Fuller began introducing the Irish ambassador ahead of them.

Fredriksen, whose face was flushed, thought only of the situation he had put himself in and felt bile rise in this throat. *I wonder if the Palestinians know who I am and what I have done,* he thought, choking back the feeling that he was about to vomit.

"Ambassador O'Regan of Ireland," said Fuller, presenting him to the colonel.

"Excellency," said Abu Khalid, beaming and pumping his hand.

Ali looked ahead, through misty eyes, at the colonel and the UN delegates lined up to meet him. His heart was beating so vigorously he thought it would be visible to others. He felt more sweat on his forehead, and his brain quivered. He was conscious that Aduan, his dear friend and mentor, was standing immediately beside him.

Alhamdulillah, he thought. *Aduan has always been with me when I needed him. And now he is here when I need him once more.*

"Ambassador Falk of Norway," Ali heard.

Ali clasped Aduan's arm with his left hand in a fierce, claw-like grip, and a millisecond later, shouted, **"FATIMA!"** as he pressed the button on his vest. A fiery explosion engulfed the hall. The room descended into hell.

CHAPTER SIXTY-NINE

NEW YORK, OCTOBER 1982

After the suicide bombing at the PLO intelligence headquarters in South Lebanon, those UN-based delegates who were injured had been flown back to New York for medical care, along with the bodies of those who were killed. Among the dead at the scene were Under-Secretary Fuller, Brigadier Kuweku, the Irish and Norwegian ambassadors, Martin Fredriksen, and from the Palestinian contingent, Colonel Abu Khalid, Ali, Aduan, and several others. More were injured.

The morning sun shone brilliantly through the large windows and lit the pale-green walls of the hospital room. "Alex, how are you feeling today?" said Salim, walking in and taking a chair beside the bed. "Are your injuries more bearable?"

"Things are coming along quite well for me, Salim. Each day seems a little better. Thank goodness the blast didn't hit me in any life-threatening areas. Elizabeth won't let me look in the mirror yet, but she says the scars will give me character."

"I am thankful, Alex. You know that I was at the back of the line and hadn't yet entered the building when the bomb went off. I gather that, when the Secretary-General announced what had happened, the entire UN system around the world was paralyzed in shock. It still is. All meetings are still cancelled. In the corridors, the suicide bombing is the only subject that anyone can talk about."

"Do they know who exactly the bomber was and his motive?"

"They now think it was an aide to Colonel Abu Khalid but have no idea what the motive was."

"I can't understand what would drive anyone to carry out such a horrendous attack, and to commit suicide doing it," said Alex.

"I am saddened to think that this incident reflects so badly on the Palestinians," said Salim. "There are always extremists who live only to die, in the bizarre hope that they'll go to paradise and further the interests of Islam. I do not believe at all that these extremists are faithful to Islam, and they do nothing for the cause of the Palestinians."

"Lying here in pain, I've had a lot of time to think, Salim," said Alex. "I want to make sure this kind of thing stops happening. When I get out of here, we must continue working with colleagues to create understanding and peace in the region. UN members must become aware of what more can be done for the people who live in those dreadful camps and have no future. They're the ones who are really suffering. They just want to work and raise their families. Only leaders start wars, not the population." Alex leaned back on his pillows in exasperation at the thought.

"You are right, Alex," said Salim softly. "The struggle continues."

EPILOGUE

In 1983, a commission headed by former Irish Foreign Minister, Nobel Peace prize laureate, and UN Assistant Secretary General Sean MacBride found that Israel bore responsibility for the massacre at Shatila.

The Kahan Commission, led by Yitzak Kahan, President of the Israeli Supreme Court, determined that Ariel Sharon bore personal responsibility. Sharon was forced to resign as Minister of Defence. However, he later served as Prime Minister of Israel from 2001-2006.

In the period following the Israeli invasion of 1982, Iranian-backed forces and clerics in South Lebanon formed the Party of God, known as Hezbollah. It is classified by many nations as a terrorist group and has carried on intensified operations against Israel for years. The party now has a political wing with seats in the Lebanese Parliament.

Some 500,000 Palestinian refugees are registered with the UN Relief Works Agency as living in Lebanon and 1.5 million are living in UNRWA camps in the region.

The struggle continues.

Printed in Canada